ChangelingPress.com

Jackal/Wraith Duet

Harley Wylde

Jackal/Wraith Duet
Harley Wylde

All rights reserved.
Copyright ©2019 Harley Wylde

ISBN: 9781086415469

Publisher:
Changeling Press LLC
315 N. Centre St.
Martinsburg, WV 25404
ChangelingPress.com

Printed in the U.S.A.

Editor: Crystal Esau
Cover Artist: Bryan Keller

The individual stories in this anthology have been previously released in E-Book format.

No part of this publication may be reproduced or shared by any electronic or mechanical means, including but not limited to reprinting, photocopying, or digital reproduction, without prior written permission from Changeling Press LLC.

This book contains sexually explicit scenes and adult language which some may find offensive and which is not appropriate for a young audience. Changeling Press books are for sale to adults, only, as defined by the laws of the country in which you made your purchase.

Table of Contents

Jackal (Devil's Boneyard MC 1) 4
   Chapter One 5
   Chapter Two 23
   Chapter Three 33
   Chapter Four 45
   Chapter Five 62
   Chapter Six 78
   Chapter Seven 94
   Chapter Eight 103
   Chapter Nine 116
   Chapter Ten 133
Wraith (Dixie Reapers MC 8) 146
   Chapter One 147
   Chapter Two 159
   Chapter Three 172
   Chapter Four 183
   Chapter Five 204
   Chapter Six 218
   Chapter Seven 231
   Chapter Eight 249
   Chapter Nine 268
   Chapter Ten 279
   Epilogue 292
Harley Wylde 296
Changeling Press E-Books 297

Jackal (Devil's Boneyard MC 1)
Harley Wylde

Josie: I spent an amazing three days with Jackal before he disappeared, back to his club, the Devil's Boneyard. He'd made it clear what we had was a temporary thing -- he never wanted the picket fence and kids. I was fine with that. Then I faced the scariest thing ever. Telling my big brother, Tank, a Dixie Reaper, I was pregnant and alone at the age of nineteen. He wanted to go after Jackal, but I wouldn't let him. I wanted this baby, and I knew Jackal wouldn't. I never expected to see him again. Funny how fate has a way of surprising you.

Jackal: I've thought about Josie often since I walked away from her over two years ago. When I'm finally back in Dixie Reapers territory, I knew I'd look her up, see if we could have some more fun. I never counted on the little girl glued to her hip, or the fact the kid was mine. So I did what I do best. I ran. But now I want something I've never wanted before. My family. Because Josie and our daughter, Allegra, are exactly what's been missing in my life. I just have to do some groveling and hope she'll forgive me. Easy, right? I've never had a woman tell me no.

Figures the one I want more than anything might be the first to send me packing. But when she gets an unexpected visitor who threatens her and our child, I'll do whatever it takes to keep them safe. Now that I'm ready to keep my woman and kid, I'm not letting anyone take them away.

Chapter One

Josie
2 years, 5 months ago

I managed to get past the Prospect at the gate, which may have had something to do with my extremely low-cut shirt and some massive flirting, and pulled my car to a stop in front of the Dixie Reapers clubhouse. Another Prospect was manning the door, which was a little odd, but I wasn't going to let a little thing like six feet of muscle stand in my way. After all, the bigger they are, the harder they fall. I stepped up onto the porch and gave him my best smile, the kind that usually brought men to their knees. I knew men found me attractive, and I wasn't above using it to my advantage. Men had been checking me out since I was fourteen, which eww, but I'd learned to turn it against them.

"I'm here to see my brother," I said sweetly.

"Sorry, doll. Members only tonight."

"My brother is a fucking Dixie Reaper and you aren't going to let me in?" I asked, stomping my boot-shod foot. My temper was spiking. I had to get in there! If I didn't talk to Tank tonight, then I was seriously screwed, and not in a pleasant way.

He shrugged.

I was about to argue my way through the door when something distracted him just long enough for me to rush past him. The door slammed into the wall as I ran through it, drawing everyone's attention my way. Just what I wanted. I tossed my hair over my shoulder like I didn't have a care in the world, and started to saunter forward, my boots clicking on the floor. I might have added a little extra sway to my hips.

"I'm sorry, Tank. I tried to stop her," the Prospect from outside said as he loomed behind me and reached for my arm.

"Don't you fucking touch me!" I said, snapping my teeth at him.

The Prospect jumped back, jerking his hand away from me. Asshole. What the fuck was wrong with guys? Like it was okay to just manhandle a woman. Bad enough they'd eye you like a piece of candy and you just knew they were undressing you with their eyes, but touching was a no-no unless I said it was okay.

Tank groaned and met me in the middle of the room. "What the fuck are you doing here, Josephine?"

"It's Josie," I said. I'd only told him that about a million and one times, and he still didn't get it. Josephine was the name of some prissy princess type, and that so wasn't me. I was high-heeled boots, black leather, and a good dose of sass all the way. "I hate that fucking name and you damn well know it."

"Fine. What the fuck are you doing here, *Josie*?" Tank asked.

"Mom has gone too damn far this time. Either you do something, or I won't be held responsible for my actions." And she had gone *really* fucking far. I was beyond livid, but I didn't know where to turn except to my big brother. Well, half-brother, but he was still the only family I had outside of Mom. That I knew of. Dad was such a horndog, it wouldn't surprise me if we didn't have siblings in every damn state. Maybe even a few other countries.

"You know your whore mother doesn't listen to a fucking thing I say," Tank said. "You're nineteen, Josie. Move the fuck out."

"And go where?" I mean seriously. Did he expect money to just magically appear? I'd tried the college thing, but it wasn't for me. I wasn't about to tell anyone I'd been stalked and attacked on campus. Mom would make it all my fault, and Tank would likely beat the fucker into the ground. Then big brother would be in jail. Now that I'd refused to go back... No, I wasn't going to think about that because big brother was going to fix it. At least he fucking better.

Tank shrugged.

I screeched and stomped my foot before marching over to the bar. The Prospect handing out drinks stared at me wide-eyed, not that I was surprised. I was acting like a fucking brat and I knew it, but dammit. I was seriously losing my shit over this mess. My life had become so fucked up in a very short time, and I didn't see any way out of it. I didn't have anywhere else to go, and I refused to listen to my mother this time. She'd ruled my life long enough. I was going to take a stand. I just preferred not to take that stand and end up living in a cardboard box behind the diner. I might not be a prissy princess, but I also knew I didn't have the skills to survive on the streets. Just the thought of not being able to wash my hair every day was enough to give me hives. Okay, so maybe I was a *little* bit of a prissy princess.

"Whiskey," I snapped at the Prospect.

"You're underage," Tank said.

"Since when do you obey the law?" I sneered. Please. As if my big, badass biker brother gave a shit about what was legal or not. I'd be willing to bet every penny in his account came from illegal dealings. Not that I'd ever asked, and I never would. I didn't give a shit what he did, as long as he stayed alive and out of jail.

Tank tossed his hands into the air and turned away from me. "Someone else can deal with this shit."

I could feel someone moving closer to me, but I was a little more interested in staring down the Prospect who still hadn't given me my fucking whiskey. I glared, and he glared right back. Little did he realize, I could do this shit all night, and I was *not* leaving until I'd had a drink or five. No way I was dealing with my fucked-up life stone-cold sober. If I had to go home to the she-beast known as Mom, I was going to need some liquid courage. Even that wouldn't likely be enough to face the fate she had in store for me. Just the thought of it made me want to puke.

"Give. Me. The. God. Damn. Whiskey."

"You're under --"

I growled and bared my teeth at him. "You're about two fucking seconds older than me and I know you're all up in here whoring and drinking your ass off every night. Don't you lecture me, you fucking prick."

I heard a chuckle to my left and turned my head in that direction, but the baleful glare I was going to blast the guy with fizzled and died when I got a good look at him. He was quite a bit older than me, probably close to my brother's age, but God was he sexy as hell. His chocolate eyes just pulled me in and promised all sorts of wicked delights. My gaze strayed down his chest, and I couldn't help but lick my lips. The material clung to him, showing off very well-defined pecs that I wouldn't mind exploring. The patch on his cut said he was part of Devil's Boneyard, an MC I hadn't heard of before now. But if he was here on Dixie Reapers property, then he must be okay.

"Jackal," he said, holding out a hand.

"Josie."

"So I heard." He smirked. "So, do you really want a drink? Because there are other, much more entertaining ways to blow off steam."

"Oh, are there?" I asked, playing along. I didn't whore around, but no one would believe me if I told them that. I dressed to kill, but I'd taken my own virginity with a vibrator when I'd turned sixteen. No way I was leaving something like that up to a fumbling guy who didn't know fuck all about pleasing a girl. Since then, I hadn't seen the reason to get overly dirty. But this guy… Yeah, I could see myself getting all hot and sweaty with him.

He reached over and trailed a finger down my bare arm, making me shiver in the most delicious way. "I bet I could keep you entertained for hours. Maybe days."

"Days?" My gaze dropped to his lap and the rather impressive cock straining against his jeans before flicking back up to his face. "You seem awfully sure of yourself."

"Oh, baby, you have no idea." He winked and I couldn't help but smile.

I'd often had fun flirting with Tank's brothers, but there was something about this guy that made me want to do much, much more. For the first time in my life, I was tempted to take a true walk on the wild side. He seemed like the type of guy who could make a woman forget her name, claw up his back, and beg for more. If I was going to let some guy fuck me, he was definitely at the top of the list of possibilities. He had this sexy smirk that made my panties damp, and the way he ran his hand through his hair had me wanting to lean just a little closer. And those tattoos peeking out from under his sleeves! Oh yeah, I wanted to explore those with my tongue.

"Maybe you should convince me," I said.

"I thought you'd never ask." His eyes blazed as he reached for my hand, tugging me off the barstool and leading me out the front door.

I didn't know where we were going, and right then, I didn't much care. As long as I wasn't heading home, I was all right with any destination, especially if Mr. Tall Dark and Sexy was leading the way.

We stopped at a Harley that made me want to drool, it was that goddamn beautiful. He swung his leg over the seat, then held out his hand. I climbed on behind him, my body fitting against his like we were two pieces of a puzzle. I wrapped my arms around his waist and held on as he pulled out of the lot and headed for the front gate. The Prospect on duty let us through, and Jackal opened up the bike on the highway, flying down the road and taking us farther and farther away from my small Alabama town.

I didn't know how long we'd been riding, but he pulled over after a while and stopped at a motel. He gave me a wink as he headed inside the front lobby and returned a few minutes later with a key in his hand. Jackal got back on the bike and drove to the last room. Butterflies were rioting in my stomach as I got off the bike and followed him inside. Jackal flipped on the lamp by the door and I took a moment to look around.

The room wasn't much, but there was a queen bed and the room seemed to be clean. He shrugged out of his cut and draped it over the dresser. His gaze latched onto mine as he pulled his shirt over his head, and I'm pretty sure I started drooling. The guy was seriously ripped and covered in ink. My favorite type. My fingers twitched as I fought the urge to reach for him, to explore every inch of his sexy as fuck body.

Jackal pulled off his boots and socks, then reached for his belt and my stomach clenched as I anxiously waited to see what he was hiding under there.

He stripped out of his jeans, and my eyes went wide at how fucking perfect he was. His cock was already hard and had pre-cum pearling on the tip. I'd never seen that many cocks, even though I'd blown a boyfriend or two. But out of the ones I had seen, his was by far the best. Long and thick, and I shivered as I thought about how wonderful he'd feel inside of me.

"You're a bit overdressed, baby," he said, moving toward me.

I let him help me out of my clothes, my nipples already hard and aching for his attention. He cupped my breasts through my lacy bra, then leaned down and nipped at the hard tips. My hand curled into his hair, pressing him closer and wanting more. He licked, sucked, and bit my nipples through my bra, and a fire started burning inside of me. My panties were soaked and I knew my jeans were quickly getting that way too.

He cupped my pussy, rubbing and pressing the seam of my pants into me. I moaned and wanted more, so much more. He made quick work of the button and zipper on my jeans, then he shoved his hand inside, his fingers stroking my bare pussy.

"So fucking wet," he said, lifting his head to claim my lips.

I'd been kissed before, plenty of times, but not ever like this. He thrust his tongue deep into my mouth as his fingers rubbed against my clit. I whimpered as sensations swept over me that I'd never felt before. Even using the few toys I'd bought had never felt this damn good. His spicy scent clung to me as he worked my pussy with his fingers, toying with my clit, then sliding a finger inside of me. My hips jerked, wanting him deeper.

Jackal pulled away and quickly removed the rest of my clothes, then he lifted me and gently laid me on the bed. The feral look in his eyes told me that I was in for the ride of my life, and I had a feeling that after being with him, I'd be ruined for other men. No one would ever be able to compare to the man about to lay claim to me, even if it was only for a night or two. I'd take whatever he could give me.

He spread my thighs wide and stared at me, licking his lips. He slid his hands up my legs, then spread my pussy open, a low growl erupting as his gaze got even hotter. Jackal lay between my legs, his shoulders holding my legs open, then his mouth latched onto my pussy and I nearly screamed with how good it felt. His hands held me open wide while his tongue licked and tasted every inch of my sensitive flesh.

"You taste so Goddamn good," he said, his voice barely sounding human, he was so turned on.

My heart hammered in my chest as he sucked at the lips of my pussy, then traced his tongue around my clit. When he grazed the nub with his teeth, I came, my hips bucking. My mouth opened, but nothing came out as I fought not to black out from the intensity of the first orgasm a man had ever given me. He thrust a finger inside of me again, stroking it in and out before adding a second.

"Jesus, baby. You're so damn tight." He lifted his gaze to mine, his fingers stilling a moment. "You're not a virgin, are you?"

I bit my lip, not sure how to answer. "Not technically?"

His eyes narrowed. "What exactly does that mean? Either you've had a cock in you or you haven't."

"Um, I took my virginity with a vibrator in high school. I've had boyfriends, and we've fooled around, but I've never…" My words trailed off as a possessive gleam entered his eyes.

"You've not had a cock filling up this pretty pussy?" he asked.

"No," I said softly.

He slid up the bed, his body covering mine. Jackal leaned in close and I could smell myself on his lips. My pussy clenched as his cock brushed against me and it took everything I had not to beg him to fuck me.

"Ever had a cock in your ass?" he asked.

"N-no."

"Given a blow job?"

"Yes," I said. "A few times."

He growled again, and then his legs were braced on either side of my shoulders, his cock pointing toward my face. "Then open up, baby, and show me what you've got. You suck me dry, then keep sucking until I'm good and hard again."

I licked my lips and opened wide. Jackal thrust his cock into my mouth, not giving me time to adjust, just driving inside of me until his cock touched the back of my throat, then slid a little deeper. I fought not to gag, but I wanted this, wanted him. He gripped the headboard and fucked my mouth with hard, deep strokes that oddly turned me on. Clutching at his ass with my hands, I encouraged him to take what he wanted.

"Fuck yeah!" he shouted as his hips jerked and he started coming, my mouth flooding with his cum as I tried to swallow it all.

He didn't stop thrusting and I licked and sucked at him, just like he'd said to do. With a groan, he pulled free of my mouth, then slid back down my body. Jackal gripped my waist and flipped me over, pulling me up onto my knees.

"Stay just like that," he said. Then he got off the bed and I heard him rummaging in his clothes.

He came back and I heard what sounded like a bottle opening. Jackal placed a hand between my shoulder blades and pushed my chest to the bed.

"Reach back and spread those ass cheeks for me, baby. You're in for a treat."

My body shuddered as I obeyed, and I felt something cool and wet drip down the crack of my ass. Whatever it was, he worked it against my tight hole, using soft teasing touches to drive me wild. When he penetrated me, his finger easing into me, I gave a muffled cry and arched my back. He chuckled and gave me more, then I felt his cock press against my pussy. But he paused.

"I always use a condom, and I'm clean. Since you're a technical virgin, I'm going to assume you are too?" he asked.

"Yes."

"Baby, I want to take you bare, but I need to know you're on birth control first. My club has this thing about kids. Darian was a fluke, but I'm not the kind of guy to have a family."

"I'm on the pill." And I was. My mom had made sure I was on it once I turned fifteen, since she was so damn worried I'd end up pregnant before I graduated high school. Never mind I'd never even had sex before now. Not really. Touching and a blow job didn't count in my book. No guy had ever seen me completely naked until Jackal.

I felt his cock pulsing against me. "I need the words, baby."

"Take me, Jackal. I want you without barriers."

His hand smacked my ass and then thrust deep into my pussy. I cried out as my pussy burned from being stretched so damn wide, but as his finger teased my ass and he began rocking his hips, that burn turned into a different kind of heat. It didn't take long before I was clawing at the bedding and begging him to take me harder. He slammed into me over and over, adding a second finger to fuck my ass while his cock drove me wild.

I reached between my legs and pinched my clit, and it was all I needed. Screaming out my release, I heard him roar behind me; then he pounded my pussy until he'd filled me up with his cum. Even after he came, he kept fingering my ass. His other hand slid down between my legs, and he toyed with my clit until I was coming again, my ass clenching down on his fingers as my pussy gripped his cock.

He pulled out and eased his fingers out of me, then hummed in appreciation.

"So damn beautiful."

I could feel his cum running out of me, and he gathered it on his fingers, then shoved it back inside of me.

"I've never seen a woman with my cum sliding out of her pussy before, and I have to say, I fucking love it. I'm going to mark every inch of you, Josie. Fuck you so good and hard all damn night and into tomorrow."

"Please," I begged, wanting that. So much.

He smacked my ass before leaning down and nipping my ass cheek with his teeth. "You're going to wear my marks by morning, baby. My handprints, my teeth marks, and my cum. And I'm going to fucking love every minute of it."

I whimpered, knowing I would too. He was exactly what I'd been waiting for, and I only wished he wasn't leaving. Being a Devil, he wouldn't hang around for long, not this far from his home. He'd said he wasn't the family kind of guy, and that was fine. But having fun for a while would have been nice. I'd be willing to bet he'd make all my sexual fantasies come true if given the chance.

He fucked me thoroughly all night and for the next two days. Then his club called and said they were heading out. I rode on the back of his bike headed back to the clubhouse, feeling used and deliciously sore. We'd nearly made it when another group of bikers surrounded us and forced Jackal to stop.

"I told you I'd seen a pretty redhead," one of them said with a smoker's voice.

It was dark and I couldn't see their patches, but I could tell by the stiffness in Jackal's shoulders they weren't Reapers or Devils. They walked their bikes closer, pressing in on us, and I couldn't stop my hands from trembling where they gripped Jackal's waist. If these men had stopped us for me, then I had a feeling things were about to get really, really bad.

I heard a gun cock, and my breath stalled in my lungs.

"Get off the bike, honey," one of them said. "You come over here and keep ol' Joker warm. And if your man there knows what's best, he'll go the other way. We see him following us, and things might not turn out so great for you."

Jackal patted my hands and I took that as a sign to obey the other biker. I swung my leg over the back of the bike and walked unsteadily toward the man who had spoken. When I got closer, I saw the patch on the front of his cut. Lucifer's Redemption. I'd heard of them before, and not in a good way. But I also knew they liked to pick on those who were weaker than them. And I was not going to be a victim!

The man who had called himself Joker helped me onto the back of his bike, then we were off, the other Lucifer's Redemption members roaring along with us. I glanced over my shoulder and saw Jackal pull out his phone, and I knew he was calling in reinforcements. It wouldn't be long before help was on the way, but I had to survive until then.

We didn't ride for long before they pulled off the road and down a bumpy drive to a house that looked like it had seen better days. I knew this wasn't their territory, which meant they were likely squatting for whatever reason. I was jerked from the back of the bike and forced to go into the house that smelled like piss and mildew.

A stained mattress lay in one corner, and the biker behind me shoved me toward it.

"You ready to spread those pretty little legs and let real men show you how it's done?" he asked, grabbing my ass.

I took a breath, then channeled the inner spoiled bitch I often showed when I was around my brother and his club. Stomping on the jerk's foot, I shoved my elbow back into his ribs.

"Do I look like a fucking piece of meat to you, shithead?" I demanded. I turned, my hair whipping around me, and I sneered at him. "Why would I want someone like you to touch me? I bet your dick is a shriveled-up useless piece of junk that can't even get hard anymore."

"Bitch!" He spat at me, then his hand cracked across my cheek, but I refused to cry and show how much it had hurt.

"I might be a bitch, but at least I'm not a worthless worm like you."

The others laughed from where they stood near the door.

"Looks like she has your number, Roach," one of them said.

I scanned Roach from head to toe. "I'm going to assume you were named after the bug. Fitting. You're just as disgusting as those little fuckers."

Roach lunged at me, but one of his brothers caught him. "Easy, man. Don't want to damage the goods too much. There's a difference in having a bit of fun and ruining the merchandise."

"Like I'd let you touch me either," I said. "I have standards, and I can assure you that none of you meet them."

It probably wasn't wise to provoke men with guns, but they seemed to want or need me alive for some reason. If I could just buy a bit of time, maybe Jackal would come and rescue me.

Joker grabbed his crotch. "I have exactly what you need. It's long and hard, and it can pound that sweet pussy all night."

I arched a brow. "You come near me with that thing and I'll break it off."

I hoped like hell they didn't see that I was shaking like a leaf. I might be talking big, but I knew they could hold me down and force themselves on me. If Jackal didn't get here soon, I had a feeling it would be too late. I didn't hold any illusions. These men would use me, then whore me out until I died. No way was I going down without a fight, though.

"Leave her alone," one of the older ones said. "She'll settle down and realize she doesn't have a choice. No point getting bitten or scratched."

They backed off, but not before Roach shoved me onto the dirty mattress. I cringed, not even wanting to think about what the stains might be. It felt like hours passed before something at the window caught my eye. I turned to see Jackal peering in at me, and I nearly breathed a sigh of relief. He winked and then disappeared.

After that, everything was chaos. Jackal hauled me out of there, and as the door slammed behind us, I heard the shouts of men I knew wouldn't live to see the morning. The Devil's Boneyard would make sure of that, and any Reapers who might have joined in the fun.

Jackal paused at his bike and kissed me hard. "You are so much damn trouble, woman."

"I thought you liked my brand of trouble."

He cupped my cheek and stared at me. "Are you okay? They didn't do anything to you?"

"I went on the attack, and they decided to let me cool off before they took turns."

He growled and glared at the house again. I reached up and turned his face back toward mine.

"Let your brothers handle it."

He took a deep breath. "Yeah. Let's get you home, baby. I'm sure your brother is worried."

I climbed onto his bike and held on tight. He wrapped his hands around mine and squeezed. I thought I felt a shudder run down his body, and I wondered if he'd been worried about me. We didn't talk, and it felt like he was putting distance between us. I hadn't thought we would have a happily-ever-after, but I'd expected some kind of emotion from him after the time we'd shared. Whoever this man was, he wasn't the same as the Jackal who had rocked my world in that motel room.

Jackal took me straight back to the Reapers. He gave me a long look as I climbed off his bike, but he still didn't say a word. I didn't understand why my chest was aching. It wasn't like I'd fallen in love with him over a few days. Maybe it was his dismissal that hurt so much, like I was just another club slut. He'd been my first and being with him had felt special in some way. When he rode off, I fought the urge to cry. I wasn't the crying type, and I wouldn't start now. We'd had an amazing time together, and he'd showed me what had been missing in my life. I'd have to hold onto the memories because something told me I wouldn't be seeing Jackal again anytime soon.

Tank came out of the clubhouse and looked me over, noticing the whisker burn, bite marks, and even the fingerprints Jackal had left on my neck, shoulders, and arms. There were others, hidden marks that only I would ever see. His gaze caught mine, and I wasn't sure what I saw as he stared at me, but something must have changed in that moment. We'd never been the hugging type, but there was concern in his eyes, and something else I couldn't decipher. It was almost a tender look before the mask slid over his face again.

"I'm glad you're back safe and sound," he said.

"You didn't ride with them to come get me?" I asked.

He shrugged and looked away. The way his jaw tensed I wondered if maybe he'd been ordered to stay behind.

"Why don't you want to go home?" he asked.

"Mom is forcing me to marry some guy. He's like fifty and balding, and his breath is god-awful. I know she's getting something out of it, but I don't know what. She said if I don't marry him, then I'm out on my ass without a dime or anything she's ever bought me."

"Why? Why now?" he asked.

"I dropped out of college and ruined her plans to have a doctor for a daughter."

He studied me and I squirmed. "Why did you leave college, Josie? And don't give me some bullshit excuse."

"I had some trouble with a guy there. The police wouldn't do anything, and I didn't want to get you involved, so I packed up and left. I was struggling anyway, so I didn't see the point in applying anywhere else."

He looked away and sighed. "I'll go to your mom's and gather what I can. You can stay with me for a while."

"Really?" I asked, hope filling me for the first time since Mom had dropped her bomb on me.

"Yeah. Fuck knows, if I don't look after you, you'll end up in a ditch somewhere. You have shit survival skills. If fucking Jackal and your kidnapping isn't proof, then I don't know what is."

My body tensed. "What's wrong with Jackal?"

"Best if you don't know. Let's just say you have shit taste in men. You know where my house is. The door is unlocked. Go get cleaned up while I get your things. You can borrow one of my shirts until I get back."

"Thanks, Tank."

He shrugged. "It's what big brothers are for, cleaning up their little sister's messes."

I smiled, knowing he wouldn't appreciate me hugging him right now, or telling him that I loved him. I got in my car and drove to his place, thinking things were looking up after all. I should have known not to tempt fate, because she's a mean-ass bitch who will kick you in the teeth when you least expect it.

Chapter Two

Jackal
Present Day

When Scratch had said the Dixie Reapers needed some help, I'd volunteered. It might have had a little to do with the tempting Josephine. It had been over two years since I'd seen her, come inside her, and fucked her until we both passed out. But I hadn't forgotten her, not for a second. I'd gotten my dick wet a few times since I'd parted ways with Josephine, but it always left me feeling empty. Eventually, I'd stopped trying to fill the void with nameless women. I hadn't had sex in nearly two years, which had my brothers threatening to change my name from Jackal to Pussy Whipped.

I didn't know how the little vixen had so thoroughly captured my attention in such a short amount of time, but I couldn't deny that I wanted to see her again, hold her, see if she tasted as good as I remembered. It had been hard as fuck staying away all this time, but I didn't know how she'd take me coming back into her life. Maybe if I'd called during the last two years, but I hadn't. At first, it was because of shit the club had been going through. After that, I was just a chickenshit.

But there was something about Josie that just wouldn't let me go. I didn't know if it was because she'd been the only woman I'd ever taken bare, or if it was something more. And that more was what scared the shit out of me. I was Devil's Boneyard and we didn't do the mushy claiming shit the Reapers did. Not a single member of my club had an old lady. Hell, Scratch was the only one with a kid, and she was full-grown.

We'd entered the Reapers' clubhouse, ready to get our orders and find out exactly what the hell was going on, and I hadn't even noticed Tank at first. Which was saying something since he was a big, mean bastard who would make King Kong look like a pet monkey. His fist met my face and nearly knocked me off my damn feet.

"What the fuck are you doing here?" he said, growling as he advanced on me, his hands clenched like he wanted to beat the shit out of me.

"I heard you needed help, so I volunteered. Something about one of your women needing protection." My gut clenched as I considered something I hadn't before. "It's not Josie, is it? She's not in trouble?"

"Like you fucking care." He snarled and came at me again, but his brothers held him back. It took three of them, and they were struggling but managed to hold on.

"Easy, Tank," Venom said. "He's not worth it, brother. Go take a walk or head over to the hospital. We'll meet you there."

"Hospital?" I asked. Fucking hell, if it was Josie and she was hurt or sick, then I might seriously lose my shit right now. I didn't like how that made me feel.

"Zipper claimed a woman who is in a shit ton of trouble. She nearly died and has been in the hospital the last few days. We're heading over there because he reserved the chapel. Wants to make it official," Venom said. "Your crew is welcome to come to the wedding, and when we get back we'll figure out logistics. Delphine is going to need round the clock protection until her psycho stepmom is caught."

I wanted to ask about Josie, but something told me that wasn't wise. I didn't know why Tank had come after me the way he did, but I'd be willing to bet it had to do with his sister. Which made me wonder if she was mad that I'd left and not called. I'd wanted to, even picked up the phone a dozen times that first week back home, but I'd decided a clean break was better. There was no place in my life for a woman. Or there hadn't been. That was then, and this was now. Things had changed with the Devil's Boneyard, and now that we had space to breathe, the thought of a hot-ass woman like Josie being by my side held a lot of appeal. I still wasn't ready to go down the daddy road, but we could have some fun. Maybe I'd even be the first Devil to take an old lady.

Venom gave everyone directions to the hospital, and we climbed back onto our bikes and headed that way. I'd have to figure out what the fuck was going on with Tank later. Right now, we had a woman to protect and I needed to stay focused. We might have been into some bad shit in the past, but if anyone in the club had ever hurt a woman, or turned away one in trouble, then Scratch and Cinder would have kicked our asses and booted us the fuck out. Since Scratch's daughter was married to a Reaper, they were like family to us now. If they needed help, then we'd be here. And we knew they'd offer the same to us. It was more than that, though. We actually liked the bastards.

The hospital chapel was packed, and I sat with my brothers on one pew while the Reapers took up the rest of the space. The bride was a gorgeous Korean girl who looked completely in love with Zipper. I had to admit the tattoo artist looked just as smitten with her. I wondered what that would be like, to love a woman that much. I'd always just hooked up and moved on, hadn't even had a girlfriend in high school. The closest

I'd ever gotten to long-term was this insane craving I had for Josie.

The wedding was short, and when we got back to the Dixie Reapers' compound, we were all assigned jobs. Or most of us were.

I frowned at Scratch. "What do you mean they want me out of here?"

Scratch rubbed his beard. "I didn't ask questions, but I'd imagine it has something to do with you fucking Tank's sister the last time you were here. You ran off with her for a few days and I don't think that went over well with big brother."

"Shit, Scratch! She's a grown woman and can make her own decisions. If she has a complaint about our time together, I want to hear it from her."

He shrugged.

"Do you know where she lives?" I asked.

"I shouldn't tell you," Scratch said. "They don't want you anywhere near her."

"We're brothers, man. Come on. I just want to talk to her. If she's pissed at me, fine. I want to hear it from her."

He watched me for a moment, then nodded. "I heard she's been living with Tank. Green two-story house about two miles down the road," he said, nodding to the left of the compound. "But if Tank beats the shit out of you for going after his sister, you're on your own. You've already been warned away."

"I'm just going to talk to her. If she wants me to leave, then I will."

"Don't stir shit up, Jackal. I'll send you packing and ask someone else to come help. You hear me?" Scratch asked.

"Yeah. I hear you."

I got on my bike and went in search of Tank's house. The car parked in the driveway of the green house looked to be the same one that had been outside the clubhouse that night over two years ago. I killed the engine on my bike and walked up the porch steps, then knocked on the door. A slightly curvier Josie opened the door, her hair up in a messy bun, no make-up on her face, but fuck if she didn't look gorgeous. Her hips seemed a little wider than before and her breasts looked bigger too. She damn near took my breath away, and I knew I was staring. There were dark circles under her eyes, and there was a yellow smear on her tank top, but I ached to reach for her.

I smiled. "Hi, Josie."

Her eyes went wide and she stepped outside, pulling the door mostly shut behind her. She cast a nervous glance into the house before facing me again.

"What are you doing here, Jackal?"

"I came to help Zipper and I wanted to see you."

She nervously looked over her shoulder again through the crack in the door, pulling it closed a little more before looking at me. Something was up, but I didn't know what. I knew Tank wasn't in there, so who was? Was there a guy in there she didn't want me to see? I hadn't really thought about her hooking up with someone while I was gone, but I should have. A beautiful redhead like Josie? She probably had men falling at her feet.

"You should go," she said.

"Go, but... What's going on, Josie? Are you pissed I didn't call?" I glanced at the door, anger burning in my gut. "Is there someone else?"

"Please, Jackal. I can't do this right now."

She stepped back inside, careful that I wouldn't see into the house, then shut the door. I heard the lock click and her footsteps wander away.

What the fuck was going on?

I'd promised Scratch if she didn't want to see me that I'd leave, but now that I'd seen her there was no way I was walking out of here without talking to her. I needed to know what the fuck was going on. If she didn't want me, if she'd moved on, then fine. The least she could do was be an adult and say it to my fucking face. Shooing me out of here with that almost fearful look in her eyes had all my alarms going off in my head. If she was in trouble, then I wanted to know, and I was sure as fuck going to fix it.

I edged around the house, checking to see if there were any Reapers nearby who might question my motives, but I didn't see anyone. Most of the blinds were closed in all the windows, except at the back of the house. I blinked, thinking I was hallucinating, but no. The room I was looking into hadn't changed. Baby bed, books and toys all over the place, pink walls… and Josie with a little girl on her hip. I didn't know shit about kids, but the girl looked like she was about a year old, maybe a bit older.

I felt like someone had hit me upside the head with a sledgehammer, and I backed away. Was that why everyone was warning me away? Had Josie hooked up with someone else? But if she was seeing someone, why did she live with Tank? My heart was hammering in my chest and fury filled me. It was stupid and irrational. I didn't have a claim on Josie, but I felt like I fucking should. Here I'd been thinking about her for over two damn years, and she'd had a kid with someone else? Let someone else touch her, fuck her?

My stomach churned as I backed even farther away, then a shadow fell over the ground. I turned to look at Tank, who looked seriously pissed. His eyes were dark, his jaw set, and if the tic by his eye was any indication, he was about to pound the shit out of me. I just didn't understand why. What did any of this shit have to do with me? Or did he blame me in some way? Did he think if I'd stuck around or taken Josie with me that this wouldn't have happened? Maybe he blamed me, thinking that if I hadn't been her first, she'd have remained a virgin longer and wouldn't have a kid right now.

"So, now you know," he said.

Not exactly. I mean, yeah, she had a kid. But that's about as much as I knew. I felt a little like I was riding one of those Tilt-A-Whirl rides at the fair. Josie. Had. A. Kid. A daughter. The little girl had her mother's pretty red hair and pale skin. For some reason, I felt like something had been stolen from me. I hadn't wanted kids, still didn't. Did I? No. I didn't. But knowing Josie had found someone to give her that little girl... that fucking hurt.

Tank narrowed his eyes. "What are you going to do?"

"Nothing."

I turned and walked off, heading back to my bike. Maybe now I could get over her, put her in my past and leave her there. I hadn't been laid in a while, thoughts of Josie always cock-blocking me. Now that I knew she'd moved on, that would hopefully change. I swung my leg across my Harley and put the key in the ignition, but a growl from Tank made me pause and look his way. I hadn't even realized he'd followed me.

"Fucking figures," he said. "Run away like the little shit you are."

"What the fuck is your problem? I'm sorry I didn't fucking call her after I left. I'm sorry I stayed away for over two fucking years, but it's not my fault that she let some asshole knock her up."

His expression cleared and his eyebrows lifted. He glanced at the house, where Josie was now standing on the front steps, the little girl clutched in her arms. The fear in her eyes, how damn pale and scared she looked, made my chest hurt. I hadn't meant to yell so loud, and now I was just as bad as the asshole who'd given her a kid and probably left her, since she was living with her brother.

"So I'm a whore now?" she asked softly. "Just spread my legs for whoever and let them plant a baby in me?"

"Josie, I…"

She shook her head and turned to go back inside, but not before I saw the tears in her eyes. Fuck. Motherfucking shit fuck damn. I hadn't wanted to hurt her.

"Nice." Tank moved past me and headed up the steps, but he stopped before going inside. "By the way, most men don't go around admitting they're assholes, so at least you got that much right."

What? My brow furrowed. I hadn't called myself an asshole. I'd called Josie's baby daddy an… My eyes went wide as I stared at the now-shut door and empty porch. Holy fucking hell. That little girl was mine?

My hand shook as I started my bike. I knew I should go after her, try to smooth shit over, but right now I was still wrapping my head around the fact I had a kid. A daughter no one had told me about. I drove through the compound, past the clubhouse, and right through the front gates. Pointing my bike toward the highway, I blew out of town and rode until some of the shock had worn off, then I turned around and went to the first bar I came across.

If ever there was a time to get drunk, it was the day you discovered you were a dad. Especially when you'd never wanted to be one. I tossed back shots for a while, then switched to beer so I wouldn't fall off my damn bike when it was time to go back. But I wasn't ready yet. Didn't know if I'd ever be ready. I ran a hand down my face and tried to figure out what the hell I was going to do. If Josie had wanted me in the kid's life, she would have said something, right? Maybe it would be better if I just went home, sent someone else to help the Reapers.

I paid my tab and got back on my bike, then kept driving until I crossed the state line. The Devil's Boneyard compound wasn't quite as big as the Dixie Reapers', but it was home. I pulled through the gates, and Cinder was waiting for me at the front of the clubhouse, arms crossed and expression neutral. That blank expression always scared the shit out of me.

"You get some sleep, then we're going to fucking talk," Cinder said. "Or more accurately, I'm going to talk while you pull your head out of your ass."

I nodded.

"Go home and sleep, Jackal. Come find me when you wake up."

"All right, Pres."

Unlike the Dixie Reapers, all our homes weren't inside the compound. The officers all had places inside the gates, but the rest of us fended for ourselves out in the world when it came to housing. My duplex wasn't the best, but it kept me dry when it rained, cool when it was hot, and warm those rare times it was actually cold enough in Florida to turn on the damn heat. Then again, I wasn't a native, so fifty wasn't cold to me. That was T-shirt weather where I came from.

I went inside and looked around the place, really studying my surroundings for once. My couch was old and beat-up, the leather torn in spots and I'd just duct-taped over it. My coffee table looked like it was ready to collapse and was covered in stains and scratches. I did have a kickass TV, though, not that a woman would give a shit about that compared to the rest. I'd never really thought about my future before, other than knowing it was with the club. But if I had a kid out there, maybe I needed to re-evaluate a few things. Just not right now.

My head fucking hurt, my chest ached, and I was bone-deep tired. I kicked off my boots, and stripped off my clothes on the way to my bedroom, where I face-planted on the bed and was out before my body even landed on the mattress.

Chapter Three

Josie

He'd left. Again. That damn asshole just up and left without a fucking word. I was so angry that I was ready to beat the shit out of someone, and maybe a little hurt too. All right, a lot hurt. He'd seen our precious daughter and had just ridden off like it was no big deal. I should have expected it, which is why I'd never told him about Allegra. He'd made it clear he never wanted kids, and I hadn't wanted to force a daughter on him. Now he knew she was here, though, that she existed, and he'd still left. I was glad that Allegra was too young to ask questions about the strange man who'd stopped by a few days ago.

Since another Devil had shown up at the gates, I was going to assume that Jackal wasn't coming back. I wasn't going to hide Allegra from his club, though. Now that Jackal knew, I could move about the compound like I normally would, even if his club was here. Every time a Devil had been on the premises, even Scratch coming to see his daughter, I'd stayed hidden, making sure no one saw Allegra. The Reapers had been sworn to secrecy. All that careful planning, and now Jackal knew anyway. It had to happen sooner or later, but I hadn't been prepared for it. Hadn't even known he would be here.

It was daytime, so there weren't club sluts hanging around the clubhouse when I walked in with Allegra on my hip. She was nearly two and didn't have as much energy as most kids her age, but she kept me busy. We'd been through a lot, from me nearly losing her before she'd even been born, then her showing up way too early, to another scare after she was here. She was small for her age and had been through hell, but we were hanging in there, and Tank and the Reapers had been wonderful through it all. Without my family, I didn't think I'd have survived. I'd never thought about being a mom, but if Allegra hadn't made it, they probably would have had to bury me next to her.

The Devils were sitting around a table near the bar and eyed me as I came through. Scratch didn't seem all that surprised as he looked Allegra over, and I worried that Jackal had already told them all, and they would be pissed I'd kept her a secret. I didn't know if it would cause problems between the clubs, that I'd kept Allegra from the Devils, and had asked the Reapers to help me. Technically, my daughter was a product of both clubs, and the Devils had every right to get to know her. I'd kept her from them, from her family, even if I'd thought I had a good reason.

One of the Devils was standing at the bar, a beer in his hand, and he eyed me up and down a moment before moving a little closer. He didn't look all that old, but the closer he got, I realized he was probably around my brother's age. Fine lines fanned out around eyes that had seen far too much. The man looked Allegra over before his gaze clashed with mine again.

"Is this why we never see you when we visit?" he asked, his voice thick with an accent. Russian maybe? He sounded like the Russian mobsters on the movies I sometimes watched.

"This is Allegra. My daughter," I said.

"I'm Stripes," he said, then grinned. "Like the big jungle cat, yes?"

I bit my lip. I could see him being a predatory kitty, with the way he moved and that sharp gaze. Ladies probably dropped their panties when he entered a room. If my poor stupid, battered heart wasn't still mooning over Jackal, I likely would have joined their ranks. But the asshole who had given me Allegra had done a number on me. I hadn't been interested in even eyeing a guy too closely since he'd left.

"And this little angel is not just yours, no? Perhaps she's part Devil?" he asked.

I glanced at the table of Devils and slowly nodded as I faced Stripes again. "Yes. She's Jackal's daughter."

He nodded. "This explains much."

With a wink, he rejoined his brothers and some of the tension left me. Maybe they wouldn't be angry that I'd kept Allegra a secret. I still didn't know what to make of Jackal appearing after so long, then taking off again. He'd seemed almost happy to see me, a playful smile on his lips, until he'd found out about his daughter. Then he'd taken off like his tail was on fire.

The newly patched Savior, who I'd known as Gabe the last few years, came over with a sippy cup in his hand for Allegra, and a virgin daiquiri for me. Ever since I'd had her, I'd given up alcohol except for an occasional glass of wine when a day had been exceptionally difficult. Tank was letting me live with him and had insisted I stay home with Allegra instead of getting a job. It meant he had to cover all our expenses, which I hated, but I loved having this time with my daughter. Especially when she'd been in the hospital for weeks after her birth, then was sickly the first few months she was home. Even now, she got sick easier than most kids.

"Thanks, Gabe," I said, giving him a smile.

His brow arched and my cheeks flushed. "Sorry. Savior."

I patted his cut, touching the stitching of his road name. He'd earned it, giving his all to the Reapers any time they'd needed help. Although, I think it had more to do with the medals someone had found hidden in Gabe's things. The man was a decorated war hero, several times over. He'd only been patched in for a few months, but he'd made the transition seamlessly, and hadn't seemed to get a big head over it. That was saying something. From what I'd heard, Coyote, formerly known as Prospect Pete, had acted like a jackass the first few months after he'd been patched in.

The Reapers always had a handful of Prospects hanging around. Some stuck it out and some didn't. Poor Johnny had been a Prospect for as long as I could remember, and he still hadn't been patched in, but I had a feeling it had more to do with his age. I'd heard he'd been prospecting since he was seventeen, and even now, he was only in his early twenties.

Savior placed his hand over mine, and I heard several chair legs scrape across the floor, then I had a bunch of Devils at my back. The one who had called himself Stripes growled and leaned toward Savior.

"Um, what's going on?" I asked, glancing at the Devil's Boneyard members.

"You're Jackal's," Stripes said. "This Reaper needs to keep his hands to himself."

Now it was my turn to raise my eyebrows as I stared at them incredulously. "Wait. The Jackal who ran off when he found out he was a dad? The Jackal who knocked me up and rode out of here without ever looking back, or calling? That would be a no. A big fucking hell no. I don't belong to him. We have a daughter together, but that's it."

The Devils didn't look too pleased with my words, and Savior's hand tightened on mine. I knew he wasn't romantically interested in me, but I could tell by the look in his eyes that he wanted to fuck with them.

His gaze met mine before he wrapped an arm around my waist and pulled me closer to his side, the three of us looking a little too much like a loving family. Ah, hell. He was going to start a fight and Tank was going to be pissed at me. Somehow, he'd lay the blame for it at my feet, even though the testosterone in here was so thick even my sharpest knife wouldn't cut it.

"Josie and Allegra are Reapers' property," Savior said. "Unless your boy Jackal wants to man the fuck up and say otherwise. But since I don't see him here... Oh, wait. That's right. He left. Again."

Stripes snarled at him and I bit my lip, hoping that if fists were going to fly, they'd let me and Allegra move out of the way first.

More booted steps came our way and I looked over Savior's shoulder to see my brother, Torch, and Flicker heading our way. Torch didn't look like he was going to put up with any shit today. I'd heard that since Isabella had come home and made him a daddy that he'd mellowed a little, but right now, he was every inch the Pres of the Reapers, and he looked a little pissed.

"What the fuck is this shit?" Torch asked. "You're guests in my fucking house, and you're going to bow up to a patched member?"

Stripes backed up a bit, but not much. "He said Josie and the little angel were Reapers' property, but they're Jackal's woman and kid."

Torch just stared until Stripes backed up a little farther. Then his gaze swung to Scratch, the VP of the other club. "Are we going to have a problem?"

"Don't think so. But just so we're clear, the little girl is both a Reaper and a Devil. Even if Jackal doesn't claim Josie as his old lady, their daughter is a product of both clubs, and we're laying claim to Allegra,"

Scratch said. Then he grinned a little. "Think of it as joint custody until Jackal can pull his head out of his ass."

Torch pushed his hands into his pockets. "I don't see Jackal here. And even if he does show up, Josie doesn't have to accept him if she doesn't want to."

Scratch nodded, and the Devils backed up and went back to their table. Torch patted Savior on the shoulder.

"I want you to keep an eye on Josie and Allegra while the Devils are here. Stripes doesn't seem all that stable, and I don't want anything bad to happen. When Tank isn't home, I want you there, or take Josie where she needs to go. You can use one of the club trucks since I doubt you're going to fit in her tiny as fuck car," Torch said.

My eyes narrowed at the man who often treated me like a father would a rebellious daughter. "My car isn't tiny. You're just all freakishly huge."

Torch winked at me. Tank kissed the top of my head as he passed by, and even Flicker squeezed my shoulder. They were all like brothers to me, even Savior. He tried to tug me toward the door, but I wasn't budging. Not yet anyway.

"I want to enjoy my drink," I said. "It's not like we can see the doctor right this second anyway."

He looked at me. Really looked at me. "What's wrong? The shadows under your eyes are darker than usual."

"Allegra had a rough night."

"Which means you did too."

I nodded.

Savior squeezed my waist, and we both sat down at the bar while I sipped on my frozen drink. A Prospect was standing between us and the Devils.

Ivan. I'd always liked him, mostly because he was nice to me, and not in an I-want-in-your-pants kind of way. Savior signaled to him and got a bottle of water.

"Water?" I asked.

"If I'm going to drive you and princess around, then I don't want to drink alcohol. Even if a cold beer does sound good," he said, giving me a wink.

"Thanks, Gabe," I said softly.

He grinned, letting me call him by his given name without a fight. I knew if a brother had done that, he'd have handed their ass to them, but I was like a little sister to all of them. He might have puffed up earlier and it made me think he preferred I call him by his road name, but I knew he hadn't really minded. They were all big, rough, and tough to outsiders or other clubs… With me? They were like overgrown teddy bears. That's the one thing I could say about every last Dixie Reaper. They didn't take shit from anyone, but once they loved someone, they'd die for them. And they treated their old ladies and kids like they were precious gems.

Ryker and Laken strolled in, and I took that as my sign to leave. Not that there was anything wrong with them, but I sometimes felt like Ryker didn't care for me too much. He'd never been overly rude, but when I'd found out I was pregnant and hadn't told Jackal, Ryker had gotten this look in his eye like he'd disapproved. He wasn't a Reaper, though, so I didn't really give a shit what he thought. I just didn't want to deal with the stress of having that disapproving stare cast my way.

"Can you come with me to take Allegra to the doctor?" I asked. "I called when they opened to see if they would take a look at her. She was fussier than usual last night, and I just want to make sure nothing is wrong."

"Did you drive here?" he asked.

"Yeah. My car is out front."

"Then let me grab the keys to one of the trucks and I'll pull it around. We can move her seat over. Torch is right. There's no fucking way I'm fitting in your damn car."

I smiled. "I didn't buy it with overgrown bikers in mind."

"You should have. You know that tall, sexy, and tattooed is your type." He winked, and I giggled. He wasn't wrong. I'd had fun flirting with the Reapers before, knowing it would never go anywhere, but even when I'd gone out on dates, I'd always liked the bad boys.

And look where that had gotten me.

I went outside to get Allegra's bag from my car and left the door open so Gabe could move her car seat over. Once Allegra was buckled, Gabe helped me up into the truck, then drove us to the doctor's office. Because of her health issues, I'd stuck with the pediatrician who had taken care of her in the hospital. Dr. Aikens was amazing, and so nice.

Gabe carried Allegra for me so I could get my daughter signed in, and then we sat and waited. Allegra rested against Gabe, clutching his cut, and I wondered if she'd do the same if her daddy were to ever hold her. My heart hurt just thinking about Jackal not wanting us. Not wanting her. How was I supposed to tell her that her daddy didn't want her? I knew one day she'd ask.

It took an hour, but we were finally called back. Gabe had offered to wait out front, but I worried I might need moral support. Every time I had to bring

Allegra in, I was anxious that it would be bad news. After her rocky start in life, part of me was always waiting on the other shoe to drop, as the saying went. I was always concerned that she'd be taken from me far too soon, and I knew my heart would break and I'd never be the same if that ever happened.

"Good morning, Josie," Dr. Aikens said as he came into the room. His ginger hair was bright under the florescent lighting, and his blue eyes twinkled. I'd never been rude enough to ask his age, but the rumor around town was that he was younger than my brother, single, and considered the most eligible bachelor in town.

"Allegra was fussy all night, and she seems more lethargic than usual," I said, as Gabe eased my daughter onto the paper-covered table.

"Let's take a look," Dr. Aikens said.

He checked her ears, looked at her throat, listened to her heart, and went through the routine stuff he always checked out when Allegra came in. When he was finished, he folded his arms and studied me.

"She has an ear infection, and her throat looks irritated. Her temperature is a little elevated, but not high enough to worry. I'll call in some antibiotics for her, and some eardrops that will help numb the pain a bit. She might run a bit of fever the rest of the night and possibly for a few days, so give her Tylenol as needed. And of course, if it goes too high, take her to the ER or call me. You have my cell number," he said, and I noticed Gabe look at him sharply.

"She has your cell number?" Gabe asked.

Dr. Aikens nodded, looking amused. "Yes. I gave Josie my number after Allegra was born in case she ever needed me. Though she hasn't used it often."

Gabe looked my way and I knew he'd have questions for me later. It wasn't that I had kept it a secret that Dr. Aikens had given me his personal number, but I'd known my brother wouldn't like it, and it seemed the other Reapers didn't either. I seriously doubted that the sexy doctor wanted anything to do with a single mom who looked like she'd been dragged backward through a cat door, and hadn't slept decently in two years. The man was just being nice, and being a concerned doctor. Nothing more.

"Usual pharmacy?" Dr. Aikens asked.

"Yes, and thank you for seeing her on such short notice," I said.

"Anytime, Josie. Call with any questions or concerns, otherwise, I'll see you at her next routine visit."

Gabe ushered me out of the room, Allegra back in his arms, but his shoulders were tense. When we got into the truck, he gave me a hard look.

"What the fuck, Josie? You know Tank would shit a brick if he knew Allegra's doctor was flirting with you. He doesn't fit in our world, and never will."

I sighed. "Give it a rest, Gabe. He's just being nice and is concerned about Allegra. Don't read anything into it. The man has never been inappropriate, and I'm sure he treats all the parents the same way."

He shook his head, and I had no doubt he'd pass it along to Tank that he thought Dr. Aikens was flirting with me. Like I needed them to protect me from a cultured, intelligent man who saved lives for a living. If they wanted to focus on keeping someone away from me, maybe they should concentrate their energy on asshole bikers. Like Jackal. Although, Jackal seemed to be pretty good at keeping himself away from me.

I actually couldn't remember the last time a man had looked at me as if I were desirable. Jackal had been the last man to touch me intimately, to kiss me, and he'd been the only man who'd ever had sex with me. Now I was just a tired single mom who looked like she'd last slept a few years ago, which was about right. Once my all day long morning sickness had kicked in, I hadn't gotten much sleep, and after Allegra arrived it had only become worse. I didn't regret having her, loved her more than anything or anyone, but sometimes I was lonely.

Yes, I had my brother and the Reapers, and I had Allegra, but that wasn't the same as being in a relationship with someone. I missed having a man's arms around me, wanted someone to lie next to me at night. Was it asking too much that I wanted a man who would love me and would love my daughter?

Gabe glanced my way a few times. "Why do you look so sad?"

"Because no one wants me, Gabe. Jackal's the only guy I've ever been with, and since he left the first time, no one else has looked at me that way. And if you, my brother, and the other Reapers have a say in it, no one ever will."

I looked out the window and watched the scenery pass. Gabe sighed, but he didn't comment. When we got back to the compound, he drove me straight to the house and helped me get Allegra inside and settled.

"I'm sending a Prospect for her prescriptions," he said. "I'll keep an eye on her for a little while. You should get some rest."

I nodded and left Allegra in his capable hands. It wasn't the first time he'd helped take care of her, and I doubted it would be the last. Each of the Reapers had doted on Allegra since she'd come home. Even though there were a half dozen or more kids running around the compound, she seemed to be everyone's favorite.

In my bedroom, I changed into some comfortable pajamas, then crawled into bed. Gabe was right about me needing some sleep. I burrowed into my pillow, pulled the blankets up to my chin, then closed my eyes. I could hear the TV in the living room with Allegra's favorite show playing, and I smiled softly as I slowly fell asleep.

Chapter Four

Jackal

I stopped my bike outside the gates of the Dixie Reapers compound and let the engine idle. The Prospect watched me, but didn't seem to be in a hurry to let me in. After the way I'd taken off, I didn't blame him. From what Scratch had said, not only was Josie pissed-off, but the Reapers were too. I'd been a chickenshit. Instead of being the man my woman and daughter needed, I'd taken off, and somewhere along the road back to Florida, I'd convinced myself they were better off without me.

I'd hauled ass back home, and Cinder had straightened me out. It had taken me nearly a week to get things ready for my new family, though. I'd broken the lease on my duplex and used some of my savings to buy a small house. It was just a three-bedroom one-bath home in a quiet neighborhood at the end of the cove. Looked like a good place for a kid to grow up. The home was older, but looked like it had been taken care of by the elderly couple who had lived there.

The family had insisted on giving me a good deal when I told them I needed more room for my daughter. The couple had already moved into one of those assisted-living places, and the house had been vacant for months without so much as one offer on the place. The outside needed some new paint, and the roof looked like it might need replacing in another year or two, but the inside had been beautiful. Hardwood floors, neutral wall colors, and a lot of windows. I'd left two Prospects painting my daughter's room pink and putting the furniture together. I wanted it to be perfect when I brought her home.

"Not letting you in, Jackal," the Prospect at the gate said.

"My woman and kid are in there," I said. "I'm here to take them home."

"They're Reapers. They are home."

Like hell. "Open the fucking gate."

He pulled a phone from his pocket and quietly spoke to someone. I didn't have to wait long before several Reapers were heading my way, and none looked very happy that I was back. Tank was in the lead and stopped at the gate.

"What the fuck are you doing here, Jackal?" he asked.

"Came back for Josie and my daughter."

He snorted. "You don't even know your kid's name, didn't stick around long enough to find out. Am I supposed to believe you suddenly give a shit about my sister or your daughter? Because your actions up to this point have proven otherwise."

"I had some things to take care of," I said. "Yeah, I ran. I never wanted kids and it freaked me the fuck out that I have a daughter and no one ever told me. So who's really at fault here, Tank? Josie could have called and said something. It's not like no one here knows how to reach Scratch or Cinder. Either of them would have given her my number."

"Why are you back?" Tank asked.

"I bought a house. The Prospects are painting my daughter's room and setting up her new furniture. I came to take my family home," I said.

Flicker threw his head back and roared with laughter. "Oh my God, that's fucking priceless. Your family? You were a one-night stand that lasted a few days, and a sperm donor. Then you take one look at your kid and run like a little bitch. Family? Family sticks by you. Where the fuck were you when Josie was put on bed rest so she wouldn't lose the baby? Where were you when your daughter was premature and nearly died?"

I could feel the blood drain from my face. My daughter had nearly died? Josie had nearly lost her before she was even born? If I'd felt like an asshole before, it was even worse now. Josie had fought for our daughter, and I'd taken off the second I'd seen her. Not my finest moment. I didn't seem to have any fine moments when it came to Josie. Yeah, we'd had a fucking great time at that motel, but then I'd left and never called or come back to see her. Left her pregnant and alone.

Fuck me. Maybe the apple really didn't fall far from the Goddamn tree since my old man had done the same to my junkie whore mother. Not that she'd ever known who the fuck my dad was since she'd been with so many men. When she'd died and left me alone at the age of twelve, a family had taken me in. It was their name I carried. I'd lived with them for two years when they'd decided to adopt me, and I'd asked if they would change my name.

No one knew that, though, not even my club.

"I need to see Josie. Need to talk to her," I said.

"She's resting," Tank said. "Savior finally convinced her to go to bed yesterday, and she's been asleep for nearly twenty-four hours."

My jaw tightened. "What the hell is another man doing sending Josie to bed? Is he in it with her?"

A red haze settled over me and fury flooded my veins. Maybe if I'd been calmer, I would have asked why she was sleeping so long. But all I could think about was Josie and some guy staying with her. If some Reaper had his hands all over Josie, I'd rip them off and beat the shit out of him. My fingers tightened on the grips of my bike, and my teeth ground together.

"Holy shit. I think I might actually see steam coming out of his ears," Flicker said. "Maybe we should let him in before he has a stroke or a heart attack out there and dies in our driveway. Moving the body in broad daylight could be an issue."

Tank sighed and motioned to the Prospect. "Let him in."

The gate slid open and I eased my bike through. Tank motioned for me to stop just inside the gate as the Prospect locked the compound down again. Tank, Flicker, and Rocky surrounded me. All of them were big bastards, but if they thought I would be intimidated, they were wrong.

"You can wait at the bar until Josie is awake. No guarantees she'll let you through the front door, though. That's all on you," Tank said.

"Fine."

I parked outside the clubhouse and went in for a drink. Stripes was already at the bar with a full beer in front of him, so I slid onto the stool next to his. I didn't see the rest of my crew, but I knew they were around somewhere. Scratch was probably visiting his daughter and grandson. Stripes gave me a nod, but didn't say anything.

I asked the Prospect manning the bar for a beer, then sipped at the cold brew while I waited. According to the clock on the wall, it was nearly nine in the morning. With a little girl in the house, I hadn't thought Josie would be the type to sleep in. Tank had said she'd been asleep twenty-four hours. Was Josie sick? Who was watching my kid? Savior? I didn't like the thought of him playing house with my woman and daughter, but until I convinced Josie to go home with me, there wasn't much I could say or do. Not without having every Reaper on my ass.

Another hour crept past and still no word that Josie was up. When it was getting closer to eleven, I'd decided I'd waited long enough. No fucking way she was still passed out, not unless she had the damn flu or something. I slapped Stripes on the back, then headed for my bike. No one tried to stop me, but then Tank wasn't around. Josie's car had been at the clubhouse, and since she wasn't up there, I hoped that meant she was home. I killed the engine and walked up to the door. In case my kid was napping, I knocked softly at first, then louder. After a few minutes, I was getting pissed.

"Josie! Open the fucking door!" I pounded on it again.

"They're not home," a voice said behind me.

I turned and saw a young Prospect walking past. I couldn't remember his name, but I'd seen him at the compound before. He was a favorite of Torch's from what I recalled.

"What do you mean they aren't home?" I asked.

"Allegra was sick. They took her back to the doctor."

"Allegra. The little girl?" I asked.

He gave me a look that made him appear much older and wiser than my thirty-eight years. All right, so I didn't know my own kid's name. It wasn't like I'd been here to learn it. And that didn't make it sound any better, not even in my own mind, so I wisely kept that comment to myself.

"Where's the doctor's office?" I asked, heading back to my bike.

The Prospect gave me directions and I took off, intent on finding out what was wrong with my daughter, and why the hell no one had told me she was sick. I pulled up outside the doctor's office a short while later and went inside, scanning the waiting room. No sign of Josie or any Reapers. The woman at the front desk was eyeing me like she'd like to lick me like a lollipop, so I turned up the charm to see what she'd tell me.

I swaggered over and gave her the smile that tended to make panties drop. "Hey, darlin'. I'm looking for Josie and Allegra."

She scanned me again. "I'm sorry, sir, but I can't give out patient information to strangers."

"Not even if the stranger is that little girl's daddy?" I asked.

Her mouth dropped open and she blinked a moment.

"What? You thought Josie had an immaculate conception?"

She napped her jaw shut. "Um, n-no. They're in room four. Just through that door," she said, pointing to the door at the end of her counter.

I winked and went through then tried not to stomp my way to room four, still feeling pissed off that no one had said my kid was sick. I didn't bother knocking, just went inside. A tall man in a white coat had his arm around Josie as my woman cried against his chest. What the fuck? A Reaper stood in the corner, his arms crossed and a stoic expression on his face as he stared at my daughter.

"Hands off her, jackass," I said, moving farther into the room.

"What is it with bikers and their limited vocabulary?" the doctor asked as he released Josie.

She wiped her eyes, but when she looked at me, there wasn't anger. Just sadness. It made my nape prickle, and I moved farther into the room, noticing the little girl lying on the table, too still. Too pale. Her eyes were closed, but they opened and focused on me. I moved across the room slowly and reached out to stroke her red hair.

The Reaper standing nearby glanced at me, but his expression was blank. I think that worried me more than Josie apparently having a breakdown of some sort.

"Hey, pretty girl. Not feeling good?" I asked softly.

She just blinked at me.

"What's wrong with my daughter?" I asked the doctor.

His eyebrows shot up and he glanced at Josie, who gave him a slight nod. Like I fucking needed permission to hear about what was wrong with my kid.

"It started as an ear infection and some redness and swelling in her throat," the doctor said. "But now she's getting weaker, and her fever has spiked to 104.3. I was going to run some tests, but with Allegra's history, I think it would be better if Josie took her to the hospital."

History? What history did my kid have that made him so worried? Was he talking about her being premature? I hadn't realized that was something that would affect her for the rest of her life. It was just a fever, right? She could take antibiotics and be good as new. Wasn't that how all this worked? I looked at Josie and I could tell she was about two seconds from falling apart again. I reached for her and pulled her to my chest. My hand pressed to her lower back while I tangled my other hand in her hair. She started crying again, her hands clutching at me.

"It's going to be fine, baby," I said, pressing a kiss to the top of her head. "She'll bounce back and be running around in no time."

"I can't lose her," Josie said between sobs.

"I can call an ambulance to take her, or you can drive her to the ER yourselves," the doctor said. "She'll be treated faster if an ambulance takes her. Those cases are always a priority."

"Ambulance," Savior said. "We'll wait until Allegra has been taken, then we'll follow. I'll call Tank and the others. I'm sure they'll come wait with us."

"You can ride with me," I said, my hand tightening against Josie's back. Fuck. She felt perfect in my arms, even if the circumstances weren't ideal. I hadn't realized just how much I'd missed her, missed holding her, until this moment.

The doctor left to make the call, and about ten minutes later, paramedics came through to get Allegra. Josie cried even harder when they walked out with our daughter, and Savior followed them. I held onto Josie, keeping her back long enough for her to pull herself together.

"Come on, baby. I need you to dry your tears. Allegra needs us to be strong if she's feeling sick, right?"

She nodded and I wiped the tears from her cheeks.

"I want to hate you. I feel like I should scream at you and throw shit, but… I'm glad you're here," she said. "I don't think I can go through this alone again."

"What happened before?" I asked.

"Allegra was two months premature. I'd been on bed rest for over a month because my placenta tore, and they worried I would lose her. Then a few days after she was born, she had an intraventricular hemorrhage. They said it sometimes happened in babies with underdeveloped lungs. She was so damn small, only four pounds. They said if she'd been full-term, she would have been a nice healthy weight."

"What's that intra... whatever?" I asked.

"She had bleeding on her brain. I don't remember all the technical stuff they said, but it was a grade two, which meant she shouldn't have long-term effects. It's possible, but not as likely. But she's not developing as quickly as she should. She didn't walk until she was over a year old, and she has yet to speak."

"I'm sorry." I smoothed her hair back. "I should have been here. Why didn't you ever call and tell me I had a daughter?"

She looked away before meeting my gaze again. "You made it really clear you didn't want kids. I knew Allegra hadn't been planned, and I didn't want you to feel like I'd tried to trap you. I'd forgotten that some medications can alter the potency of birth control pills. About two weeks before I met you, I'd gotten sick and taken some antibiotics. My doctor said that the birth control pills would have needed a month to build back up in my system before being effective."

"You should have called, Josie. I don't know that I would have reacted any better than I did when I showed up on your doorstep last week, but at least I would have had the option of being part of her life. Of being part of yours." I slowly lowered my head, and when she didn't pull away, I pressed my lips to hers in a brief kiss. "I missed you."

"We should go to the hospital and wait for news on Allegra."

I nodded and took her hand. "Come on. We can take my bike."

When we got outside, she hesitated before she climbed on back of my Harley. "This doesn't change things, Jackal. You left us. Pretty much called me a whore when you did show back up. I'm vulnerable right now, but if Allegra wasn't sick, I wouldn't be getting on this bike with you. Wouldn't have let you kiss me in there."

"I'm not leaving Alabama without you, Josie. You or Allegra. We can talk as much as you want, but I'm taking the two of you home with me. It's why I took so long to come back after finding out I was a dad. I had a few things to take care of, make sure Allegra would have a nice home."

She just stared at me a moment before sliding onto the back of my bike. With her arms around my waist and her body pressed to mine, I was taken back to that first night we'd met. I'd never been hotter for another woman, and hadn't met her equal since then. For two years, the part of me that had been missing was Josie. I'd just been too stupid to admit exactly how much I wanted her in my life. I'd thought it was something I'd eventually get over. Even when other women hadn't appealed to me I'd thought maybe one more taste, and then she'd be out of my system. I should have known better. A woman like Josie only came along once in a lifetime.

I pressed my hand over her clasped ones, then I pulled out of the parking lot and drove to the hospital. Hopefully, the doctor was just being overly cautious and Allegra was fine. I wouldn't admit to anyone just how fucking scared I felt, having seen her so pale and lifeless on that table. I'd lost nearly two years with my daughter, and if something was seriously wrong with her, then I could lose out on having her in my life completely. And that scared the shit out of me.

When we got to the hospital, I parked near the ER entrance and walked inside with Josie. Savior was already there, along with Torch, Venom, Tank, Flicker, and two other Reapers. Even a few Prospects were leaning against walls or sprawled in chairs. I didn't know if the show of support was for Josie or because of how much everyone loved Allegra. The doors opened behind us and a hand landed on my shoulder. I looked over at Scratch, who gave me a nod, then Stripes and Phantom came in behind him. I wondered if Shadow was coming too, or if he'd stayed behind to help guard Zipper's woman. If that's why my club was even still here. No one had said whether or not the threat was over.

We all moved farther into the room, and Josie went to sit with her brother. Tank wrapped an arm around her, then glared at me. As much as I wanted to sit with Josie, hold her hand, it was obvious the Reapers didn't want me here. They closed ranks around her and I was left standing on the outside. Instead of telling them to fuck off, I gave Josie some space. She was stressing over our daughter, and I didn't want to upset her even more. I'd done that enough already.

It felt like we'd waited forever before a doctor came through.

"Family for Allegra Baker?" the doctor asked.

Josie stood up and I had a what the fuck moment. My kid didn't even have my last name? Had she listed me on the birth certificate at all? Or was Alabama one of those states where I had to be legally aware Allegra existed before that could happen? Just another thing to deal with later. I moved in closer to stand by Josie and hear what the doctor had to say.

"Ms. Baker, Allegra is resting comfortably. We gave her something to help her sleep. The best ENT in the state works at this hospital, and he'll be taking over Allegra's care until she's released to go home. Her ear infection is pretty severe, and she has strep. From the tests we've run, there don't seem to be any other issues," the doctor said. "Because her fever is still high and doesn't seem to be dropping, we're going to admit her for observation. With her medical history, we don't want to take any chances."

"Can we see her?" Josie asked.

"You may. If the father is here, he can go with you. Everyone else will need to remain out here," the doctor said.

Josie looked over at me and I reached for her hand. It surprised me when she didn't pull away. We followed the doctor through the ER doors into the back, and he showed us to a curtained-off area where Allegra was asleep, looking way too small on the big bed.

"You can talk to her," the doctor said. "She's just sleeping, but maybe hearing your voices will assure her that she's not alone."

"Thank you," I said, shaking the man's hand as Josie claimed the only chair by the bed. I placed my hand on her shoulder and gave it a little squeeze.

"I'm sorry," Josie said softly. I thought she was talking to Allegra until she looked up at me. "I wasn't trying to be a bitch by not telling you about her. I genuinely thought you didn't want either of us, and I thought I was doing you a favor by not telling you that I was pregnant."

"What's done is done, Josie. The question is how do you want to move forward?" I asked. "Because I want the two of you to move in with me. I know your family is here, that the Reapers have been a big support system for you, but Devil's Boneyard will treat this little girl like a princess too. If you give us a chance."

"I don't have anything against your club, Jackal. I'm not sure moving Allegra away from her doctors is a good idea, though. She's been a sickly little girl. I told you about her slow development, but there's more. She gets sick very easily because she has a weakened immune system. This isn't her first ear infection. I just didn't realize what was going on because she wasn't pulling at them like she usually does."

"Just think about it, Josie. Please. I've missed out on almost two years of her life. If we live in separate states, how much more will I miss?" I asked. "I know we don't have women in the club like you do here, but we can figure everything out. Don't shut me out. I know I was an asshole, a really big one, and I'm sorry."

"I can't think about this right now," she said, rubbing at her forehead.

She was right. This wasn't the time or place, but we did need to talk, and soon. I'd stay as long as I could, but Cinder would eventually need me for a job. Not to mention, I had no idea where I was going to sleep while I was here. I didn't think the Reapers were going to welcome me anytime soon.

Josie talked to our daughter, rubbing her arm, and soothing her. I didn't have the first clue about being a dad, so I mostly stayed out of the way, but close enough Josie would remember I was here, in case she needed me. We stayed in the ER for over an hour before they found a room for Allegra in the pediatrics ward. An orderly rolled the bed up to that floor and we followed. Josie sent a text to her brother once we were settled and the nursing staff had checked on Allegra. It didn't take long for the Reapers and my brothers to make their way up to us, but they hung out in the hall, only two coming in a time.

"She's tough," Tank said. "She's going to be fine, Josie."

"I know. I just hate seeing her here, all sick and pale. Makes me remember those first days."

He gave her a hug and I hung back. Savior had come into the room with him, and the man was eyeing me like he hadn't decided yet if he should toss me out the nearest window or let me keep breathing. I didn't know what his connection was to Josie and my daughter, but I wanted to ask. As beautiful as my woman was, I knew that other men wanted her. It wouldn't surprise me if someone had made a move on her in the nearly two and a half years I'd been gone from her life. And that was my fault, not hers. She was right. I'd made it clear that I never wanted kids those days we'd pretty much stayed in bed, fucking like rabbits. She'd had no reason to believe that I would want anything to do with her or a kid when she found out she was pregnant.

"We're going to have a Prospect here at all times," Tank said. "It will likely be Ivan since you seem to like him. Not in the room with you, but in the waiting room down the hall. You text or call him if you want or need something, even if it's just some coffee or something. They'll take turns hanging out for a few hours at a time until our little angel can come home."

"You don't have to do that," Josie said.

"Are you going to leave her long enough to go eat?" he asked.

She pressed her lips together and he smiled a little.

"Yeah, that's what I thought. So humor me. I want to make sure you pass out while you're at her bedside." Tank looked at me. "And I guess you're staying too?"

"Yep." I nodded toward one of the recliners in the room. "I'll sleep there."

"I guess Ivan can bring you food too," he said, stared at me hard, then kissed Josie on the cheek before he left.

Savior lingered a moment and gave Josie a hug, then kissed Allegra on the forehead. "You need anything, you call. If the Prospects are falling down on the job, you let me know."

"Thanks, Gabe," Josie said softly, her gaze still on Allegra.

The man didn't seem to care that Josie had just called him by his given name, but it pissed me the fuck off. She'd never called me anything but Jackal, even when I'd been balls deep inside her. I didn't like that the two of them seemed close. Closer than I was with Josie. It wasn't right.

He stepped out, and for the next hour it was a revolving door between Reapers and Devils coming to check on Allegra and give their support. Josie looked overwhelmed so I shut the door and dimmed the lights. She gave me a grateful smile as I pulled one of the recliners a little closer to the bed and urged her to sit. There were shadows under her eyes and she wore a pinched expression that told me just how worried she was about Allegra.

"They said you slept an entire day," I said. "You sick too?"

She shook her head. "Just tired. I haven't slept more than maybe an hour or two a day lately. Even before she was fussy and showed symptoms of being sick, she was having trouble sleeping. It was easier to just stay up and try to nap when she did."

"You can't do that, Josie. You're going to run yourself down, and when you collapse, who will watch Allegra?" I asked.

"Savior helped me the last few days."

I growled. I tried to hold it back, but I couldn't, and she looked up at me in surprise.

"I'm not yours, Jackal," she said.

"Eric."

"What?" she asked, her brow furrowing.

"You can call that asshole, Savior, by his given name, so you can damn sure use mine. Call me Eric when we aren't around the others."

"Eric," she said, then stared at me. "You never told me your name."

"Never?" I asked, trying to think back to our few days together. And I realized that she was right. I'd never given her my name. No wonder my kid didn't have my name. She hadn't even fucking known it. Christ. I really was a fucking asshole.

"Guess we were too busy doing other things," she said, her cheeks flushing.

It made me wonder how many times since, then she'd done those other things with other men. I didn't have a right to feel jealous. I'd walked out, never looked back. There was no way a gorgeous woman like Josie had been single all this time. I was just glad she hadn't married someone, or become an old lady for one of the Reapers.

I had a lot of shit I needed to fix. I'd fucked up badly when it came to Josie and my kid. I had no doubt that if Allegra weren't sick right now, Josie would have slammed the door in my face this morning when I showed up at her house. And maybe she would have been right to do that. I'd fucked her, gotten her pregnant and abandoned her, and never even told her my name or gave her my number. Assholes did shit like that, and when it came to her, I didn't want to be an asshole. She wasn't some club slut, and she deserved a hell of a lot from me.

I just hoped I hadn't figured all that out too late.

Chapter Five

Josie

Jackal being here with me was a little surreal. When I'd found out I was pregnant, I'd wanted to call him several times, wanted him by my side, holding my hand. I'd convinced myself he'd never want me or our daughter, and so I'd thought I was doing the right thing and left him alone. He'd made it abundantly clear he didn't want kids, and I hadn't wanted him to feel trapped and obligated to hang out and spend time with us. Maybe I'd been wrong, though. If I'd told him, at least he'd have had a choice about being part of our lives.

It was nearly three in the morning and he was passed out in the other recliner, even though he cracked his eyes open every time a nurse came in to check on Allegra. Her fever was down some, but it still hadn't broken. I worried that something else was going on, something they hadn't discovered yet. It should have dropped more, shouldn't it?

I quietly got up and went into the adjoining bathroom and shut the door. Then I sagged against the wall in the shower area and started crying. The stress of Jackal being back, of Allegra being sick, it was all too much for me. I wanted to believe that he was here to stay, that he meant what he said, but I was scared and angry. The way he'd walked out the first time and never called had hurt, even though he'd been clear up front it wasn't anything long-term, and then he'd taken off when he found out about Allegra had infuriated me. I wanted to strangle him, scream at him, throw things. But I was so damn tired. Emotionally and mentally drained from fighting for so long on my own.

I had Tank, and I was grateful for him, but it wasn't the same. Your brother holding your hand while you were pregnant, or hovering in the waiting room while you gave birth, wasn't the same as the father of your child holding your hand and being with you through it. And all Allegra's illnesses had taken their toll on me. I didn't know how much longer I could keep going on my own like this. Jackal was here, and I wanted to reach out and grab onto him, hold on and never let go, but at the same time I was terrified he'd change his mind and take off again. He'd proven that he was a runner.

The door opened and Jackal stepped inside, his eyes cloudy with concern as he shut the door behind him. He moved toward me, not stopping until we were toe to toe. Gently, he reached up and wiped the tears from my cheeks. I stared up at him, wanting to melt against him, to beg him not to leave again, but refusing to be that damn weak. When his head lowered, I braced myself for that jolt I always felt when he kissed me, like lightning had reached out to stroke me. His lips brushed against mine and something inside me broke. I didn't want to face anything alone anymore, didn't want Allegra to not know her father. I wanted Jackal, needed him. Not just for my daughter, but for me too. I gripped his biceps and clung to him as he deepened the kiss, his hands squeezing my waist and pulling me closer.

I hadn't been with a man since Jackal left, and my body was starved for attention. My nipples hardened, and I felt my panties grow damp. Tightening my grip on him, I pressed closer, rubbing against him like a cat in heat. I couldn't even remember the last time I'd had an orgasm. I sometimes snuck a waterproof toy into the shower with me, but it wasn't the same as being with a man. Jackal began unfastening my pants and my heart started to pound.

My body was different from the last time he'd seen it. My hips were wider, my breasts were bigger, and I had stretch marks across my belly, breasts, and thighs. I was nervous about him seeing me, but I wanted him too much to push him away. My hands trembled as I clutched at him, but he pried me off him and slowly lifted my shirt over my head. When it hit the tiled floor, I forced myself to watch his reaction. Heat flared in his eyes as he reached up to cup my breasts, his thumbs rubbing across my hard nipples.

"Fuck, Josie. You're so damn beautiful."

I tried to hide the marks across my stomach, but he pulled my hands away.

"There isn't a part of you that I don't want to worship with my tongue. These marks," he said, caressing them softly. "They're part of you. Your battle scars from carrying my kid. You think seeing them is going to turn me off?"

"Maybe," I said. "No one's seen them. They're ugly."

Jackal dropped to his knees and pressed a kiss to my belly, right across the silvery stretch marks. "They're not ugly, Josie. No part of you could ever be ugly. You're beautiful inside and out."

He tugged at my jeans, stopping to remove my shoes, then peeling the denim off me. My bra and panties didn't match, and were far from sexy. My bra was just a plain black satin, but the panties were pink-and-black-striped cotton. I called them my mom panties because there was no way they were going to make any man want to rip the clothes off me. Not compared to the sexy things I used to wear.

Jackal ran his hands up and down my thighs, then leaned in close and breathed me in. He tugged at my panties until they fell to my ankles, then I stepped out of them. He gripped one of my legs and placed it over his shoulder, opening me up. My breath caught as he moved in closer, his tongue lapping at my pussy. I moaned and bit my lip, trying to stay quiet since our daughter was asleep in the other room.

"You taste as good as I remember," he said. "Maybe better."

"Jackal…"

He drew away and gave me a heated look. "What did I tell you?"

"Eric," I said softly.

He winked, then went back to tasting me, teasing me with that wicked tongue of his. The tip circled my clit before brushing across it and I nearly screamed as my knees buckled. Oh yeah, a flesh-and-blood man was way better than my toy. Or maybe it was just this man in particular. The first time I'd seen him I'd wanted him with a hunger I'd never felt before, and after all our time apart, that hadn't diminished even a little. I still craved him like a woman with PMS craves chocolate.

Eric held me open as he feasted on my pussy with his lips and tongue, his teeth occasionally grazing my clit, making stars burst across my vision. He kept me on edge, getting right there and then not letting me fall. I wanted to come so bad, and I was seriously close to begging. When he pulled away and stood up, I wanted to cry in frustration, but I was quickly silenced by his mouth as he kissed me hard and deep. I heard his belt buckle and the rasp of his zipper. Before I could even process what was happening, he had my legs around his waist and he was balls deep inside me.

I cried out, my head tipping back as he drove into me over and over. He curled an arm around my waist, holding me tight as he took what he wanted from me. I was more than fine with it since I hadn't experienced pleasure this incredible since the last time we were together. It felt like Eric was consuming me, and our passion burned so hot, I worried it would scorch us.

His thumb brushed across my clit, and it was enough to set off the best orgasm I'd had in years. My toes curled and I nearly blacked out. I felt the hot splash of his cum inside me and my eyes went wide.

"Eric! We forgot protection."

He smirked, his cock still pulsing inside me. "Didn't forget. I wanted to feel you bare again. Never been bare with anyone but you."

My heart nearly broke because I knew there had been women after me. I'd been celibate since he left, but a guy like Eric? Yeah, no way he'd not been with other women. He must have noticed the look on my face because he kissed me softly and nuzzled my ear.

"I haven't been with a woman in about two years, Josie. And there were very few since you. None could compare after I'd had a taste of you. If I could do things over, I would. I'd have stayed, or taken you with me," he said.

"That doesn't change the fact you could have just gotten me pregnant," I said.

"I'm okay with that, if you are," he said. "I'm sorry, Josie. I'm sorry I fucked up, more than once. But I want you and Allegra in my life, want to take you home with me, be a real family. If other kids come along, then I'm all right with that too."

"What if another baby is just as sickly as Allegra? What if it's born too early, or I have a miscarriage?" I asked, fear taking over.

"Hey." He smoothed my hair back from my face and forced me to focus on him. "Whatever happens, we can face it together. I'm not leaving this time. Even if you pushed me away right now, I'd just come back."

Tears gathered in my eyes and he slid from my body, gathering me close and holding me tight. I cried against his chest as his hand rubbed my back and he murmured comforting words in my ear. When I was finished, I sniffled and wiped my eyes.

"Get cleaned up and sit with Allegra. I'm going to head down and see if the cafeteria is still open. You should probably eat something. You've barely picked at your food today," he said.

"All right. A sandwich from the vending machine would be fine, though."

Eric kissed me again. "You need better food than that. If I have to leave and hit a twenty-four-hour place, then that's what I'll do, but you need a hot meal."

He zipped up his pants and left me to clean up. When I got back to Allegra's bedside, he was gone and our daughter was awake. She blinked at me, then smiled softly, reaching for my hand. I wished she could talk to me, tell me what she was thinking, how she felt about meeting her father. Now that her eyes were open and she seemed alert, she'd get to officially meet Jackal for the first time. She'd seen him at our house when he'd found out he was a dad, but I hoped she didn't remember the words that had spewed from his mouth that day.

"Baby girl, there's someone I want you to meet if you can stay awake long enough, okay?" I said.

She nodded, the smile never leaving her face. I hoped, for her sake, that what Jackal had said was true, that he was here for the long haul. That he really wanted us, wanted a family. If he broke her heart, I didn't think there was a force on Earth that would save him from me. I'd tear him apart one piece at a time with my bare hands. I just hoped that putting my trust in him wouldn't backfire.

He returned a half hour later with a fast food bag in his hand. When he saw Allegra was awake, his smile was nearly blinding. Jackal handed the food to me, then knelt at his daughter's bedside and reached for her hand. She gave him a look before turning to me, a question in her eyes.

"Allegra, sweetheart, I'd like you to meet Jackal. He's your daddy."

Her little eyes went wide, and then she turned to look at him again. She reached for his beard, tugging on it before exploring his face with her fingers. Jackal reached up and pressed her hand to his cheek before kissing her palm.

"Hey, sweet girl. I'm so glad I finally get to meet you," he said. "I wish I could have been here sooner."

She just stared, seeming fascinated by him.

"When you're better and able to go home, we'll sit down with your mom and have a talk. I bought a house for us where I live in Florida. I think you'll like it. There's a playset out back and you have a room with toys. It's a pretty pink like your room at your Uncle Tank's house," he said.

My lips twitched. "She doesn't call him Tank."

Jackal glanced at me. "Then what does she call him?"

"She doesn't call him anything since she can't talk, but I always refer to him as Uncle Zach. And she loves her Uncle Zach, don't you, angel?" I asked.

Allegra nodded slowly, her gaze still locked on her father.

My heart squeezed at the look in her eyes. I hadn't realized until this moment just how much she'd wanted to know her father, and I felt horrible for not having reached out to Jackal. I don't know that she understood enough to really wonder about Jackal all that much, but I could tell she'd noticed the other kids had both a mom and dad when we went out places. Jackal should have known about Allegra. If he didn't want her, then it would have been his choice. When she asked why he hadn't been in her life the first two years, I'd have to admit that I'd kept her from him, and I didn't know how she'd handle it. We had a lot of years before that happened, or so I hoped. It would give me time to figure out exactly what to say. She didn't need to know that I'd thought he didn't want either of us. No child ever needed to hear that their parent didn't want them.

"Eat your food," Jackal said, tossing me a glance before looking back at our daughter. He seemed just as mesmerized by Allegra as she was by him.

I dug through the sack and pulled out a grilled chicken sandwich with a side salad. I didn't know how he'd guessed that I liked honey mustard dressing, though. I held it up and looked at him, my eyebrow raised.

"Tank. I called to see what you liked to order from that place. He suggested the salad with honey mustard. And I thought the chicken would be better for you than a greasy burger."

"Thank you," I said. "Aren't you going to eat?"

He shook his head. "I ate earlier when you were picking at your food. I'll be fine until breakfast. Besides, I'm pretty good at living off coffee."

I snorted. Yeah, coffee and probably a heavy dose of alcohol if he was anything like the Reapers. I loved my brother and his club, but they could drink an Irishman under the table. Jackal spoke softly to our daughter, telling her about his home and a little about himself. I smiled as he talked about the antics he'd gotten up to as a little boy, and tears misted my eyes when he talked about losing his family.

Allegra eventually fell asleep, but I could tell she was fighting it. I smoothed her hair back and kissed her brow.

"Rest, my little angel. Your daddy will still be here tomorrow," I told her. Before, I would have worried about making such a promise, but the way Jackal was watching his daughter, I knew he wasn't going anywhere. Not by choice.

Jackal moved his recliner closer to mine and reached for my hand. It felt nice, sitting with him and just holding hands. Comforting. I'd always associated Jackal with being wild and only thinking about sex, but it seemed there was another side to him that I'd never seen before. Of course, maybe if we'd spent our time together somewhere other than a motel room, I'd have seen this other side. I had a feeling that getting to know Jackal would be worth it. I'd written him off as another oversexed biker, but maybe I was wrong. Not that he'd done anything before to dissuade me from that idea.

"What are you thinking?" he asked, rubbing my hand with his thumb.

"I'm thinking that there's more to you than I realized," I admitted.

"We have a lifetime to figure each other out, Josie. All you have to do is say yes to moving to Devil's Boneyard territory."

"What would this move entail, exactly?" I asked. I had a feeling it was more involved than just moving to his house. He'd said something about wanting to keep us, be a family, but I hadn't been thinking clearly at the time.

"You'll be mine. My old lady. Mother of my children," he said.

"So, I'm good enough for a patch you can rip off, and good enough to fuck, but not good enough to marry?" I asked, unable to resist teasing him a little. Watching men squirm when the M word was mentioned was always entertaining.

"Married?"

I bit the inside of my lip so I wouldn't smile at the slightly panicked look on his face. He let go of my hand and rubbed his palms up and down his denim-clad thighs. He glanced from me to Allegra a few times before looking around the room. I could almost see the urge to bolt, but he stayed put. I had to give him points for that. The Jackal I'd come to know would have run in terror by now, and probably headed straight for home.

Jackal ran a hand through his hair. "You want to get married? Like stand before a priest and say vows?"

"Well, I'm not Catholic so a priest wouldn't be necessary."

He was so twitchy that it was hard not to laugh, but I decided to stop being mean and put him out of his misery.

"Eric," I said softly, drawing his attention back to me. "We don't have to get married. But if I'm not living with Tank, then I'm going to need to figure out health insurance for our daughter. She's on the state insurance here, but you don't live in the state, so…"

"I hadn't thought about that," he said softly. "The Devils have healthcare, but I don't think I can add the two of you to mine."

"Unless we're married," I said, waiting for that panic to cross his face again, but instead I saw… resolve?

"Okay," he said. "Let's do it."

"Um, what?" I asked, knowing I had to have misheard. "We don't even know each other and you want to marry me? Seriously? What if I move in with you and we can't stand each other? I was just teasing about getting married."

"Maybe you were, but I need to make sure Allegra is taken care of. Cross all the t's and dot all the i's. That sort of thing."

"And marrying me will do that?" I asked.

"I want to know that both of you will be taken care of. The future is uncertain, especially with the shit that seems to rain down on my club, but I don't want anyone to question whether or not you're entitled to keep the house, any vehicles we get, and my life insurance money. And no, I don't have a policy right now, but I'm going to get one."

"Eric, slow down," I said, smiling slightly. "We'll move with you, when they clear Allegra. I'm not taking any chances with her health, though, so you'll have to wait. Even when they discharge her from the hospital, we should probably stay a little bit to make sure she's really in the clear."

"You're good at this," he said, waving a hand toward our daughter. "Being a mom. I never saw you in this role, but I can tell she loves you and that you've taken good care of her. It's obvious she comes first for you."

"I've had nearly two years to practice. I was scared shitless when I found out I was pregnant. Thankfully, Tank let me live with him so I didn't have to deal with my mother. If it weren't for him and the Reapers, I'd be married off to the highest bidder and our daughter would likely have been adopted out to someone."

"What?" Jackal's eyebrows slammed down into a hard line and his jaw clenched. "What the hell does that mean?"

"The night we met I was furious and acting out. My mom had given me an ultimatum. I either went back to college or I did what she said. Which happened to be marry some balding guy who was like thirty or forty years older than me. He wanted an heir so my dear, sweet mother was going to auction off my virginity and my womb."

"That's what the outburst was about that night?" he asked. "Is that why you ran off with me? To get back at your mom?"

"No. I went to the clubhouse that night to demand that Tank do something to help me, but meeting you… that was just a bonus of being there. I'd never been tempted to ride off with someone before, but one look in your eyes and I was hooked."

He winked. "Yeah, I'm sure it was my eyes that hooked you."

"Shut up," I muttered, my cheeks burning. "All right. So I checked out the rest of you."

"That's okay. I couldn't take my eyes off you. The second you walked through the door, storming in like you owned the place, then putting that Prospect in his place? I was a goner. I was used to women using their bodies to get a leg up in the club. I'd never seen anyone like you, acting like the queen over her domain and demanding shit from guys three times your size."

"I knew Tank and the Reapers wouldn't hurt me. If anyone there had grabbed me with the intention of harming me, Tank would have ripped their heads off. He likes to be all gruff and blustery, but deep down, I know he loves me."

"You don't look anything alike," Jackal said.

"We have the same dad. Different moms. Our dad tended to get around. He was a Nomad for another club. I guess the biker gene is in our blood. Tank is one, and I seem to gravitate toward them."

Jackal narrowed his eyes. "Speaking of that. What exactly is your relationship with Savior? He seems to be a little too familiar with you."

"Down, Cujo. Savior is like a brother to me. All the Reapers are, except Torch. He's more like a dad to me. Don't ever tell him I said that, though, since his wife is about two seconds older than me."

"How old are you?" Jackal asked. "I mean, I know I'm probably robbing the cradle, as they say, but you were legal the three days we spent together, right?"

"You don't remember Tank announcing to everyone I was nineteen? Relax, Eric. I'm twenty-two as of six months ago."

"Still robbing the cradle," he muttered.

"How old are you?" I asked. I'd pegged him at being around my brother's age that first night we'd met, and I wondered how close I was in getting it right.

"I'm thirty-eight. For another month," he said. "Too damn old to be claiming a twenty-two-year-old."

"Really? So there's something wrong with the relationship between Isabella and Torch?" I asked. "Or between Bull and Darian?"

He held up his hands. "No. They all seem to be perfect for each other."

"My age wasn't an issue when Allegra was conceived," I pointed out.

He smiled a little. "No, it wasn't. I guess I just felt like you'd get tired of being with someone so much older. I'll be fifty and you'll still be young and ready to take over the world."

"Eric, I have a toddler. I can barely function most days, much less plot world domination."

He chuckled and leaned back in his chair. "I was serious, Josie. I think we should get married. If for no other reason than for Allegra. I want her to have my name."

I chewed on my lower lip for a moment, thinking things over. He seemed sincere, and I didn't want to push him away, not after he seemed to be making a genuine effort where his daughter was concerned. Maybe for me too, even though he'd claimed it was for Allegra. But marriage? I hadn't been serious when I'd brought it up. Just having him sit here and not take off was huge enough. I never really expected a ring out of this. After having Allegra and the way men avoided me, I'd figured I'd be single until she was out of high school. Maybe forever.

"I'll make a deal with you," I said.

"What?"

"Stay here long enough for Allegra to regain her strength, get to know the both of us, and if you still want to get married we'll talk about it again. But you're going to have to figure out a place to stay. I don't see my brother offering up a spot in his house."

He snorted. "No, probably not. He gave me a black eye first time I came back here. All things considered, I'm surprised he didn't do far more. His brothers held him back, but Tank is a big bastard. If he'd really wanted to break free and beat the shit out of me, I'm sure he'd have managed it."

"No doubt. You'd knocked up his baby sister and ran off, never to be heard from again. Well, until recently. He wanted to go after you when I found out I was pregnant, but I wouldn't let him."

"Why?" he asked.

"You didn't want kids, and I didn't want you to feel trapped."

Jackal ran a hand down his face. "I'm so fucking sorry, Josie. If I hadn't stressed the fact I didn't want kids when we were together, then maybe you'd have reached out. Sometimes I can be an asshole."

"Just sometimes?" I teased. "Come on, Jackal. You have that alpha biker thing going on. Trust me, you're an asshole most of the time."

"Yeah, maybe." He smiled at me. "But I promise I won't be an asshole with you. Not anymore. If you'll give me a chance, I'll prove that things can work between us."

"Two weeks. After they release Allegra, you're to remain here two weeks and show that you can be the man we need. After that, I'll check with her doctor and see when she can move, if you've proven yourself. And I'll prove myself too. I didn't exactly act all that grown up and responsible when I kept your daughter from you, even if I did think I was protecting her. Neither of us is perfect."

He lifted my hand and kissed it. "Maybe not, but perhaps we're perfect together."

I felt hope for the first time since finding out I was pregnant with Allegra. I just hoped that fate didn't fuck me over. That fickle bitch had a way of screwing with my life.

Chapter Six

Jackal
One Week Later

I'd done everything Josie asked of me. With some help from the Reapers. After a long conversation with the officers of the Dixie Reapers, I'd convinced them I really did want a chance with Josie and my daughter. They'd let me stay in a furnished duplex inside the compound so I'd be close enough to spend time with my family. It hadn't been easy. Allegra had stayed in the hospital for two days, until they were convinced her fever was gone for good and she was on the road to recovery. Since then, I'd done my best to show Josie that I wanted to be a good dad for Allegra, but I seemed to always fuck shit up. Didn't help that I knew jack about kids.

The toy in my hand was the first I'd given my daughter, and I worried she wouldn't like it. I'd spent enough time with her to know she loved her dolls and books, but I'd thought maybe she'd like something a little different. I'd found some plastic blocks that were a lot bigger than Legos and thought she might enjoy putting them together. Now that I stood in front of Tank's house, I was second-guessing myself. I'd played with blocks, cars, and trains as a kid, but I didn't have a clue if a little girl would be into those things.

The door opened and Josie leaned a hip against the doorframe. "Are you going to stand there all morning or come inside?"

I went up the steps, brushed a kiss on her cheek, then stepped into the house. We hadn't been intimate since that one night I'd found her crying in the bathroom at the hospital, but I'd caught the heated looks she threw my way. I'd decided to arrange for an adults-only night, and I hoped she wouldn't think I'd overstepped. Tank had offered to watch Allegra, but I'd sworn him to secrecy. Something told me it had been a long while since anyone had surprised Josie, and I wanted to be the first.

"A present for Allegra?" Josie asked, nodding to the gift bag in my hand.

"Yeah. I wasn't sure how well she did with wrapping paper, and my skills at that kind of thing are pretty shitty. Gift bag seemed easier for both of us."

"She likes presents." Josie smiled and tugged me into the living room, where Allegra had already made herself comfortable on the floor and her favorite cartoon was playing on the TV. She was sitting on a blanket with unicorns on it, a few toys scattered around her.

I hunkered down next to her and touched the wisps of hair around her face, smiling at the little angel. She blinked at me, then stuck her thumb in her mouth. Josie had said it was something she did when she was nervous or upset. I didn't like that I made my daughter feel either of those things, but I knew it would take time for her to get to know me. I was trying, but some days it didn't feel like enough.

"Morning, baby girl. Daddy brought you something," I said. Handing her the bag, I watched as she pulled the package of blocks out, but she seemed confused.

I took the bag from her and unzipped it, then pulled out some of the brightly colored blocks. I put a few together and showed her how it was done. Allegra's eyes lit up and she grabbed the blocks and started making stacks of them. When she'd put them all together, I showed her how to take them apart and she started all over again.

"I think she likes them," Josie said.

"So, I had a question for you," I said. "And you can say no, but I'd really like for you to say yes."

"You're being cryptic, Jackal. Just spit it out."

"Eric," I reminded her. I was Jackal to everyone else, but to her I wanted to be Eric. Jackal was the name the club sluts had screamed, and Josie was different from them.

"Fine, Eric. Just tell me whatever it is."

"I've arranged for Tank to watch Allegra tonight." I cleared my throat. "All night."

Her eyebrows did that slow climb that was honestly a little frightening. I'd seen her do that right before losing her shit a time or two since I'd come back, and I hoped I wasn't about to have something launched at my head.

"All night?" she asked.

"I thought we could go to dinner, maybe catch a late movie…" I shoved my hands into my pockets. "Maybe you could stay over."

She rose from the couch and moved closer, the sway of her hips mesmerizing me. Josie reached out and trailed a finger down my chest, not stopping until she reached my belt buckle, and fuck if my cock didn't stand at attention.

"Are you saying you want in my pants?" she asked softly.

"Will you throw me out if I say yes?"

She glanced at our daughter, who wasn't paying us the least bit of attention, then Josie turned us so my back was facing our kid. There was a playful look in her eyes as she unfastened my belt, then unzipped my pants. My heart nearly stuttered and came to a halt as she plunged her hand into my underwear and gripped my cock, giving it a firm stroke. I braced my hand on the wall behind Josie and leaned into her touch.

"Christ, woman. Is now really the time for this?" I asked, my voice deeper than usual as that soft hand worked my cock.

"I think you need a little relief before tonight." She smirked at me, then looked over my shoulder. Allegra must have still been ignoring us because her gaze latched onto mine again as she stroked me harder and faster.

"You're going to make me come in my pants," I warned. "Then I'll have to go home and change."

She looked at Allegra once more before pulling me around the corner, just out of sight. She tugged my pants down, then dropped to her knees. The second her lips wrapped around me, my legs turned to jelly. She sucked, licked, and teased. It didn't take but a minute before I was coming, filling her mouth with my cum. Any other time, I'd have been embarrassed, but my woman just had that effect on me. I'd gotten off every night by my own hand while picturing her on her knees just like this. It was like a wet dream come true.

Josie swallowed it all, then licked her lips and gave me a sassy look. As she got to her feet, I pinned her to the wall and growled.

"Woman, if our daughter weren't right around the corner, I'd fuck you so damn hard you wouldn't be able to walk for a week."

"Later." She winked, then disappeared back into the living room with Allegra.

I breathed hard for a moment, then zipped up and joined them. Allegra seemed oblivious, thank God. Not that she would have had a clue what was happening at such a young age, but I didn't want to scar her for life either. Josie had already claimed one corner of the couch, but I knew if I sat next to her, I'd never keep my hands to myself. I eased down onto the opposite end, and she winked at me. Damn woman. She knew she was turning me inside out, and I had a feeling she was enjoying every second of it.

I spent the morning with my girls, went out to grab some lunch for us, and stayed until Tank walked in the door. He might have agreed to give me a night with Josie, but I knew he was still pissed at me for taking off. Both times. Couldn't blame him. If I had a sister, I'd probably feel the same if some douchebag ran out on her. I'd had my reasons, but looking back, they'd sucked. My first priority should have been my daughter, the moment I'd found out about her. Instead, I'd been a chickenshit.

I gave Tank a nod, then headed out to my bike. A glance back at the house made me smile as my little girl had her nose pressed to the window. She gave me a wave and I returned it before getting on my Harley and heading to my temporary home. As I drove through the compound, I had to admit that the Reapers had the right idea, keeping everyone behind the gate. There was around-the-clock protection for them and their families. The Devils had a decent amount of land but nothing like this.

I walked through the door of the duplex, and shut it before pulling out my phone. I wasn't an officer with my club, but I hoped that our Pres would listen to me. Now that I had a family to think about, I wanted to see some changes in my club. Josie would be the only old lady, and Allegra the only kid. Scratch was the only other brother with a kid, and his was an adult, near Josie's age.

The phone rang a few times before Cinder picked up.

"Any trouble?" he asked.

"No. Are we expecting any?"

"Not at the moment. Is this a social call?" Cinder asked.

"I'm calling because I think the Reapers have the right idea. On some things anyway. Their compound is fucking huge, and they all live inside the gates, which means their women and children have twenty-four-hour protection. I know the bad shit we've been dealing with is finally over, but if more comes to our door, Josie and Allegra could be targeted."

"And you want me to what? There's no way we're fitting a bunch of houses inside our gates like the Reapers have. Or are you suggesting that we move the club? Because we've had this clubhouse for over fifty years, ever since the Devils moved to this town."

"I don't know," I admitted. "I just don't like the idea of Josie and Allegra being in danger. I just bought that house before I came here. I mean, I haven't signed the papers yet, but the previous owners let me move in and pay rent until everything goes through. I've already asked the Prospects to make some changes to the house."

"When you get back, we'll throw some ideas around and put it to the club. Maybe we could put up some sort of apartment building inside the compound that could be used as a safe house when trouble comes knocking."

"Thanks for listening, Cinder. I'm just worried about Josie and Allegra. I'm still trying to convince Josie to move back with me, and she's seriously thinking about it. She said she wanted time to get to know me better, and I appreciate you giving me the time away from the club," I said.

"Honestly, I'm hoping this goes well for you. You're not the only one who would like to have an old lady. Let's just say that you're my guinea pig. If it works out for you with Josie and your kid, then maybe there's hope for the others," Cinder said. "It's time for things to change around here."

I couldn't have agreed more, but I was happy to hear my Pres say that. We talked a few more minutes, and then I hung up. Tossing my keys and phone onto the bar that separated the kitchen from the living room, I sprawled on the couch and stared at the ceiling. I'd been with more women than I could count since the age of sixteen, but only one had ever made me feel nervous. Josie. She was the only one I'd ever wanted to keep, had ever thought about for longer than a night. She mattered when all the faceless women from my past were a blur. And because she mattered, I was worried I was going to fuck this up. Royally.

I had a feeling that tonight was extremely important. I'd been in town long enough now that she had to have some idea as to whether or not she wanted to leave with me. Allegra had a doctor's appointment scheduled in five days to see how she was doing. It was my hope that he would give her the all clear to move, and Josie would start packing to go back to Florida with me. I had a really big obstacle in front of me, though. Not only my habit of running on her, but she had family here. Not just her brother by blood, but all the Reapers treated her like a sister or daughter. And they all doted on Allegra. Taking her from here wouldn't be easy, but I was a Devil and I needed to go home.

The minutes ticked by, slowly at first, then faster. When it was creeping up on time to pick up Josie, I took a long, hot shower, then dug through the small amount of shit I'd packed, but it was all the same. Black or gray tees, jeans, and my boots and cut. Not that I really owned anything nicer back home. I was a pretty basic guy when it came to my clothes, and since I'd never done the dating thing, not since high school, I hadn't had a need for nicer shirts. Fuck. I should have used my time to go shopping.

The clock mocked me, showing I only had enough time to oil and comb my beard, put some shit in my hair, and head out. I felt like a fucking girl, worrying over my appearance, but this was my first official date with Josie, and I wanted everything to be perfect. I wanted to win her over and prove that she wouldn't be making a mistake by moving back with me. It was a lot of pressure to put on one night, but I knew my time was running out.

When I was as presentable as I was going to get, I grabbed the small box I'd hidden in my bag, and drove over to Tank's house. I knocked on the door, and he answered with Allegra on his hip. He looked me over and shook his head before stepping back and letting me inside.

"What?" I asked.

"You look like you do any other time. I'd thought you'd put some effort into this."

Go ahead. Kick me while I'm down.

Josie came down the hall, and my cock got hard just looking at her. She had on some sort of black pants that molded to her curves, and a fitted top that left nothing to the imagination. Calf-high boots clicked on the wood floor as she came closer and fuck if I didn't want to see her wearing those, and nothing else. She smirked and I wondered if she'd read my mind.

"Ready?" I asked.

She nodded, then gave Allegra a kiss and her brother a hug. My daughter waved at me and I reached out to grab her hand, giving it a kiss. No way I was getting close enough to Tank to do more than that. He might have agreed to watch Allegra so I could take Josie out and keep her out all night, but I could tell he wasn't thrilled over the idea of me and his sister being together.

I got on my bike and Josie swung her leg over the seat behind me. Her body pressed against mine, her thighs gripping my hips. When she wrapped her arms around my waist, she clasped her hands right over my belt buckle and I fought back a groan. I backed the bike down the driveway, then headed for the front gate. As we turned onto the main road, her hands dropped a little lower and she gave my cock a squeeze.

I damn near wrecked the bike and I could feel her laughing behind me, but she did pull her hands back up to my belt. No woman had ever gotten to me the way Josie did. I hadn't decided if that was a good thing or bad thing, because it meant she could easily wrap me around her finger. I'd hated seeing her cry at the hospital, and I'd do anything to keep a smile on her face. Was it wrong I hoped that involved multiple orgasms every night for the rest of our lives?

The little Italian place I'd discovered was crowded, but not overly so. I was able to park not too far from the door and I reached for Josie's hand, tangling our fingers together as we walked inside. The hostess settled us at a table by the window and I admired Josie as she sat across from me. I'd seen other guys checking her out as we'd passed, and I didn't hold it against them. As long as all they did was look. First man to flirt with her or touch her would be going home minus a few teeth.

"This is nice," Josie said. "I haven't been here in a while."

I looked around and noticed most of the customers were older. "Not a hot date place?"

She shrugged. "It's a little pricey for the younger crowd. I came with my mom a few times, but it was usually for special occasions. You did realize this is one of the most expensive places in town, right? Because we can leave and go somewhere else."

"Josie?"

She blinked. "What?"

"Shut up." I smiled to soften the words. "I can afford to take you out for a nice meal. The Devils pay me well. I not only handle any jobs Cinder assigns, but I work with Scratch at the garage too."

"Garage?" she asked, sounding skeptical.

I shrugged. "Okay, so it's more of a chop shop. We aren't exactly the kind of club that walks the straight and narrow. But we're not into hardcore shit, and we don't sell women. Not anymore."

"Anymore?" Her eyes went wide.

"Before Cinder took over, the old Pres kept a few whorehouses in the county. We dismantled them when Cinder took over. Our old Pres got us into a lot of bad shit, had people knocking on our door wanting our blood. Cinder has worked hard to clean things up and put all that in our past. The chop shop stays, and we also own a few bars in our county. Sometimes we deal in guns, and we have a small pot field inside the compound. But we don't sell to minors."

She opened and shut her mouth a few times, then nodded.

"Not going to read me the riot act about breaking the law?" I asked.

"Can't really do that when I've been living with the Reapers, now, can I? It's not like they don't do illegal shit too."

I tried not to laugh, but I couldn't stop the smile that spread across my face. Josie was made for this life, meant to be a biker's woman. She'd had a problem with the harder stuff, but didn't care that we broke the law. I had a feeling she'd fit in well with the Devils, if she gave us a chance. And I knew my brothers would love the fact that she could be sassy and sweet. They'd adore Allegra, and she'd get spoiled rotten as the only kid in the club. But first things first…

"Have you thought more about going with me when I leave? If Allegra's doctor says she's okay."

She nodded and stared at the table a moment. "I've had Tank in my life for a long time. I didn't know about him at first, but he found out about me and made sure I knew to come to him if I had any problems. He's been my rock for as long as I can remember. Leaving him won't be easy."

"But?" I was hoping there was a but in there. If not, I was screwed and not in a pleasant way. More in the bend over and take it without lube kind of way. I needed Josie. Wanted her. I just didn't know if her love for her brother would trump whatever we could have together.

"I want to go with you," she said softly. "You've shown me that you're not going to run this time, and that you really care about Allegra. She needs her father in her life. I just want to know that I'll have the freedom to come visit my family whenever I want."

I reached across the table and took her hand. "Josie, I'm not chaining you to my bed. Although, now that the thought is in my head, you tied down and spread open for me is rather pleasant. But no, I won't keep you from your family."

I released her hand and rubbed my hands up and down my thighs before I stood up. I hoped like hell my hands weren't shaking as badly as it felt like they were, then I knelt next to her and pulled the small box out of my pocket. Her eyes went wide, and she stared at me unblinking.

"Josie. I know that we don't know much about each other still, but we'll have a lifetime to learn. I don't just want to be a father to Allegra. I want to be a friend to you. A lover." I opened the box. "A husband."

Her eyes started to tear and she blinked rapidly to hold the tears back. "Jackal, I…"

"Eric," I reminded her. "Only you get to call me that."

"Only me?" she asked softly, staring at the ring.

"Only you, sweetheart. Will you be mine in all ways?" I asked.

She paused, staring at the ring before locking her gaze with mine. After a moment, she nodded and held out a trembling hand. I slid the ring onto her finger and applause broke out around us as I kissed her. As much as I wanted to fly her to Vegas and make her mine right this second, I'd give her as much time as she needed, now that she'd agreed to make things legal. I wanted both my girls to have my last name. Wanted us to be a real family. Something I'd never really had, unless you counted the Devils. My adoptive family had tried, they really had, but I'd been a screwed up little shit by the time they got me and I'd given them hell. I hadn't realized until it was too late that I'd fucked up something good.

My childhood with my junkie mom had been pretty fucked-up, and I was determined that Allegra wouldn't face any of the shit I had to. The people who adopted me had tried their hardest to give me a normal upbringing, but by then, the damage had already been done. I wanted her to have a fairy-tale kind of life, just with Harleys instead of knights on horses. Horses were overrated anyway. They crapped everywhere and could bite.

We broke apart and I retook my seat. Josie kept looking at her ring, making it shine in the light. When our server came to take our order, I wondered how long it would take for the food to arrive and for us to eat, because I was more than ready to take my woman home and celebrate. Preferably naked and with her screaming my name all night long. By the time I got the check and paid for our meal, I was so fucking hard from watching her lips wrap around her fork and the teasing looks she'd been giving me, that I didn't know if I'd make it home before I fucked her.

I was holding it together, mostly, until she grabbed my cock halfway to the compound. I pulled down a darkened alley between two strip malls, and checked out the space to make sure it was dark enough and there weren't cameras.

"What are you doing?" she asked.

"Off. Get off the bike, Josie."

She released me and stood, giving me a confused look. I swung my leg over the bike and reached for her pants. They were made of some stretchy material, and I jerked them down her hips until the tops of her boots stopped them from going any lower. She gasped and her mouth dropped open, but I didn't give her time to process what was happening. I unfastened my pants, then bent her over the seat of my bike.

With one hard thrust, I was buried balls deep inside her, and Josie was moaning for more.

"Fuck, Eric! That feels so good."

I gripped a handful of her hair and pulled her head back. "When you tease me, be prepared to have my cock inside you. Doesn't matter where we are or who we're with. I'll find somewhere to take you."

She whimpered and pressed back against me.

I released her hair and gripped her hips with both hands, driving myself into her hard and deep. She was so fucking wet, and so damn tight. It only took a few minutes before I was coming inside her, filling her pussy with my cum. Some of it leaked out around my shaft and I gathered it on my finger, then teased the tight hole between her ass cheeks. Josie gasped and I felt her tighten around me.

I kept teasing, using light strokes, before I pressed my finger into her slowly. My dick was still hard as a fucking post and I gave her pussy a few strokes as I teased her ass. As she relaxed, I gathered more of our mingled release and added a second finger, stretching her out. This wasn't the ideal place for this, but she looked too damn beautiful spread across my bike.

"You like that?" I asked, working her ass with my fingers.

"Y-yes. Oh, God. Eric, anyone could…"

"Could walk by and see us? See you filled with my cock, my fingers in your ass?" I asked.

"Yes." She whimpered, then it turned to a moan as I added another finger.

"I think you like that idea. The thought that we could be caught."

"Maybe," she admitted.

I used more of my cum to slick her tight hole, then I pulled out of her pussy and spread her ass cheeks wide. Her breath caught as I pressed against her, slowly pushing into her tight ass. I stroked in and out of her slowly, watching as she stretched tight around my shaft.

"Fucking beautiful," I said. "One day, I'm going to record this so you can see how gorgeous your ass looks taking my cock."

"Eric, I…"

I took her a little harder, a bit faster, and soon I was driving deep. I reached around her to play with her clit, pinching it tight. It was all she needed and she screamed out her release. Little shockwaves made her tremble. Her ass tightened on my cock and I pounded into her until I came. My cock twitched and I slowly pulled out, holding her open so I could watch my cum slip out of her. Fucking perfection.

I helped her right her clothes, then zipped up my jeans. Giving her a hard kiss and a smack on the ass, we got back on the bike.

"Now that the appetizer is out of the way, we can go home and get to the meal," I said.

"Appetizer? I'm not sure my legs work anymore," she said.

I chuckled and revved the engine, then headed back to the Reapers compound. If she thought her legs wouldn't work now, wait until I was done with her. I had her all to myself tonight, and I planned to fuck her all night long. When my cock wasn't inside her, I'd be teasing her with my tongue, making her come over and over again. By morning, she'd be hoarse and wouldn't be able to walk. But who knew when we'd get another chance to have a night to ourselves? I was going to take full advantage.

Something told me she wouldn't mind, not with the way she was clinging to me. When we got to the duplex, the bike had barely come to a stop when she'd hopped off and run for the door. I smiled and went after her. Once the door shut, our clothes came off, and we didn't even make it as far as the bedroom the first two times. I took her hard and fast against the door, making it rattle on its hinges, then the wall in the hallway was christened. By the time we made it to the bed, my dick needed a break, but my tongue was in perfect working order, and I was more than ready to make her come for hours.

Best. Fucking. Night. Ever.

Chapter Seven

Josie

Holy hell! Jackal had kept me up all night and well into the morning when we'd gone on our date. When his cock hadn't been in my pussy or my ass, his head had been between my legs, and that talented tongue of his had me screaming his name. I was sore, but in a way that had a permanent smile on my face. Yeah, I looked thoroughly fucked even three days later. Tank said I was glowing, and I was convinced that nothing would burst my bubble of happiness. But you know what they say about tempting fate…

Jackal was in the living room playing with Allegra, and Tank was in the kitchen sucking down coffee like it was the elixir of life, when a knock sounded at the front door. I went to open it, thinking it was a Reaper looking for Tank. And came to face to face with a man I didn't know, but I recognized his eyes. Because I saw them every morning when I looked in the mirror. He had the same dark hair as Tank, though.

His gaze scanned over me before he looked me in the eye. "You've grown up, Josie. Not going to give your old man a hug?"

My heart hammered in my chest and I gripped the door tight. "Why the fuck should I give you a hug? You're just a sperm donor."

He rocked back on his heels and nodded. "Guess I deserve that."

I raked my gaze over him again, stopping at the cut he wore. He'd been a Nomad, or that's what Tank had told me when I'd asked about our father. A drifter who didn't belong to a chapter, wandering from place to place. But he'd never once said which club our dad belonged to, just that he wasn't a Reaper. I stared at the patch and his name. *Demonic Reign -- Abraxas*. I'd heard of them before. Everyone had. They brought terror and chaos everywhere they went. And my father was one of them? No wonder Tank had kept that little tidbit to himself.

"Tank!" I yelled out.

I heard the scrape of his chair and his booted steps as he came closer. He pulled the door loose from my iron grip, and then I heard him growl.

"Told you not to come here anymore," Tank said.

I looked up and his gaze was narrowed. His lips were firm as he glowered at our father. Or maybe father wasn't the right term. He'd fucked our moms and ridden off into the sunset, leaving a piece of himself behind and not much else except broken hearts. I'd wanted to meet him when I was little, but then Tank had found me and I'd settled for having a big brother. Now I was glad I'd never met the man before. A chill went down my spine at the cold look in his eyes as he stared at Tank.

"Son," our father said.

"I don't know why you're here, but you can turn the fuck around and leave," Tank said, trying to slam the door, but our dad caught it.

"Now is that any way to treat family?" our dad asked.

"You're not family," Tank said.

Jackal came up behind me, our daughter in his arms. "Everything okay?"

"Our sperm donor was just leaving," I said. "Right?"

Our dad looked at my daughter, then his gaze landed on Jackal's cut and that's when everything went to shit.

"A fucking Devil is in your house?" our father said through clenched teeth. "And holding what? My granddaughter?"

"Uh, no," I said. "You will never be considered her grandfather. Not even if hell froze over."

"Over my dead body will I let you hook up with a Devil," my father said. "He leaves. Now."

I folded my arms over my chest and pressed a little closer to Tank, trying to block our dad from coming inside. "You don't get a say in who stays and who goes. This isn't your house. Not your town. Not your club. Get the fuck out and stay gone. You're not wanted."

"You're my daughter. Since you're not attached to a Reaper, that makes you Demonic Reign property." My father gave me a cold smile. "And I don't agree to you being with him."

"Are you fucking serious right now?" I asked. "I've never laid eyes on you before today. If I'm property of any club, it's the Reapers. They've been my family for years. I've lived here at the compound for over two years. What is it they say? Possession is nine tenths of the law? Guess that makes me a Reaper. Until I marry Jackal. Then I'll be a Devil."

"And you condone this?" our dad asked Tank.

"She seems to like him, and he's good with their daughter. Besides, Devils and Reapers are family, but Josie is right. You aren't. You've never been a father to either of us, and all the other siblings that we have out there. You're just a piece of shit drifter who can't keep his pants zipped." Tank leaned in closer to our dad "Now get the fuck off my property. I'm calling the gate and if you aren't out of here in the next three minutes, I'll have your carcass put on display as a warning to any who want to fuck with my family."

Our dad's face flushed red, and I would be willing to bet he would pop a blood vessel if he didn't calm down. Not that I cared. Let him stroke out on our porch and drop dead. Wouldn't bother me any. Or Tank. Like I'd said. Abraxas was no family of mine. Never would be. Seemed Tank felt the same way since he'd just threatened the man.

"This isn't over," our dad said. "She's my kid and I don't agree to her being with a fucking Devil."

Tank shrugged. "Don't care. It's never been up to you what any of us did."

He stepped back, pulled me with him, and slammed the door in our dad's face. Then he twisted the lock into place.

"Any of us?" I asked. "Do you know something?"

"Yeah. There are others, but they aren't very pleasant. Dad had a total of twelve kids. Nine of us are still alive. And out of those nine, you and me are the most well-adjusted of the group. We have a brother in Devil's Fury, two other brothers in clubs out west, two more brothers in prison, and our sisters are part of the world's oldest profession."

My eyes went wide. "How do you know all that?"

"Had Wire do some digging a while back. When I found out about you, made me wonder who else might be out there. What I found out about them made me take a step back. I didn't want any of those little shits coming to your doorstep."

"I've asked several times and made comments about Dad having more kids. You should have told me," I said.

"Now you know," Tank said.

We moved to the living room and looked out the front window. Dad was standing by his bike, phone to his ear, and casting hateful looks at the house. I had a feeling that things were going to get really bad. I looked over at Jackal and he seemed just as concerned, our daughter held tight against his chest.

"Maybe you should call your brothers?" I asked. "I don't know what he's planning, but it can't be good."

"I'll talk to Torch. We may have to ask Ryker to bring in some Hades Abyss too," Tank said. "I'm not taking any chances with you, Allegra, or the other women and children here. Dad can be a mean bastard, and he's cold as ice. Won't hesitate to kill a woman or kid."

"How do you know that?" I asked. "You've always said you didn't have much contact with him."

"Dad did some time. Rape and attempted murder. His lawyer eventually got him an appeal and he got out on a technicality. There's a reason I've kept the two of you apart. He came here about five years ago, but that was the last I'd seen of him. For a while, he stopped by once a year. Then nothing for two years until that last visit. I'd forgotten that he was given the okay to be inside the compound or I'd have revoked that right when you moved in with me," Tank said. "I'll take care of that now."

Tank hesitated, then kissed my cheek and brushed his fingers through Allegra's hair.

"I'll keep them safe," Jackal said.

"I know you will," Tank said. "And so will everyone else inside the compound. Hopefully, we'll have reinforcements by nightfall."

Jackal handed our daughter to me and pulled his phone from his pocket. "I'll call in some brothers now.

I know that Cinder will give the okay. Josie and Allegra will be the first old lady and kid to live with the Devils, and he will give everything he can to keep them safe."

Tank nodded, then headed out of the room. Jackal gave me a kiss, then left as well. Allegra and I watched as my dad got on his bike and left, then we settled down to watch her favorite cartoon. She didn't seem upset by what had happened, and I was grateful she was too small to really understand. All she'd likely picked up was the anger in everyone's voices.

I tried to keep Allegra occupied while Tank and Jackal worked on keeping us safe. Something was bothering me, though. Why did our dad show up now, after all this time? Had he wanted something in particular, or had he just been passing through and it was rotten luck that he'd seen Jackal and my daughter? Something told me there was more going on than we realized, and that scared the shit out of me.

I dug my phone out of my pocket and stared at it. Did I dare make the call that could save us? Or would it only destroy us? Tank didn't know about the friends I'd made while I was living with Mom or during my year of college. Well, friends was using a bit too broad of a term. I'd dated a few guys and had kept in touch with them until Allegra was born. Not because I had feelings for them, but because I'd thought they might be able to help me at some point. I'd kept Tank in the dark on purpose, knowing it wouldn't go over well. But if there was ever a time to call in a favor, it was now, right?

I looked up the one number I knew would piss my brother the fuck off, and likely the rest of the club too.

"Agent Becker," said a deep voice.

"Drey, I need help," I said.

There was a pause. "Josie?"

"Yeah. I know I stopped returning your calls and texts, but I'm in trouble. And so is my daughter," I said.

"Daughter? So you're married now?" he asked.

"Um, engaged. There's more. It's… my fiancé is part of Devil's Boneyard, and my brother is a Dixie Reaper. It's part of why I kept things casual with us."

He cursed. "Josie, what the hell do you want? I can't step foot inside that compound and you know it."

"Look, Drey, my dad showed up. The one I'd never met? Well, he's part of Demonic Reign MC. I think I'm in some serious trouble. He got really pissed when he saw Jackal and found out we're together."

"What's your dad's name?" Drey asked.

"Abraxas."

The silence on the line scared me more than anything else had this morning.

"Josie, you're in more shit than you realize. Talk to your club. I need permission for me and Logan to come by. You know we'll always have your back."

"Thanks, Drey."

I hung up and gathered my courage, then went to find Tank. My brother was staring out the kitchen window, his shoulders tense and his back stiff.

"Tank, I need to talk to Torch," I said.

Allegra squirmed and I set her down. She toddled over to Tank and pulled on his leg. He smiled down at her and picked her up before facing me.

"Why do you need Torch?" he asked.

"Because I called in my own reinforcements. And they need permission to enter the compound." I swallowed hard. Knowing what his next question would be, I tried to brace myself for his reaction.

"Who did you call?" he asked.

"Agent Drey Becker. He wants to come here, with Agent Logan Pierce."

I could feel the temperature dropping in the room.

"You want to bring two DEA agents inside the compound?" he asked, his voice deceptively calm. "How do you even know them?"

"We dated for a short time when I was in college. It only lasted a few weeks, and nothing happened between us, but we stayed friends. Until I got pregnant with Allegra. I cut off contact at that point."

Tank kissed Allegra's cheek but kept staring at me.

"I'll talk to Torch. If you think those men can keep you and Allegra safe, then have them come to the gates in two hours. We'll talk to them and decide if we're letting them inside. But, Josie, we're going to talk later. You shouldn't have kept that from me."

"I know, and I'm sorry. They're part of my past, Tank. Once I moved in here with you, I made sure I never said or did anything that would harm the club. You know I love all the Reapers. I'd never do anything to bring trouble to your door. Not on purpose anyway."

He nodded, then handed Allegra back to me. "You need to tell Jackal."

I sighed, knowing that wasn't going to go over well. "I'll tell him."

"Call your friends back. Two hours, Josie. If they're a minute late, then they won't be coming inside. And they will be patted down, relieved of all weapons, and searched for wires."

"Fine," I said.

I went back to the living room with Allegra, then called and relayed the information to Drey. Then I sat and waited, hoping my entire world wasn't about to implode. I had no idea how Jackal was going to handle this, but hopefully he would listen and not lose his shit. Dating DEA agents was a big no-no in the world Jackal and my brother lived in. I'd never live it down once they found out I'd dated the guys at the same time.

I just hoped Drey and Logan had learned to keep their mouths shut over the years, but I doubted it. No doubt fists were going to fly.

Chapter Eight

Jackal

I stood next to Tank, my arms folded and my feet braced a shoulder's-width apart, as we stared at the two DEA agents that my fiancée had brought into our midst. I still couldn't believe she'd dated these fucksticks, or that she was still in touch with them. Obviously, we had some talking to do. This was the kind of shit I needed to know about her past. Yeah, she'd been a virgin when I'd taken her that first time, but I'd known she'd been out on dates. Just hadn't expected this.

At least they had ditched their suits and had shown up looking like bikers, complete with Harley Davidsons. It seemed Josie had a type even before she'd met me. One of them had a tattoo on his bicep. A fucking SEAL. Jesus. She'd gone from clean-cut American heroes to climbing into bed with me?

"Where's Josie?" the one on the right asked.

"At home with our kid," I said.

That got their attention. Both of them scanned me head to toe, and I knew they found me lacking from the matching sneers they wore. Too fucking bad. I was Josie's choice, and I wasn't letting her go. But if they could help me keep her safe, then I'd listen to what the jackasses had to say. Couldn't promise more than that, though. What I really wanted to do was beat the shit out of them, just on principle.

"You search them?" Torch asked the two Prospects guarding the gate.

"Yeah, Torch. They're clean," one of them said.

"Good. Come on, then. We'll go talk about this like civilized men. Can't guarantee your safety after the talking's done, though," Torch told the agents.

I heard footsteps behind us and glanced over my shoulder to see Josie and Allegra heading our way. I cursed and went to her, hoping to stop her before she got any closer.

"What the fuck? I told you to stay home," I said.

"What am I? Your dog? Move out of the way, Jackal."

I narrowed my eyes but stepped aside. She walked right up to the two dickhead agents and gave each a one-armed hug, then introduced our daughter to them. Both men softened as they met Allegra, but the steely-eyed glares were back when they looked at me again.

On the plus side, none of the Reapers looked too happy that Josie had associated with the DEA agents. At least it wasn't just me. I knew they'd been together before she'd even met me, but it still pissed me the fuck off. I didn't want to analyze too closely why that was exactly. But I also wasn't stupid. The way they carried themselves, their jobs, their good looks -- yeah, I had to admit they weren't ugly -- I was sure that women fell at their feet. Made me hate them even more since my woman had been one of them.

"It's good to see you both," Josie said. "Thank you for coming."

"You know we've always got your back, Josie," one of them said. "Even if you did pick a fucking Devil over us."

"Be nice, Logan," she said. "I told you guys before that we could only be friends. Sorry, but there just wasn't a spark."

The second one gave a chin nudge in my direction. "But you found a spark there?"

She sighed. "Yes, Drey. I mean it, you two. Play nice. Don't make me regret asking for your help. If I'd thought you would come in and try to pee on me, I would have rethought that call."

Logan snickered, and Drey smiled a little at Josie. "We'll be good," Drey said.

"Park your bikes in front of the clubhouse, then come inside and we'll figure out what the fuck is going on," Torch said. "Devil's Boneyard is sending more men. They should be here soon. Hades Abyss is sending some help too, but it will take them longer to arrive."

Drey focused on Torch. "The three clubs are working together?"

Torch stared, and Drey lifted his hands, backing down. "Got it. Not my business."

"Just remember you're here for Josie, not for a bust," Torch said. "The second I think you can't be trusted, you're out on your asses. Inside these gates, your badge don't mean shit. Not without a warrant."

Drey and Logan both lifted their shirts, showing they didn't have badges clipped to their belts. I watched Josie, seeing whether or not she noticed the ripped bodies the two men were showing off, but she wasn't paying them any attention. Her gaze was locked on me and she came to stand next to me. Allegra reached for me and I pulled her into my arms.

"You should have stayed home, Josie," I said.

"They're here to help me, Jackal. I'm not romantically interested in them. I haven't even spoken to them in about two years, but I didn't know what else to do. I'm scared, okay?"

Her eyes filled with tears and I felt like an asshole. I shifted Allegra so that I could pull Josie against my side. She burrowed into me and sniffled as she fought not to cry. The thought of her with the agents made me a little crazy, but if she said she wasn't interested in them, I would believe her. As far as I knew, she'd never lied to me. While she'd kept my daughter a secret, she'd done it for what she believed were the right reasons. Josie didn't seem to have a mean bone in her body, and I didn't think she'd do anything to intentionally hurt me. Unless she was pissed, then I wouldn't put it past her to throw shit at my head.

"I need to go with them," I said. "Why don't you come sit in the clubhouse with Allegra? I'm sure someone's running the bar and will get you a cold drink."

"All right," she agreed.

I kept my arm around her waist as we walked to the clubhouse and stepped inside. I got her and Allegra settled at a table not too far from the bar, then followed the Reapers into Church. It was a little strange to be in a room filled with Reapers, but if they could help Josie, I was more than happy to hear what they had to say. Even the DEA agents, who looked a little too comfortable.

"What do you have for us?" Torch asked the agents.

Drey didn't shift position or expression. "The man Josie says is her father, Abraxas, has been on the government's list for a while. He's not only dealing massive amounts of drugs, but he's headed up some arms deals, and we believe he's in charge of a sex-trafficking ring. Any evidence we've been able to gather against Demonic Reign seems to always unravel before we can arrest anyone, or things just disappear completely."

"He's also a known rapist, even though no one has been able to get the charges to stick, not permanently," Logan said. "Anytime we get one of them behind bars, they find a loophole and they're out in no time. Demonic Reign has a tendency to make people disappear. If Josie's dad says that he won't allow her to be with Jackal, then I'd take him seriously and expect the unexpected. Asshole is crazy enough to come in guns blazing and try to take her by force."

"Tank?" Torch called out. "He's your father too. Thoughts?"

"The man is bad news, there's no doubt about that. I'm not sure how far he'll go to get Josie. He's never had any interest in her before now, which makes me wonder why he'd show up out of the blue like this. There has to be something in it for him, or for his club. If we can figure out what that is, then maybe we can find a way to stop him," Tank said.

"And if we stop Abraxas, then we'd be taking out a key player for Demonic Reign," Drey said. "It would hit the club hard, maybe even hard enough for them to falter. Even if they don't fall, it might at least spook them enough that they slip up and don't cover their tracks as well."

"Or we can try to get Abraxas to roll on them, but that's doubtful. He hasn't cracked when he's been picked up before," Logan said.

"So how do we find out what they want?" I asked. "Josie said she'd never met her dad before today, but it seemed like he'd come specifically to see her. I don't want anyone to take this the wrong way because I'm crazy about that woman, but what's so special about Josie that he'd come for her? He's never shown interest before. Why now?"

"Wire, were you able to gather any information before this meeting?" Torch asked. "I know we didn't give you much time."

The clicking at the end of the table drew my attention and I saw Wire with a laptop in front of him.

"Still working on it," Wire said. "But what I can tell you is that Demonic Reign doesn't have children, not officially. We know Abraxas has fathered quite a few children, but they're all…"

"Complete and total fuck-ups," Tank said. "You won't hurt my feelings if you speak the truth. The only one who might not be too bad is my brother in Devil's Fury. He did a short stint in the state pen, but that was a while back."

"So maybe he wants Josie because she isn't a fuck-up?" Logan asked. "Does he have other daughters or is she the only one?"

"She's not the only one, but the others are whores," Tank said, putting it bluntly. "And I mean that literally."

"You think he needs Josie to complete some sort of deal?" I asked. "Since he's now seen Allegra, he has to know she's not a virgin. Whatever he needs for her, apparently that isn't important. Unless he plans to take our daughter too."

The Reapers all started cursing and a few banged fists on the table. Whether I liked the Reapers or not, I had to admit they cared about my little girl and about my woman. And I likely would have gotten along with them just fine, if I hadn't knocked up Josie and taken off. Of course, I'd like to think that if I'd known she was pregnant that I would have come back for her. As scared as I'd been of being a father, there were no guarantees, though.

"What are your intentions with Josie?" Drey asked. "Is that ring on her finger the real deal, or are you just jerking her around?"

"What the fuck do you care?" I asked, getting pissed that he felt like he had a right to know. He might have been a part of her past, and he might be here to help, but I didn't like the guy. The only thing that had kept me from putting my fist through his face was the knowledge that I'd been Josie's first.

Tank looked from Drey to me, his gaze somber but thoughtful. "My sister has been wearing an engagement ring ever since your night out. I think I see where Drey is going with this. If you were to marry her now and not later, then if my dad did try something, he'd taking another man's wife and not just an unwed mother and sister of a biker."

"You think your dad is going to give a shit if we're legally married or not?" I asked.

"No," Logan said. "Abraxas won't care about that. But the Feds will. Demonic Reign isn't staying in Alabama, so if he takes her and crosses state lines, then the Feds will be all over it. Especially if he takes your daughter too."

"And the Feds will pay closer attention if she's married? Isn't it their job to give a shit when someone is kidnapped whether they're married or not?" I asked.

"Is there a reason you don't want to marry her right now?" Torch asked.

"She asked me for time. I want to honor her wishes and give her as much time as she needs, and I want her to have the wedding she's dreamed of. All little girls plan their weddings, right? At least, that's what the movies say," I said.

Tank sighed. "Yeah, she has a notebook filled with crap about weddings. She's had it for a while I think, but I didn't see it until she'd moved in with me. I found it in her closet when I went looking for something I thought I'd left in that room."

"Can you get that notebook?" Torch asked. "Maybe if the women can help her create her dream wedding on short notice, she'll still get what she wants, but she'll officially belong to Jackal."

"And Devil's Boneyard," I said. "She'll be our first old lady, and my club is willing to defend her at all costs. Her and Allegra both."

"We just sent your damn club home and now they're coming back," Flicker grumbled. "It feels more like a biker resort around here these days than a damn club. Maybe we need to just put in a hotel out back."

Zipper glared at him. "If it weren't for the Devils, then Delphine would still be in trouble, so keep your bitching to yourself. They helped keep my woman and unborn child safe."

Flicker gave a nod, but didn't look pleased. As far as I knew, he hadn't had an issue with the Devils before so I wondered if something had happened. Not that it was any of my business. Flicker was an officer for the Reapers, and I was just a patched member for Boneyard. I'd leave the political shit to those who held more power.

"Oh, shit," Wire said, the clicking coming to a halt.

"What?" I asked.

"Demonic Reign just received a shit ton of money from some known human traffickers in Colombia, Japan, and Russia. It looks like the mafia families in those countries are expecting a big shipment from Demonic Reign. And there's a wish list in the Pres's email," Wire said. "They really should learn to cover their tracks better. This is all kinds of fucked-up."

"Wait, did you just hack into their accounts?" Drey asked. "You've only been sitting here like fifteen to twenty minutes."

Wire shrugged.

"That's because Wire is the number one hacker in the country," Torch said. "And yes, your government is aware of him."

"What's on the wish list?" I asked, almost dreading the answer.

"The Russians specifically asked for a redhead," Wire said, his gaze meeting mine. "A young, fertile redhead. Josie fits the bill. I think dear ol' dad is going to sell her if he can get his hands on her."

"Can you get that information to me?" Drey asked. "Somehow drop it into my email anonymously where no one can track you? I think we need to get the Feds in on this and add more firepower to our ranks. But I don't want them asking questions about you if that can be helped."

Wire nodded. "I can do it. You'll have it within a half hour. I want to do a little more digging to see what else I can find first. Might as well nail these guys with as much as we can."

"You sure you don't want to work for Uncle Sam?" Logan asked. "We could use someone with your skills."

Wire snorted. "Yeah, thanks but I'll pass. I do enough of your dirty work already."

What the hell was that about? Wire worked with the government? I glanced at Torch, who didn't seem the least bit shocked. The Reapers were just full of surprises. It made me wonder if our own hacker, Shade, provided his services outside the club. I'd never really asked him about the type of work he did, but now I was curious.

"Jackal, I'm going to have Ridley, Isabella, and Darian come over and talk to Josie. It would probably be easier to do that here at the clubhouse. They can take over a table or two and discuss wedding plans. Preacher can marry the two of you so you won't have to worry about that part," Torch said.

"Not Kalani?" Tex asked. "You know she's not as skittish as she was before."

"I was hoping that Kalani and Delphine would offer to watch the kids. They're both pregnant and it would do them some good to see what they'll be getting into," Torch said. "Rocky, think Mara would be up to helping?"

Rocky nodded.

"Preacher, what about Kayla?" Torch asked.

"Morning sickness," he said. "She'll probably stay home with the twins and stay close to the bathroom. Hopefully, it will pass soon."

"Kayla's pregnant again?" Bull asked. "Damn. I'm falling behind. Foster was born before your twins."

Venom smirked. "Considering how long it took you to have Foster after having Ridley, I think you have plenty of time."

Bull flipped him off, and everyone started laughing. I didn't know what the story was there, and I wasn't sure I wanted to know.

"Oh yeah? When are you making me a grandpa again?" Bull countered.

"When your granddaughters stop being hellions so Ridley doesn't threaten to geld me if she ends up pregnant again," Venom said with a snort. "Damn woman asked the doc to put her on birth control."

"Wonder why?" Torch asked. "It's not like Mariah climbs trees, then jumps out pretending to be a ninja, or Farrah decides to cook while everyone is otherwise occupied and nearly blows up the kitchen. Why wouldn't you want a few dozen more?"

Venom scratched his beard with his middle finger.

"All right, assholes. Meeting adjourned," Torch said. "After Hades Abyss and Devil's Boneyard are both here, we'll meet up again. Maybe Wire will have more news for us by then."

Everyone filed out and I went straight to Josie and Allegra. My woman looked worried and I hated that. She should feel safe, especially behind the gates of the compound, but she didn't. Her father had ruined that for her. I pulled out a chair and took Allegra from her.

Everyone seemed to think we needed to get married right this second, but I didn't know how Josie felt about it. It didn't bother me since I wanted to marry her anytime she was ready. But if she needed more time, I didn't want her to feel pressured into doing this now. I was trying to be the man she needed me to be, and that meant listening when she said she needed time, space, or whatever the hell else she asked for.

"Torch thinks we should get married," I said. "As in now."

"How do you feel about that?" she asked.

"I'll marry you anytime you want. You just pick a time and place, and I promise to show up."

She smiled a little. "This is because of my dad, isn't it? Torch thinks I'll be safer if we're married?"

"Something like that. I honestly don't think it will make a difference either way. Your dad won't care about a piece of paper claiming you're mine."

"What do you want to do? And be honest. Don't tell me what you think I want to hear, Eric."

I smiled. "You used my name. It's been Jackal all fucking day."

"Yeah, well, no one else is paying attention to us right now. I figured in front of the guys you'd prefer to be Jackal. Tank has heard me call you Eric, but with the entire club here…"

I nodded and appreciated that she'd thought of that. But then she'd been around the Dixie Reapers for a while now. She'd probably learned what was and wasn't acceptable. Made things a little easier when I made her my old lady. Yeah, there would be differences between our clubs, but the basics she would already know. Not like adding a woman to the family who didn't know shit about bikers or clubs. She'd be the first Devil's Boneyard old lady so some things we'd have to figure out along the way.

"Torch is asking some of the old ladies to come help you plan a wedding, but if you want to wait, just say the word," I said. "I'm not pushing you into marrying me, Josie. You said you needed time and I want you to have it."

"It's fine, Eric. You asked me to marry you and I said yes. I'm not backing out. If Torch thinks we should go ahead and get married, then I'm okay with that."

I kissed her cheek, then smoothed Allegra's hair. "My beautiful girls. I promise you won't regret choosing me, Josie."

"How could I regret it, Eric? You gave me Allegra and she's the most precious thing in the world to me."

I kissed her again, this time on the lips, then made my way outside. I knew my brothers were on their way. It was only a few hours from the Devil's Boneyard compound to the Dixie Reapers' territory. They should be arriving any moment. Only a few had met Josie, and I wanted everyone to like her. I didn't see how they couldn't, but I was a little nervous. I had Cinder's permission to claim her, but if the others disagreed with him, then it could cause problems within the club. And I never wanted that to happen, not over a woman. Josie wasn't just any woman. She was mine, and the mother of my kid, but if the Devils wouldn't accept her I'd have to make a choice, and it wouldn't be an easy one.

I pulled a pack of cigarettes from my pocket and lit up. I had given up smoking years ago, but I still kept a pack on hand for stressful times. And if ever there was a day that qualified, this was it.

Chapter Nine

Josie

After brainstorming most of the day with the Reapers' old ladies, I woke the next morning with a pounding head and blurred vision. It wasn't often I got a migraine, but this one felt like elves were hammering on the inside my skull… and poking my brain with ice picks. I picked up the medication I kept on my nightstand and started to shake out two pills when something made me pause. Setting the bottle down, I reached for my phone and clicked on my calendar… and my stomach dropped.

I'd been so preoccupied with everything going on with Allegra and then my dad showing up, that I hadn't even realized I was late. My period was nearly two weeks late. There was no way Jackal had knocked me up that fast a second time, right? I'd probably just skipped this month because of all the stress in my life. I'd heard that could happen. But what if that wasn't it? I placed a trembling hand against my belly, then texted Darian. I knew she'd been wanting another baby and it was my hope that she had a stash of pregnancy tests in her bathroom. I'd heard she'd been buying them in bulk and took one a week in hopes it would show positive.

My phone chimed a moment later.

Darian: *On my way. Bringing two.*

My stomach flipped, and I hurried to the front of the house, hoping I could open the door without waking up Allegra or Tank. Thankfully, Jackal was asleep on the other end of the compound in the duplex Torch had loaned to him during his stay. Darian's car pulled into the driveway a few minutes later, and she jogged up the steps and handed me two boxes.

"Want me to stay for moral support?" she asked. "Bull is awake and listening for Foster so I have some time."

"Yeah. That would be great. Then at least if I have a meltdown someone can calm me down. Or at least keep me from scaring the crap out of my daughter."

Darian nodded and followed me into the house. We went to the hall bathroom, and she leaned against the wall while I stepped inside and shut the door. My hands shook as I opened the tests, and then I peed on one stick, then the other. When I was finished, I capped them and set them on the counter before washing my hands and flushing the toilet. When I opened the door, Darian stepped inside and we shut it again, staring at the sticks.

"So are we hoping to see two lines on one and a plus on the other, or are you hoping you aren't pregnant?" she asked. "Because I have no problems crossing my fingers and toes, but I need to know what outcome you want so I can send out the right vibes."

I choked on a laugh that sounded a little hysterical even to my ears.

"Right." Darian wrapped an arm around my shoulders. "Whatever happens, it's going to be fine. That man of yours is crazy about you and wants to marry you. I doubt he'll run away if you tell him you're pregnant."

"Yeah. He's here this time and not leaving," I said, more for my benefit than anything. Maybe if I said it often enough, I'd believe it. Part of me still worried he'd up and leave again. As the results showed up on the sticks, I let out another hysterical laugh that ended in a sob.

"All right, Prego, let's get you cleaned up, and I'll check on Allegra while you call Jackal. Everyone needs to know they aren't just protecting you anymore, but you have a baby on board." Darian patted my shoulder. "I'll start the shower, then you get your ass in there and clean up. I'll bring some clothes in and leave them on the counter for you."

"Thanks, Darian."

She shrugged. "What are friends for?"

She started the water and then stepped out of the room, pulling the door shut behind her. I got under the hot spray, and I heard her set my clothes down a few minutes later. The steaming hot water beating down on my head eased the migraine I'd woken with until it was just a dull ache. As much as I wanted to hide in the bathroom all day, I knew I had to face reality. After I dried off, I pulled on the clothes she'd set out for me, then grabbed my phone from the bedroom before wandering to the kitchen. Darian was making breakfast and had a pot of coffee already brewed. I knew from past experience I couldn't have the coffee so I got a glass of juice before sitting down.

Darian pointed a spatula at me. "Call him."

With a sigh, I took the chickenshit way out and sent Jackal a text that we needed to talk. He didn't respond and I figured he was still asleep, or out looking for my dad. The Devils had arrived the previous day, as well as Hades Abyss, and everyone was taking turns not only patrolling the inside of the compound, but keeping an eye out on the town for any Demonic Reign members. Darian scrambled a bunch of eggs, then fried some bacon. I got myself together enough to make some toast to go with it.

The front door opened and shut rather loudly, then I heard booted steps rushing toward us. Jackal stopped in the doorway, his hair disheveled and his expression panicked.

"What's wrong?" he asked.

Darian gave me a look. "You didn't tell him?"

"I said we needed to talk," I said defensively.

She rolled her eyes, plated everything, then gave me a pointed look. "Sit down and talk to your man before he rips out his hair. I'll check on your daughter again, and then I'm heading home."

Jackal sank onto a chair and I set breakfast in front of him before sitting down as well. My hands fidgeted in my lap and I bit my lip, a little worried how he would handle the news. When he'd found out he had a daughter, he'd bolted. Would he take off again or was he really here for the long haul? If he ran, I didn't think I could handle it. Not right now.

"Josie, just tell me what's going on because I'm losing my damn mind right now. Did you see your dad? Did you receive a threat of some sort?" he asked.

"No, nothing like that. I…" I bit my lips again. "I'm pregnant."

He blinked, then blinked again before slumping in his chair. "Pregnant?"

I nodded.

"You're sure? We were only together twice."

"That one night we had sex more than once, but it was probably the night at the hospital," I said. "I should have started my period two weeks ago and I didn't, so I think I must have been super fertile or something that night. The timeline seems to fit that night better than the other one."

He ran a hand down his face, then got up and paced. "Pregnant," he muttered.

I was ready for him to run for the door and never look back, but he surprised me. He came to me, knelt next to my chair, and cupped my cheek. Slowly, gently, he kissed me. The smile on his face wasn't what I'd been expecting. Horror. Panic. Those things I had anticipated. I wasn't sure what to make of the man who was happy that I was carrying his child, not after everything I'd been through with him.

"You're okay with it?" I asked.

"I'm more than okay with it. This time I get to be there for the entire pregnancy and see my kid being born. I missed all that with Allegra, and I don't blame you for it. That's on me."

"I'm scared," I admitted. "It was bad enough before, knowing my dad wanted me and might get Allegra too, but now… What would they do to our baby if they get their hands on me?"

"That's not going to happen, Josie. I won't let it, my brothers won't, and neither will the Reapers and Hades Abyss." He grimaced. "And neither will Logan and Drey."

I fought not to smile. "You really don't like them, do you?"

"No, but you consider them friends, so I'm trying not to beat the shit out of them. The thought of you dating them makes me a little crazy."

Tank clomped into the kitchen, already dressed even though he looked like he hadn't slept much. He raked a hand through his hair and looked at Jackal kneeling next to me and shook his head, then went straight for the coffeepot. He poured a cup and sat across from me.

"It's too early for this shit. Why the hell are you on the floor?" he asked Jackal.

"Just celebrating the fact I'm going to be a dad," Jackal said.

"You're already a dad, asshole," Tank said.

"Yeah, well, I'm going to be one again," Jackal said.

Tank froze with his coffee cup halfway to his mouth, his gaze locking on mine. "You're pregnant?"

I slowly nodded.

"Jesus. You two really need to consider birth control or you're going to breed like fucking rabbits. Either Jackass has super sperm, or you got Dad's fertility," Tank said. "I'd rather not think of either really."

"We have to stop Demonic Reign," Jackal said. "No way they're getting their hands on my family."

Tank nodded. "Wire sent everything he had to the DEA agents, but I doubt they'll get anywhere with it. I think the Feds haven't picked those assholes up yet, they aren't going to do it now. I have a feeling they're waiting on something bigger to happen, or Demonic Reign is a small piece of a bigger puzzle, and they're really after a big fish."

"So what now?" I asked.

"Now I handle things my way," Jackal said, rising and moving to the chair next to me. "I know it can't blow back on any of the clubs, but I'm not letting them get away with this shit. It's not just my family at stake, but what about the other women on that list? Shit, I bet some of them are just kids."

"They are," Tank said. "Wire said there's some fucked-up demands on that list he found. The problem is that putting Demonic Reign out of commission won't stop human trafficking. But we can at least try to save some of the women, starting with Josie."

Jackal nodded.

"What if you used me as bait to lure Dad out of hiding?" I asked.

"No," Jackal said, his eyes narrowed and his nose flaring. "You're not putting yourself in danger."

"You said it yourself, Eric. There could be kids in danger. I trust you to keep me safe, you and the others. I can't just sit here and do nothing," I said.

"Josie --"

Tank cut him off. "Let her do it."

Jackal glared at my brother, but I shot Tank a thankful smile.

"She's a grown-ass woman who has been through a ton of shit," Tank said. "We can make it look like she's alone in town. Maybe near the diner or something. If anyone is watching the area, they'll be looking for bikers. So we'll try to blend in with everyone else."

"I don't like it," Jackal said.

"I'm not asking for permission, Eric. I'm doing it," I said. "And I think the sooner we do it, the better. Like today."

"Christ!" Jackal shot up from his chair, raking a hand through his hair. "Josie, no one expects a pregnant woman to put herself in danger. Not even to save kids. What's going to happen to our baby, to our daughter, if your dad takes you before anyone can jump in and save your ass? Ever think of that? If you get shipped off to Russia, what are the odds I'll ever get you back?"

"Eric, please understand that I need to do this. It's my dad who is causing other people pain. I can't look at myself in the mirror every morning knowing I did nothing to stop him. Do you think our daughter would be proud of her mom for hiding when I could have made a difference?" I asked.

I could tell by his agitated state that he didn't care what Allegra thought when she was older. He was worried, and I could understand his concern. But I also had faith in him, my brother, and the three clubs who were here to help. I didn't think for one minute that my dad would get past them and actually have a chance to abduct me. I thought he would try, if he didn't see any bikers and thought it was safe. But I knew everyone would have my back and keep me safe.

"Tank, please make him understand," I said. "You know I'm right. I can't let anyone else suffer if I can put a stop to it. Even if I just save one or two people, it will have been worth it. Think of their families. Those women are someone's daughters, maybe someone's wives or mothers. Someone's sisters."

Tank ran a hand down his face, and he looked over at where Jackal was pacing. "You and I will stay in colors. Dad wouldn't buy it if she were out alone, but if he sees us, then he'll think we're just arrogant and think we can keep her safe on our own. Everyone else can go in without their cuts, blend into the background. I'll ask the other officers to stay here with the women, so that if we do fall, the entire club won't."

"I can't believe you're letting her do this," Jackal said.

Tank snorted. "You don't know Josie half as well as you think you do if for even one moment you believe you can stop her from doing something once she puts her mind to it. You either give her your support and keep her safe, or she'll put herself out there unprotected."

My brother wasn't wrong. I might have been a spoiled princess, only thinking of myself, when I'd first met Jackal. Having Allegra had changed me. I was older now, but not just in years. I'd had to mature quickly, and it had been good for me. I'd thought my mom would be an issue, but Tank had told her I was under his protection and that she needed to back the hell off. Amazingly enough, she'd listened. She'd also dumped all my shit out on the lawn and set it on fire, but it was a small trade-off for not being under her thumb anymore.

Since that day, I'd grown up, started thinking of someone other than myself. And I wasn't going to shut that off and go back to being spoiled and selfish just because Jackal was worried I would get hurt. I appreciated his concern. I loved that he cared enough about me to worry like that. But I couldn't bow to his demands, not when other people would suffer if I sat back and did nothing.

I stood and walked over to him, placing my hand on his arm. He came to a stop, and the anguish in his eyes nearly took my breath away. I cupped his cheek and softly pressed my lips to his.

"I know you're scared, and so am I, but I need your support. You have to see that this is the right thing to do, the only thing to do. If there's another way to put an end to this quickly, then let me know. Wire has been working nearly twenty-four hours trying to fix this mess, and he can't. The Reapers are my family and I trust them to protect me, just like I trust you to keep me safe. Now I need you to trust *me*," I said.

"I can't lose you, Josie," he said, then placed a hand on my belly. "Either of you. I may not have wanted a family, or thought I didn't, but there's not another woman out there who can compare to you. Don't ask me to give you up when I've finally come to my senses and decided to keep you."

"You don't have to give me up," I said. "But you do have to let me do this. You have to let me try. If my dad doesn't take the bait, then fine. I'll come hide behind the gates again until this all blows over, but don't ask me to sit here and do nothing."

He pressed his forehead to mine and wrapped an arm around my waist.

Tank stood and took his cup to the sink. "I'm going to get Allegra and we're going to give the two of you some space. We'll go over to Bull's and she can have her breakfast with Foster."

I heard him walk out, and it wasn't long before the front door opened and shut. Jackal still gazed down into my eyes, looking conflicted. I hated putting him on the spot, but I wouldn't back down from doing what I believed was the right thing, and he shouldn't ask me to.

"I need you, Josie. I won't stop you from doing this, even though I think you're wrong, but before you go off putting yourself in danger I need to feel you under me again. Maybe it will calm the emotions raging inside me right now," he said.

I backed up and took his hand, leading him to my bedroom. I closed the door behind us, even though I doubted Tank would be back anytime soon. I even twisted the lock just to be sure we wouldn't be disturbed. Then I turned to face Eric and slowly removed my clothes. His gaze nearly devoured me as he looked me over from head to toe. My nipples hardened and I felt myself grow slick with need.

"Eric," I said, reaching for him.

He growled a little, then quickly pulled off his clothes and boots. When he was naked, he pulled me against his hard body and kissed me until we were both breathless. I moved around him and reached into the bedside table drawer, digging to the back where I hid my vibrator and lube, then I dropped them onto the bed. We hadn't had a chance to play with toys any of the times we were together, but there was always a first time for everything.

He glanced at the items, then went to my closet and rummaged inside for a minute. When he shut the closet door, he had two belts in his hand. My heart kicked in my chest and I swallowed hard. Jackal prowled closer and pointed to the bed.

"Hands and knees in the center but close to the headboard," he said.

I gave him a sassy look and fought not to smile. "Yes, sir."

He swatted my ass as I climbed onto the bed. "That might be a game you aren't ready for yet."

If he thought his words would scare me, they didn't. Intrigue me? Yes. Scare me? Not a chance. I'd read enough erotic books to know that I wouldn't mind experimenting with a few things, if he ever asked. I didn't think we were quite to the part in our relationship where he was ready to find out just how freaky I was, at least in my mind. He'd been the only man I'd ever had sex with, and we hadn't experimented too much. Mostly because we hadn't really had the opportunity. But the way he was rubbing the leather of my belts between his fingers and eyeing me like a hungry tiger about to pounce, I had a feeling he would be open to trying new things in the future.

Once I was in position, Jackal used one of the belts to fasten my hands to the headboard. My pussy clenched at the possibility of what the other one might be used for. He climbed onto the bed behind me and pressed his hands against my inner thighs, spreading me wide. I felt his finger trail down the lips of my pussy and he hummed in appreciation.

"So fucking beautiful. I dreamed about this pussy, the years I was gone. Every damn night I remembered our time together. I even woke sometimes reaching for you."

"Eric, please… I need you."

His hand cracked against my ass and I yelped.

"No demands," he said. "In case you missed it, you're at my mercy. I'll make you feel good, but it will be on my terms. Understood?"

I couldn't help myself. I looked at him over my shoulder. "Yes, sir."

His eyes narrowed and he smacked my ass again. "Keep it up and I'll switch to the belt."

His words sent a shiver of excitement down my spine. I'd always been fascinated with spanking romances, even the ones where they used a paddle. He was just turning me on more and probably didn't even realize it. I wondered just how far he would go this time. I already knew from experience that he was dominant both in and out of the bedroom, but I wasn't sure if he was dominant in the *I'm an alpha biker* kind of way, or in the *I will tie you up, spank you, and make you call me Sir* kind of way. I was fine with either.

He picked up the vibrator and switched it on, sliding it across my clit a few times. It was enough to make my body tighten and make me want to beg for more, but not enough to make me come. He chuckled as he teased me with it again.

"So the question is do you want to this little toy in your ass while I fuck your pussy? Or do you want it in your pussy while I fuck your ass? Either way, I'm riding you hard and deep."

I whimpered and my pussy clenched at the thought.

He ran the toy over my clit again and this time pressed it tighter against me. He held it in place until my skin felt like it was tingling and I was so close to coming that I was holding my breath and straining for release. Then he took it away again, making me cry out in frustration.

"Which is it, Josie? Where do you want my cock?" he asked.

He spread my ass cheeks and I felt his finger lightly stroke the tight little hole hidden there. I cried out again, this time in pleasure, as every nerve in my body was buzzing.

"Guess that answers that question," he said with a smile in his voice. "But not just yet."

He got off the bed and went over to my dresser. I heard him pull out several drawers before the bed dipped. I looked over my shoulder at him, but all he did was grin and hold up one of the few scarves I owned. My eyes went wide and I faced the headboard again. Jackal slipped it across my face, making sure I couldn't see, then tied it off at the back of my head.

"Next time we do this, I'm getting you ear plugs too. Then you'll have to only rely on what you can feel, and you'll never know what's coming next," he said.

A shiver raced down my spine, but it was the good kind.

He touched the toy to the top of my ass and slid it down between my cheeks, teasing me with the vibrations as he did it three more times. Then he placed it against my clit again and I heard the bottle of lube pop open. I jumped when the cold liquid splashed between my ass cheeks, then moaned as he began rubbing that forbidden spot with his finger. As the vibrator buzzed against my clit, he slowly worked first one finger into my ass, then another. Every time I got close to coming, he pulled the vibrator away long enough for my body to calm again.

I heard the lube pop open again, then the wet sound of him stroking his cock. He pressed in closer to me, his thighs brushing against mine. He spread me open with his palms, and then I felt his cock press against my tight hole. I relaxed and pushed out as he slowly sank into me. It burned as he stretched me wide, but it turned quickly to pleasure when he pressed the vibrator against my clit again.

Jackal began thrusting, his strokes slow and deep, as if he were trying to draw out the moment as long as possible. The toy buzzing against me was sending waves of pleasure through my body. I came hard, screaming his name, and I faintly heard him groan before he started fucking me harder.

"So fucking tight," he said. "Jesus, Josie. You're about to squeeze all the cum from my balls. But not until you come twice more."

The toy was merciless as he pressed it against my clit, and it didn't even take a minute before my first orgasm was rolling into another. I hadn't even come down from my high yet when he plunged the vibrator into my pussy and fucked me with it while he took my ass hard and deep. Jackal pounded into me, grunting with every thrust. When my third orgasm hit, I bit my lip and stars burst behind my closed eyelids. I felt my ass clench on his cock, and then he was filling me with his cum.

He pulled the toy from my pussy and rubbed it against my clit again. His cock twitched and pulsed inside me, and I was a little surprised that he was still really fucking hard. Jackal removed the toy from my clit and rubbed it against my nipples, and I couldn't hold back my moan, or stop myself from pressing back against him.

"Tell me what you want, baby," he said.

"I want you to fuck me," I said, my voice breathless from how damn good he was making me feel.

"Fuck you where?" he asked, pressing against my ass.

"Fuck my ass again, Eric. Fuck me hard."

His hand cracked against my ass cheek. "Want me to ride this ass? Take what I want?"

"Yes!"

He teased my nipples some more before putting the toy back against my clit. I felt him withdraw nearly all the way out of me before slamming in deep. His hand gripped my hip as he drove into me again and again, taking his pleasure and making me crave more.

"Beg me for it," he said.

"Please, Eric. Fuck me. I want to feel your cum in my ass."

I gasped as he growled and slammed into me harder and faster. I could hear his hips slapping against me with every stroke of his cock, and as I felt his cum splash inside me, I started coming again too. He slowly withdrew from my body, shut off the toy, and I felt him get off the bed.

"Don't move," he said.

The door opened, and then I heard water running in the bathroom across the hall. When he came back, he shut the door and re-locked it before climbing back onto the bed. His shoulders pressed against my knees, spreading me open even more, and as his hands gripped the insides of my thighs, I realized he was lying on his back.

"Eric, what…"

I didn't get to finish my sentence before his mouth was on my pussy. Licking. Sucking. Nipping at my clit. He picked up the toy again and turned it back on, then pressed it between my ass cheeks. He slid the toy deep into my ass and fucked me with it as his lips devoured my pussy. I was shaking, my limbs trembling I needed to come so bad. He pulled several more orgasms from me, not even giving me a chance to take a breath between them.

Eric shifted and his hand tangled in my hair. "One of these days, I'm going to come down your throat, fill up your pussy, then claim that ass of yours. You'll be dripping with my cum and when you think you can't handle anymore, we'll start all over again. Maybe I'll keep this toy handy and fuck you with it again while my cock is shoved deep inside you. All fucking night long."

I wanted that. So much. I'd always been curious about being with more than one man, having every one of my holes filled at the same time, but Eric didn't seem like he'd be into sharing. What had happened between us just now was probably the closest I'd ever get to having two cocks inside me. And I honestly couldn't think of anyone I'd want to bring to the bedroom with us. As hard as he made me come, and as many times, I probably wouldn't survive more than one man at a time anyway.

He fucked me for what felt like hours, taking turns licking me and fucking me. My pussy and ass were filled with his cum when he finally released me and I collapsed onto the bed. He trailed kisses down my spine, then bit my ass before pulling me into his arms.

"Shower," I mumbled, nearly half asleep.

"Nope. If you're going to put yourself in danger, you're doing it with my cum all over you. Maybe then you'll remember what you'll be losing if you do something stupid and don't come back home."

I turned in his embrace and snuggled against his chest. "I'll always want to come home to you."

"You better. I don't think I'd survive losing you, Josie." He hesitated, then I felt his lips touch my ear. "I'm falling in love with you."

I smiled sleepily. "I'm already there."

His arms tightened around me, and I slowly drifted to sleep.

Chapter Ten

Jackal

Josie sat on the patio of her favorite coffee shop, sipping whatever syrupy drink she'd ordered, while Tank and I stood at the counter waiting on our coffees. To the casual observer, we weren't paying attention to anything but the barista making our drinks. But that was a lie. We were both completely tuned in to everything going on around us, and I knew the moment Josie's piece-of-shit dad made an appearance outside. I fought to remain loose and seem oblivious, but my muscles wanted to lock and tense as I thought about him getting his hands on my woman.

I'd introduced her to the Devils who would be watching over her today. Scratch was in town but wouldn't be with us today. We'd decided he might be too recognizable as often as he hung around the Reapers. So Havoc, Phantom, and Renegade were on Josie watch today, as well Flicker, Johnny, Savior, and Coyote with the Reapers. Hades Abyss were so damn well-hidden even I couldn't see them, but Bear, Diablo, and Marauder were lurking somewhere nearby. We weren't taking any fucking chances with my woman and kid. The other Reapers and Scratch were back at the Reapers' compound keeping an eye on the other women and children.

"He brought backup," Tank murmured, not turning or even so much as blinking. "I see at least four Demonic Reign members with him. I don't think he's seen any of our men yet, though."

My gaze shot up and I saw what he was talking about. We could see the entire street in the reflection of the signs over the counter. Josie's dad approached her, even sat down like he was coming for afternoon fucking tea and not to kidnap her. She sipped her drink, but I noticed her hand tightened on the cup. She was scared, even though she'd insisted on doing this. I hadn't decided yet if she was incredibly brave, or crazy. It was probably some mix of the two because it took a set of brass balls for her to dangle herself in front of her dad like that, but I didn't think anyone who wasn't at least a little insane would ever risk themselves and their unborn child for a bunch of strangers. At least, no one I'd ever met would do something like that. But then, Josie wasn't like other women in my life, and that's why she'd stood out.

The asshole reached across the table and grabbed her arm. When he stood and tried to pull her with him, I knew it was time to make our presence known. Tank and I headed out the door and approached Josie's table. Abraxas had managed to drag her around the table and toward the street by the time we reached them.

"Hey, asshole! Get your hands off my fiancée!" I moved faster, my boots pounding on the sidewalk with the force of my fury.

Abraxas sneered at me over his shoulder. "She's my daughter. We're just going for a little ride."

"Right. To the airstrip? I know all about your plans for Josie. Let her the fuck go," I said.

Abraxas looked over at Tank. "Tell him, son. I just want what's best for your sister."

"You're not my dad, and you're sure as fuck not hers," Tank said. "You can let her go, or we can do this the hard way. Personally, I'm hoping you choose the hard way, so I can kick the shit out of you."

Abraxas smirked. "You really think I'd come here alone?"

The other four Demonic Reign members closed in. Tank shrugged.

"You really think we'd come here alone?" he countered.

Abraxas' smile locked in place as his gaze darted around. Like shadows, the Reapers, Hades Abyss, and Devils all moved in, forming a circle around us and Demonic Reign. I looked at Josie, trying to decide if she was in distress, but mostly she looked pissed. While her dad was distracted, she stomped on his foot, jammed her elbow into his ribs, then spit in his face. Before the biker had a chance to retaliate, she moved away from him, but another Demonic Reign member grabbed her.

I didn't know who he was, but he'd just sealed his fate.

"You like having fingers?" I asked him.

His brow furrowed, but he didn't say anything.

"Because if you don't let my woman go, I'll fucking break them to the point they'll never work right again."

He sneered and pulled Josie tighter against his body, grabbing her breast and squeezing. Before I could react, Josie leaned over and bit the man through his T-shirt before shoving the heel of her hand up against his nose. The way he screamed and his eyes watered, I figured she'd broken it, and I couldn't help but smile at her spirit.

Tank charged forward, going after his dad, and I went after the asshole who had just copped a feel. That fucker didn't get to touch my woman without an ass beating. Out of the corner of my eye, I saw Johnny grab Josie and pull her to the side. They cleared the ring of bikers and disappeared from view, but I knew he'd keep her safe. Torch vouched for him and that was good enough for me. After that, it was complete chaos as Reapers, Devils, and Hades Abyss all kicked the shit out of the Demonic Reign members.

No one pulled a weapon except the pussy-ass Demonic Reign. Two had guns and the other three had knives. Not that any of that was going to hold us back. They'd threatened one of our women, a pregnant one at that, and the sister of a Reapers officer. The fury of the men fighting at my side was far greater than that of Demonic Reign. They just wanted a paycheck, but we wanted justice.

My fist collided with the nose of the jackass who had touched Josie, then I hit him again, knocking out two of his teeth. Blood poured down his face and one of his eyes was swelling shut, but the fucker wouldn't go down. He came at me with a knife, but he was sloppy and missed by a mile. With a kick to his wrist, I not only made him drop the knife, but I heard his bones snap. He screamed out and cradled his wrist, dropping to his knees.

It was the moment I'd been waiting for. I moved in closer, nailed him in the balls, watching as his face turned dark red, then I reached for him. Twisting his arm behind his back, putting extra pressure on the wrist I'd likely broken, I listened to him blubber and whine like a little bitch, I grabbed his fingers and jerked them back hard. They jutted out at an odd angle and I knew they were broken, but that wasn't good enough for me. I did the same to his other hand, then ground my boot heel down on all ten fingers, one at a time while he screamed and writhed on the ground.

"Told you not to touch my woman," I said.

I heard sirens in the distance and an unmarked car skidded to a halt. Logan and Drey hopped out and leapt into the fray. They weren't breaking it up, though. Instead, they both launched into an attack on the Demonic Reign members, throwing punches and kicking out a knee or two. If they were worried about a reprimand from their boss, it didn't show. I went after another one who was trying to slip away when I heard more sirens getting close. Two more cars showed up, the officers breaking up the fight, and soon the Demonic Reign members were in cuffs and eating pavement. Thankfully, the Reapers, Hades, and Devils weren't in trouble, thanks to bystanders telling them how we were trying to save Josie from being abducted.

"Which one of you gave us the intel on these assholes?" a deep voice said from the outer edges. Two Feds came through, surveying the scene.

"None of us," I said.

"Well, you tell whoever it was that we owe them one. And don't tell me you had nothing to do with it. Logan and Drey can't lie for shit," the agent said.

I smirked and looked at the two DEA agents, who were standing a little too close to Josie for my liking. I went to get her from Johnny, who was protecting her like a pit bull, glaring at the two agents whenever they tried to move closer. I hoped Torch patched that kid in soon because he was a real asset to the Reapers. I'd let him guard my family any day, and from what I'd heard, Torch relied on him heavily to protect Isabella and Torch's daughter, Lyssa.

"Now that we have some key players in Demonic Reign, we should be able to dismantle them," one of the Feds said. "And all that shit your man sent will definitely be looked into and stopped if we're able."

The Feds, Drey, Logan, and the cops all got into their cars and left. I didn't like the longing look that Logan and Drey gave Josie, but it was obvious they knew she was mine and I could live with that for now.

If they came near her again, though, I might not be able to hold back from putting my fist through their faces.

The Demonic Reign were hauled off, and the rest of us made our way to our bikes and trucks. Josie clung to my arm and I felt her hand tremble. I stopped and pulled her into a tight hug, just holding her a moment. I breathed in her scent and closed my eyes, thankful that she was safe and hadn't been harmed.

"That was harder than I'd thought it would be," she said.

"It could have been a lot worse, baby."

"I know. I'm sorry I was so stubborn about doing this, but I'm not sorry we might have saved some other women. Do you think they'll be able to gather up all the Demonic Reign and put an end to their human trafficking?" she asked. "I know they said they would try, but I'm worried they won't be able to do it."

"I'm sure they have enough firepower at their fingertips to make it happen."

"Take me home, Eric."

"We'll be at the Reapers' compound before you know it."

She tugged on my arm. "No. Take me to our home. The one you bought for Allegra and me. I love the Reapers, and I'm going to miss my brother, but I'm ready to start the next part of my life. With you. If Demonic Reign comes after me again, then I trust the Devils to keep us safe."

I cupped her cheek and kissed her softly. My tongue stroked hers as she parted her lips, but I pulled back before I forgot we were standing on the sidewalk and I lost control. Josie had that effect on me.

"Think Allegra can handle a car ride today? We'd need time to pack your things, and I brought my bike so if everything doesn't fit into your car, then we'll need to make other arrangements," I said. "And she hasn't had her appointment yet."

"I wasn't thinking about having to pack. I don't have much, but most of Allegra's things will need to go. Some can stay here for when we visit my brother. That way she'll have familiar things around her," she said. "As for the doctor, I can make a call and see if they can work her in before we head out of town. She seems to be feeling better so I don't think they'll say she has to stay."

"You know, I tried to set up her room in Florida so that she wouldn't need much except clothes and shoes. Maybe we could pack her favorite things and her clothes and shoes? After you get settled in, if there's anything you want that got left behind we can arrange to have a Prospect pick it up, or invite Tank for a visit and let him bring it," I said.

She smiled and leaned into me. "I like that plan."

I swatted her ass. "Come on, baby. Let's go give your big brother the news."

"Your club won't have an issue with him coming to visit?" she asked. "I know Scratch comes to see his daughter and grandson rather frequently."

"Nah. Besides, we don't live inside the compound like everyone does here. Our house is on a nice quiet cove. It's an older home, but I think you'll like it. And you can change anything you want. I bought the basics, but I didn't really do any decorating."

A hand landed on my shoulder and I looked over at Renegade. He was the Devil's Boneyard Road Captain, and close to my age. We were not only brothers, but we'd become good friends. If I had a best friend at home, I'd say it was Renegade.

"Heard you talking to your woman," he said. "We'll give you an escort home, just to make sure no one fucks with you. Just because the Feds arrested the Demonic Reign who were here today doesn't mean others aren't lurking."

"Thank you," Josie told him softly.

He winked at her, then patted my shoulder before he walked off.

"Let's go get our daughter, pack your shit, and head home," I said. "I'm ready to make you mine, Josie, in every way possible. I won't push you to have a quick wedding, but I will ask you to wear a property patch. Cinder is having one made. I asked Tank for your size so Cinder could put the order in."

"I will gladly wear something that says I'm *Property of Jackal*."

I climbed onto my bike with Josie wrapped around me and drove back to the Reapers' compound. We went straight to Tank's house, and he was already there with Allegra on his lap watching cartoons.

"Took you two long enough," he said we entered the living room.

"I'm leaving," Josie said.

He stared at her hard for a moment, then gave a nod.

"Tonight," she said.

"All right," Tank said. "Knew it was coming. Need help packing?"

"No, but if you could keep Allegra entertained that would be a huge help," she said. "Maybe call her doctor and see if you can get her an appointment while we're packing up? She hasn't had her follow-up visit yet."

"That I can do. I'll miss this little angel," Tank said.

Josie's lips tipped up on one corner. "Maybe you should have one of your own."

He flipped her off, and Josie laughed as she led me to her bedroom. She pulled a suitcase off the top shelf of her closet and started throwing things inside. I helped where I could, but mostly I felt like I was in the way. It took her a few hours to get all their things together, at least the things they were taking right now, and then came the goodbyes. Allegra had gotten the all clear from her doctor and now she clung to her uncle. She didn't want to let go of Tank, even when she was told she was going to see her new home. I hated that she was so upset, but I was anxious to get them home, where they belonged.

When we were ready to hit the road, Renegade rode at my side with Josie behind us in her car, and Phantom and Havoc rode behind her. Scratch was remaining behind to visit his family, and to lend an extra hand if Demonic Reign did reappear and cause trouble. It wasn't an overly long trip home, but it did take a few hours, and at least three stops for Allegra. By the time I pulled into my driveway with my brothers stopping on the street out front and Josie pulling up next to me, I was more than ready to get them inside, settled, and see Allegra's face when she saw her room.

I also wanted to break in the new bedroom furniture I'd bought before heading to the Reapers' compound, if Josie was up for it. There were dark circles under her eyes, and I knew she had to be exhausted after the day we'd had. My brothers helped unload her car, and I carried our daughter straight back to her room.

Allegra's eyes lit up when she saw the pink walls and white furniture. I set her down and she went straight to the wooden toy box and began pulling things out before she spotted the bookshelf and decided to check that out too. Josie leaned against me, a smile on her face as we watched our daughter. I heard my brothers leave and knew they would give us some space for a few days. After that, the entire club would want to meet Josie and Allegra, and I couldn't wait to show them off.

"She'll be occupied for a while," Josie said. She pulled out her phone and took a short video along with a few pictures. She tapped on her phone, then smiled at me. "I figured Tank was missing her by now, so maybe that will hold him over for a bit."

"So what do you want to do while she explores her room?" I asked.

"You could show me the rest of the house," she said. "Help me put everything away. And after Allegra goes to sleep, you can show me how comfortable the bed is."

I winked at her, then led her on a short tour. And she was right, by the time we put our clothes away, Allegra looked about ready to drop. I ordered a pizza so my girl wouldn't go to bed hungry, and after dinner, I put my angel to bed before leading my woman to our room.

As loud as she screamed every time she came, I'd probably have to soundproof the bedroom at some point. Hopefully, the neighbors wouldn't think I was killing her. That would be a fun conversation with the police.

No, officer. I wasn't killing my fiancée, unless you count death by multiple orgasms.

As I twisted the lock on our bedroom door, I let my gaze roam over Josie. She was fucking perfection, and she was mine. My woman, my old lady, the mother of my children... and my soon-to-be wife. I didn't know what I'd ever done to deserve such a great family, but I was going to make sure they knew they were loved. Which meant I should probably tell Josie that sometime soon. She deserved to hear the words.

I just didn't know if this was the right moment.

The heat in her gaze promised a night filled with passion, and my cock stood at attention as she began undressing. I pushed away from the door and started toward her, removing my clothes along the way. When we were both naked, I couldn't help but stare at her. Ever since the first moment I'd seen her, I had thought she was the most beautiful woman in the world. I still felt that way.

Fuck it. She needed to know.

"Josie, there's something I need to say."

"What? It can't wait until we're panting, sweaty, and cuddled in bed?"

"No, it's important." I reached for her and pulled her tight against my body, my cock trapped between us. "Remember when I told you I was falling for you?"

She nodded.

"I lied. I wasn't falling. I've already fallen. I think I fell for you those three amazing days we spent together when Allegra was conceived, but I was too blind and stupid to realize it. I love you."

She smiled and happiness shone in her eyes. "I love you too."

I kissed her long and deep, wanting to remember this moment forever. When I was eighty and riddled with arthritis, unable to get it up without a blue pill, I wanted to remember the look on her face when I told her I loved her, and I wanted to remember how amazing it felt when she said it back.

Whatever it took, I would give her and our kids the best life I could. They were my entire world, and I was pretty sure I'd die without them.

I eased her down onto the bed, then knelt on the floor between her splayed legs. I spread her pussy open and admired how pretty and pink she was, before I leaned in closer and breathed in the musky scent of her arousal. I licked and sucked at her clit until it was hard and standing up. Her thighs squeezed me as I took my time tasting her. Every time she got close to coming, I'd back off, then build her back up again. Her hands clenched the bedding and her hips lifted, silently begging for more.

When my cock felt like it might explode, I stood and gripped her hips. Lifting her, I sank my cock into her sweet pussy, filling her up. She was so damn hot and wet, wrapping around me and pulling me in. For the first time in my life, I made love to a woman slowly, gently, savoring the moment. My woman. I teased her clit as I thrust in and out of her with lazy strokes, until she was begging for more and her body was tight as she strained for her release. She came hard and kept coming as I teased the hard little bud between her pussy lips, my cock going deeper and harder.

I groaned as I came, but I refused to shut my eyes, no matter how intense it felt. I wanted to watch the emotions play across her face as she came again, her body flushed and her breasts heaving. Her hard little nipples were just begging to be licked, sucked, and bitten, but there was plenty of time for that. We had the rest of our lives to have sex in every way we could imagine.

"Mine," I said, as I leaned down and kissed her hard.

"Yours," she said. "Now fuck me you like mean it."

With a grin, I gave her exactly what she'd asked for. I took her hard, fast, and damn near broke the bed as I kept her screaming my name all night long and into the morning hours.

Somehow, I'd gone from being a fuck-up, a man who never took a woman to bed more than once, to being a fiancé and a father. And it was the happiest I had ever been.

Now that I knew how amazing it was to have a woman in my life, in my bed every night, to give her children and make a home with her, I was determined to see every single one of my brothers just as happy.

Wraith (Dixie Reapers MC 8)
Harley Wylde

Rin -- My mom died when I was little, and my dad followed when I was fifteen. My half-brother, the nastiest being I've ever met, convinced the state to grant him custody. My life has been hell since then. Every time I try to run, he finds me. This time will be different. I'm asking the Dixie Reapers for help. If they turn me away, I'm as good as dead, but even that's preferable to what my half-brother has planned for me next.

I didn't count on the sexy man with the dark, brooding eyes. The man who makes me want things I've never wanted before. When he rejects me, I run. Discovering he left a little part of himself inside me is even more terrifying than my half-brother finding me.

Wraith -- I'm not the settling-down type. Maybe once upon a time, but not anymore. Now I'm faced with Rin, the strongest, most beautiful woman I've ever met. She needs a protector, and I'll gladly be that for her. I want her. Want to keep her and make her mine. I've fucked my share of women over the years, but I've never made love to one. Until Rin. But I'm no good for her, or anyone else. She thinks she's not worthy of me, but it's the other way around.

When she runs I feel like a piece of my soul has been ripped out. I need Rin back, and I'll do anything to make her mine.

Chapter One

Rin

I knew my time was up, had been up for a while, and it was past time for me to leave. If I'd been smart, I'd have taken off after my mom died, maybe after I'd become a teen. Living on the streets might have been safer than staying with my dad and brother. Then Dad died and my life had become hell. The problem was that I had no money, no car, and no way of escaping the nightmare I'd been living since the age of fifteen. Somehow, my brother had convinced the state to award him custody of me, and I'm sure it had to do with him calling in favors or paying people off. At first, my brother -- well, half-brother -- had just let his clients grope me, or they'd stared at me while they did other things. By the time I was eighteen, he was using me as a bartering tool to sweeten whatever deal he had going at the time. The last few years, though? Yeah, those were the worst.

Now I was twenty-three, and while there were days I contemplated ending my life rather than living through the shame and horror I dealt with on a regular basis, deep down I was a fighter. I'd learned the hard way not to struggle and fight my fate while my brother had control of me, and I'd tried to escape a few times, only to be hauled back in worse shape than when I'd left. I'd been fighting my own personal war, and I had the scars to prove it. Emotional, mental, and physical ones.

As if things weren't bad enough, I'd overheard Joe's conversation with someone about having the perfect little whore for a brothel down in Mexico, and he'd described me so well I'd known who he meant. There was no way I would ever survive such a thing, and I knew no one would come looking for me. Big brother had made sure of that. Maybe I'd outlived my usefulness, or maybe he was tired of me running. No, my only means of survival was to get the hell away from Joe and find someone to keep me safe. Most people in this town were in his pocket, or terrified of him. I needed someone who wouldn't back down, someone who would retaliate if he came after me. I needed a badass, and those were in short supply.

Not many people in this small town would attempt to take down Joe Banner. He paid enough of the cops that evidence always went missing if he was arrested. I knew Officer Daniels had picked him up a few times, but the charges never seemed to stick. I'd seen the concern in the officer's eyes the last time he'd come to the house, and it was that moment, knowing that someone gave a shit what happened to me that had prompted me to leave, even if I hadn't been able to do it right then. But Officer Daniels couldn't stop my brother any more than anyone else around here could. Except for one possible group of men. The Dixie Reapers.

I'd seen the bikers around town, and knew of at least one woman from my neighborhood who had escaped my brother and was now married to one of the Reapers. Kayla and her twin brother, Johnny, had been in some of my classes at the high school. We hadn't exactly been close, and we certainly hadn't kept in touch after graduation, but I was hoping we had enough of a connection that maybe they would offer to help me. The things my brother had forced me to do were bad enough, but being shipped to a brothel wasn't on my list of things to accomplish in my life. I knew women who were sent there never came back. Taking my own life was different from dying of disease in some hellhole. I didn't think I was the type to take the easy way out, but if I had no other option I might consider it, only if I knew that all hope was lost. I wasn't going to let either of those things happen, though, not without fighting. Now that I'd decided I wanted to live, that I wanted to escape, I wasn't backing down. This time, if he caught me, I'd fight until he killed me. I was done doing whatever Joe Banner ordered.

Approaching the gates, I rubbed my hands up and down my denim-clad thighs. I shivered in the cold air despite the sun shining brightly. It might be the south, but it was also five weeks until Christmas and cold as hell. Thanksgiving had passed just two days ago, and the weather had changed drastically almost overnight. My threadbare coat didn't provide much protection as the wind whipped my hair around me and sent icy chills down my body. A man was leaning against a booth near the gate, and when I approached, he straightened to a rather imposing height. Then again, I was barely five feet tall, so pretty everyone was taller than me.

I didn't recognize him, but I did know the look he had in his eyes. It was the same one I saw every time my brother had introduced me to someone he deemed important. I hated that fucking look, but I bit my tongue because I needed help, and I'd do almost anything to escape my brother. It's not like this guy would ask me for something I hadn't been forced to do already.

"I need to see Johnny or Kayla," I said as I stopped in front of the gate.

His gaze took me in from head to toe. "Are they expecting you?"

"No, but it's important."

He stared at me for what felt like forever before opening the gate. As I stepped inside, his hand closed around my arm and he drew me to a halt.

"Need to check you for weapons," he said with a leer.

Yeah. I just bet he did. I spread my arms out, even though it made me colder. His hands went under my coat and lingered a little too long at my breasts before working down my body. When he pushed my legs apart and brought them up the insides of my thighs, I clamped my legs shut before he could go too high.

"Have to check everywhere," he said.

"Robby, what the fuck are you doing?" a man asked as he came toward us.

"She asked to see Kayla and Saint. Making sure she's not carrying any weapons," Robby said.

The guy eyed me up and down and shook his head.

"First of all, Preacher isn't letting an unknown person anywhere near his wife and kids. Second, if you think Saint can't handle a tiny-ass woman like her, I'll be happy to let him know it."

Robby paled. "Sorry, Gears."

The man I now knew was called Gears held out a hand to me. And from that little bit of conversation, it seemed Johnny was now known as Saint. It fit him. Even back in high school, he'd tried to save people. I was counting on that, hoping he'd be willing to save me too.

"Come on, darlin'. Let's get you out of this cold weather and I'll find Saint for you," the man called Gears said.

"Thank you," I mumbled, trying to stop my teeth from chattering.

He led me up the steps of a building across the lot and held the door open for me. Heat made my cheeks sting and it felt like thousands of needles were stabbing me as my body adjusted to the toasty air. Gears led me over to a small table near the bar and pulled out a chair for me.

"Sit here and I'll see where Saint is. Who do I tell him is here?"

"Rin. From the old neighborhood," I said.

He nodded and went to the other side of the room before pulling out his phone. I couldn't hear anything he said, but he cast a few glances my way. While I waited for him to come back, I surveyed the area. I'd always wondered what the Dixie Reapers compound looked like from inside the fence. This building wasn't quite the way I'd pictured it, and I could imagine a lot of wild parties within the walls. I knew those parties had never used the girls my brother pimped out, though, so whatever women hooked up with the men here did so of their own free will.

The door opened again and two more men came in wearing the leather vests all the bikers wore around town. One in particular drew my attention. His hair was dark, and he had a beard that made me itch to feel it, see if it was as soft as it looked. But his eyes were hard, the kind of eyes I'd seen on soldiers and men who had killed for a living. He moved with lethal grace and came to tower over me. I'd learned long ago to let my shoulders droop a little and hunch a bit to seem smaller when confronted with large, scary men.

"Who the fuck are you?" the man next to him asked.

My gaze jerked over to him and widened a little. The man was huge and more than just a little intimidating.

"Rin," I said softly.

"No outsiders allowed," he said. "If you're here to party, you're shit out of luck. It's family time until the holidays. Whores can come back after the new year."

I swallowed hard and lowered my gaze. Of course he'd call me that. It's what my brother had made me, and I struggled to get up. I couldn't seem to make my legs work quite right, those prickling needles still stabbing me as my body thawed out, and I kept falling back into the chair.

"Why are you here?" the other man asked, his tone softer.

"Does it matter, Wraith?" the bigger man asked. "She's trespassing."

I heard Gears come up behind me. "She's looking for Saint, but he's not answering his phone, and no one has seen him. Even Preacher and Kayla don't know where he is."

"Why do you want to see Saint?" Wraith asked.

"I need help. We went to high school together. I knew…" I stopped and looked at each of them. "I knew that Kayla escaped our neighborhood and that she was living here. I thought maybe the twins could keep me safe."

Wraith hunkered down in front of me, his gaze assessing. "Safe from what?"

"My brother," I said softly. "Half-brother. He's not a nice man and he… he plans to sell me to a brothel in Mexico. I overheard him on the phone."

"Son of a bitch," Gears muttered. "I knew you looked familiar."

My eyes widened as I looked up at him. He knew who I was? Who my brother was? Did that mean he would help, or would they ask me to leave? My heart started to race and my hands clenched. If they kicked me out, I had nowhere else to go.

"How do you know her?" the big, scary man asked.

"She's Joe Banner's sister," Gears said. "She's the one Officer Daniels was worried about. Tank, we can't send her back out there."

"Officer Daniels talked to you about me?" I asked, my brow furrowed. That didn't make any sense. Why would he come to them?

"Who is Joe Banner?" Wraith asked.

"The local pimp. He runs things on the other end of town," Gears said.

I wanted to curl into myself and disappear, especially when Wraith focused on me again. I'd never felt so dirty or ashamed as I did in that moment. A gorgeous man like him wouldn't want to be near someone tainted like me. I would have tried standing again, but he was too close. I wouldn't be able to get up without touching him.

"You work for your brother?" Wraith asked.

Tears burned my eyes but I refused to let them fall as I nodded.

"Told you she was a whore," Tank said.

Wraith pushed my hair behind my ear and forced me to look at him. "You work for him willingly? Or does he have some sort of hold over you?"

"He was my guardian until I turned eighteen, but every time I try to run, he finds me. This was my last chance to get away. I don't…" I swallowed hard. "I never wanted to work for him. I didn't ask for any of those things to be done to me, but I wasn't given a choice."

"She's not a whore, Tank," Wraith said as he stood. "She's a victim. You going to turn your back on a woman in need?"

Tank muttered something under his breath, then shook his head. "I'll call Torch and see what he wants to do with her until we can locate Saint."

"We have a bunch of empty rooms here at the clubhouse right now. She could stay in one of those," Wraith said.

Gears shook his head. "I don't think so. Not with the way Robby was groping her when he let her through the gates. Claimed he was patting her down for weapons, but it looked like more to me. She was trying to stop him from touching anywhere overly intimate."

Wraith's eyes went dark and his jaw tensed. Without a word, he turned and left the building, the door slamming shut behind him.

"Should we go after him?" Gears asked.

"If he wants to defend the whore, let him," Tank said.

Gears scowled at him. "You heard what she said, what Wraith said. She didn't choose that life, Tank. She was a victim. What the fuck is wrong with you? Normally you're the first one to go after abusive assholes."

Tank shrugged, but there was a look on his face that made me think he had a good reason to treat me the way he was. Or at least he thought he had a good reason. I'd be willing to bet that under all his bad attitude was a man who was hurting. Made me wonder if a woman had broken his trust. Or maybe... had he gotten mixed up with one of Joe's girls without knowing it? They'd been known to pick pockets when the clients weren't looking. It would certainly explain the hostility.

Wraith came back in, dragging Robby with him. He had a grip on the younger man's collar, then dropped the guy at my feet. Robby gave me a hateful glare as he struggled to his knees.

"Apologize," Wraith said.

"Sorry," Robby said caustically.

Wraith landed a punch right across Robby's jaw, knocking him out cold.

"Damn. Don't think he'll be apologizing now," Gears said. "Or eating. I think you broke his jaw."

"Shit," Wraith muttered. "We'll need someone else at the gate."

"I'll call in one of the new guys," Tank said.

"Almost makes me sorry we patched in Johnny, Gabe, and Ivan. They were our best Prospects," Gears said.

"I'll get King to watch the gate and have Diego try to find Saint," Tank said. "We're going to need new blood if we keep getting shitty Prospects."

Gears snorted. "You mean like Tommy and Carter? Yeah, I have a feeling Robby will be escorted out of here when he wakes up. Torch won't stand for him getting handsy with someone who came asking for a brother. And then getting attitude when Wraith made him apologize."

"She can't stay in the clubhouse, not after what happened at the gate," Tank said. He looked at Wraith. "Can you take her to your place for now? I'll have Torch head that way as soon as he's able, and we'll figure out what to do with her. We don't seem to have the best luck with Prospects these days, and I can't guarantee she'd be safe here."

Wraith nodded and held his hand out to me.

Gears patted my shoulder. "He'll keep you safe, darlin'. No one would dare try to go through Wraith to get to you. Not even your dumb-shit brother."

"Half-brother," I said.

Gears smiled faintly. "I figured. I've seen Joe Banner, and you two look nothing alike. He's light-haired and definitely white, and you're…"

"Half-Japanese. Dad found my mom in Japan, married her, and brought her back here," I said. "I was born a year later."

Gears squeezed my shoulder. "Go with Wraith, Rin. You don't have to be scared anymore, all right? We'll get it figured out."

Wraith wrapped his hand around mine and led me out of the clubhouse. The icy air bit into me again and I shivered, causing him to stop and stare at me. The man only had on that leather vest thing and a long-sleeved gray thermal shirt. Wasn't he freezing his ass off?

"I don't live far," he said.

He climbed onto a Harley parked out front, then patted the seat behind him. I swung my leg over and clutched at his waist, both thrilled and scared over my first bike ride. The engine turned over, and the bike rumbled between my legs. I held on tight as he eased out of the parking lot and headed to the right down a road that wound through the compound. He was going slow, which I was eternally grateful for, and eventually stopped in front of a white house with blue shutters and a blue door. It was cute, and not at all what I would have expected a rough biker to own.

He turned the bike off and I climbed off, my legs shaking. Wraith got off and went up to the front door, pushing it open. He gestured for me to step inside, and I hurried up the three steps and into the front entry.

The house wasn't all that big, but it was cozy. And warm! The short ride had made my nose get ice cold again, and my fingers were numb.

Twinkling lights drew my attention to the corner of the living room. I went toward the pretty tree and stopped to stare when it was mere inches from me. The multicolored lights blinked, making the ornaments look like they gleamed and glowed. Mom had put up trees when I was little, but after she'd died, so had all our holidays. I leaned closer and breathed in the fresh pine scent, closing my eyes as I remembered better times in my life.

"Ridley's kids made everyone get a tree," Wraith said. "Then Ridley and Isabella brought all the kids ages two and up to every house and let them decorate the trees."

Well, that explained why the ornaments were in clusters and none reached the top of the tree. Kids always seemed to do that, especially the younger ones. To me, it just made the tree more special.

"Who are Ridley and Isabella?" I asked.

"Ridley is married to our VP, and Isabella is the Pres's wife. There's a lot of kids here now that everyone seems to be pairing off."

I was still mesmerized by the tree but couldn't help asking my next question.

"And are you? Paired with someone?"

He gave a rusty chuckle, like he didn't laugh often. "No. No one wants to saddle themselves with me."

I had a hard time believing that. A guy who looked like him? Not to mention, he'd come to my rescue and knocked a guy out for disrespecting me. I'd think any woman would be lucky to have a guy like him, but what did I know.

"I think there's still some hot chocolate packets in the kitchen from when the kids were here," Wraith said. "Or I could make coffee. You look like you could use something warm to drink."

"Anything is fine. Whatever is easier for you to make. You don't have to go to any trouble over me."

He grunted. "If Torch is coming, I'd better brew a pot of coffee. And, Rin?"

I turned to face him.

"Any man who isn't willing to go that extra step for you isn't worth your time. Got me? You should never feel like you're a bother to someone. I can only imagine what life has been like for you, but get that shit out of your head right now."

"Thanks, Wraith."

He scratched at his beard. "Call me Will. Just not in front of anyone else."

I was confused by his request, but nodded. He walked out, leaving me alone once more with the prettiest tree I'd ever seen. For the first time since my mom had died, I felt like my life was my own. There was hope welling inside me, or maybe it was wishful thinking that Joe was in my past and couldn't hurt me anymore. But I knew how much that asshole hated to lose, and he'd try to get me back, no matter what it took. I only hoped the Reapers could keep me safe.

Chapter Two

Wraith

Call me Will... What the fuck had I been thinking? Jesus, it wasn't like I'd never seen a pretty woman before. Looking into her eyes, I should have been reminded of all that I'd lost, not felt this protective urge rise up inside me. Or maybe my past was why I felt so protective toward her. Rin was nothing like the sister I'd lost, except for their circumstances and dark hair, but she reminded me of Elisa just the same. If I'd been home and not off fighting for my country, then maybe I could have saved my sister. I'd failed Elisa, but I refused to fail Rin too. She needed help, and if Saint wouldn't give it to her, then I would.

I made a large pot of coffee, then poured a cup for each of us. I tended to make mine strong enough to strip paint off the walls, so I added some milk and sugar to hers. When I carried the mugs into the living room, she was still staring at the tree, a wistful expression on her face.

"Happy memories?" I asked, handing the cup to her.

She nodded, wrapping her hands around the mug. "My mom used to put up a tree every Christmas, and she'd put spooky decorations out for Halloween. She decorated for every holiday, inside and outside the house. I lost her when I was only five and nothing was the same after that."

"Sorry for your loss, and I'm damn sorry that anyone ever gave custody of you to your half-brother. I wish someone had protected you when you needed it most."

"They say that you're never given more than you can handle, that everything life throws your way just makes you stronger," she said. "If that's true, then I should be a damn hundred-year-old oak. Or maybe a female version of Hercules."

I smiled a little. "Tank scared you at the clubhouse, didn't he?"

"Yeah, a little. I learned the hard way to make myself small when big, scary men are around. It was the only way to survive."

"You said your brother dragged you back when you tried to run." I gripped her arm lightly and turned her to face me. "What did you mean, Rin? I don't for a second think he just hauled you home and that was the end of it."

She worried at her lip a moment, then set her mug down on a table. Before I knew what she was doing, she'd whipped her shirt over her head and my breath froze in my lungs. It wasn't the perky bare breasts that made breathing damn hard. It was the carnage that was now displayed. I'd seen horrors that I could never shake from my mind, but the pain that asshole had etched into her body infuriated me unlike anything I'd experienced before. I reached out slowly and gently ran my fingers along some of the deeper scars. Even her breasts were scarred. She turned and lifted her long hair, and I damn near threw up.

"What the hell did he do to you?" I asked softly.

"It's what happened when I misbehaved. Not all of it was inflicted by my half-brother, though. Sometimes men paid to hurt me. There's more," she said, reaching for her pants, but I stopped her.

"You don't have to undress, Rin. I'm so damn sorry, sweet girl. No one should have suffered the way you have. As long as there's breath in my body, I'm not letting him near you. No one will ever harm you again."

"You can't promise that, Wraith," she said. "You can't keep me safe forever. There's too much ugliness out there."

She wasn't wrong about that, but if she thought for one second I wouldn't do everything in my power to keep her safe, then she was wrong. No one had helped Elisa, but I was going to make damn sure someone helped Rin. And that someone was me. Unless Saint showed up and wanted the job. They apparently had some sort of history, but the thought of his hands on her body made me want to punch something. I rubbed at my chest, having no clue why I felt so savage over a woman I'd just met. Yes, she reminded me of Elisa, but it was more than that. There was something simmering just under my skin that I didn't want to analyze. Something I'd never felt before.

Rin put her shirt back on, then picked up her cup and sipped the coffee I'd made for her. When there was a knock at the door, she tensed and I could see her retreating again. I squeezed her shoulder and brushed a kiss against the top of her head before I could think better of it.

"It's just my brothers. No one will come to the door who isn't part of the Dixie Reapers or trusted by us, all right? You're safe inside these gates."

Or at least she was supposed to be. It wasn't that long ago that a conniving woman had slipped past the front gate and nearly killed Zipper's woman. I'd like to think something like that wouldn't happen again, but I knew better than to tempt fate. She was a fickle bitch and would kick you in the balls when you were already down.

I pulled open the front door and saw Torch and Venom on the front steps. Taking a step back, I let them into my home and noticed the second they spotted Rin. She'd tried to hide around the side of the Christmas tree, tucking herself between the pine needles and the wall. She'd seemed calm enough around me, but I could understand her hesitance to trust strange men. After everything Joe Banner had put her through, it was a miracle she'd even come to us for help at all. A compound full of large men? That had to be her version of hell.

"Rin, it's all right. This is my Pres, Torch, and the VP, Venom. Neither of them are going to hurt you. They're both married and have kids, and I can assure you they would never hurt a woman," I said, trying to get closer to her.

She stared at them with fear in her eyes, but when I held out my hand, she grasped it and let me pull her from her hiding place. Rin pressed her body tight to my side and I felt her shaking. With an arm around her waist, I stared at Torch and Venom, hoping they wouldn't move too quickly and scare her more. I had no doubt they would offer her the protection of the club. Anyone could see that she'd been traumatized by men and needed our help.

"You came looking for Saint," Torch said. "It's odd that you should show up and he's suddenly missing. Don't suppose you know anything about that?"

She shook even harder as she mumbled a no.

"Joe Banner is her half-brother," I said. "She's been abused and needs our help. Saint went to school with her. She didn't just ask for him, she asked for Kayla too."

Venom nodded. "Preacher isn't going to let Kayla anywhere near her until we know more about why she's here. And Saint really is missing. He's not answering calls. Wire is trying to get a location by tracking Saint's cell, but for now, we don't know if he's in trouble or not."

"Rin," I said softly. "They aren't going to hurt you, okay? They need to see what your half-brother did when you tried to escape. I'm just going to show them your back, all right?"

She nodded and turned a little. I lifted the hem of her shirt just to show the lower half of her back, and both men hissed in a breath at the damage they saw. I let the shirt drop back into place and held her close again.

"She's not lying when she says she needs our help," I said. "That's just a small taste of what he's done to her. He also forced her into prostitution."

"I'll call Dr. Myron," Venom said. "Get her there now. He needs to check her over and run some tests, make sure she's clean and that there's not any damage we can't see."

"You all right with that?" I asked Rin. "I can stay with you the entire time, if you'd like. I promise that Dr. Myron isn't scary, and he'll do whatever he can to help you. He's treated Kayla and all the other ladies in the club."

"Okay," she murmured. "If you go with me."

"That coat all you have?" Torch asked.

"Yes," Rin said.

"She looks to be close to Isabella's size before Lyssa was born. I think she still has a few things. They're about four years old, but she's kept them stored and they should be fine. Bring her by on your way home and I'll make sure there's some stuff set aside for her. She'll need clothes and a warmer coat," Torch said. He glanced down at her feet. "And better shoes. What size are you, sweetheart?"

"Seven," she said softly.

He nodded. "I'll see what I can find. If Isabella doesn't have something, I'm sure someone else will."

"Thanks, Pres. Could I use one of the club trucks to get her to the doctor? I don't want her riding around town on my bike in this cold weather," I said. Not to mention she'd be an easier target on the back of my bike than safely surrounded by the metal frame of a truck. If Joe Banner was looking for her, I didn't want to make it easy on him.

"Sure. We're down to two Prospects right now, and both have been assigned jobs, so I'll see if one of the brothers can bring one over for you," Torch said. Then he focused on Rin. "I'm sorry if we scared you. You'll be safe here, and the man who disrespected you has been dealt with. He's no longer prospecting for us, and Wraith broke his jaw so he won't be talking shit to anyone for a while."

I wasn't the least bit sorry about breaking the asshole's jaw. And I certainly wasn't sorry to see him go. I just hoped for the well-being of the club that we could find some decent new blood. It wasn't like we were hurting for numbers, but with the shit we seemed to keep facing there was no telling when we'd need more guys at our back. Not to mention the Prospects meant the brothers didn't have to do the shit jobs, and I was all for not having to scrub toilets or run bullshit errands.

Rin relaxed a little at my side. Even when Venom came closer she didn't tense back up. The VP stared down at her for a moment, as if he were trying to assess her. His gaze flicked to mine and a faint smile graced his lips. I didn't know what the fuck that look meant, but I had a feeling he knew something I didn't, and I wasn't sure I liked it.

"Welcome to the family, Rin," Venom said before giving me a wink and walking off.

What the fuck? Welcome to the family? I looked at Torch, who just chuckled and followed the VP out of my house. Did they think I was keeping Rin? Or did they think Saint would keep her once he returned? For some reason, I didn't like the idea of her in his arms, which was ridiculous because I certainly didn't have a claim on her. I'd never met a woman I wanted to make mine. While I had to admit that I was reacting to Rin differently than I had anyone else, it didn't mean she was mine. After the hell she'd been through, I doubted she wanted a man to touch her intimately anytime soon, and I was far from being a monk.

I took a good look at Rin while we waited for the truck to be delivered. Her coat was so thin she might as well have not been wearing one, and her shirt molded to her slender curves. The jeans she wore were those skinny ones that left little to the imagination, but her shoes looked like they would fall apart at any moment. She didn't dress like a whore and I wondered if she had her clothes, then a set of working clothes Joe forced her to wear. The shadows under her eyes spoke of many sleepless nights and it made me realize that she likely never felt safe in her own home, not long enough to truly relax and get the rest she needed.

I heard the rumble of the truck in the driveway and held my hand out to her.

"Ready to see Dr. Myron?"

She nodded and slipped her hand into mine. Gears was leaning against the truck when we stepped outside and he gave us both a nod, but his gaze was locked on Rin. It wasn't the look of a man interested in a woman, but more the look a brother would give his little sister. I could tell that Gears would protect her if he needed to, and I was glad that she had him on her side. It was doubtful she had many friends.

Gears opened the passenger door and helped Rin into the truck. After he shut the door, he leaned against it and stared at me.

"What?" I asked.

"Wire is doing some research. On your girl and on Saint. He's still not answering his phone, and Wire said he couldn't track his cell. I'd keep her close if I were you. I don't believe for a second she had anything to do with Saint disappearing, but I also know her half-brother won't let her go that easily. Be vigilant when you're in town today, in case he pops up and decides to grab her."

Why did everyone think Rin was mine? And why the hell did Gears think I needed lessons from him on protecting her? I'd served my country for eight damn years. Being shot at by insurgents and staying alive was a damn sight more difficult than keeping a tiny-ass woman safe.

"She's not my girl."

Gears snorted. "Did you see the way she looked at you? The way you went after Robby, then knocked him out cold, you're her hero. I don't think she's had one of those before. She needs you, and honestly, I think maybe you need her too."

I went around to the driver's side and got into the truck, ignoring Gears and his words of wisdom. At least, he probably thought they were words of wisdom. All they did was piss me off. I didn't need her. I'd never needed a woman and I never would.

The drive to the doctor's office was short and I blasted the heat the entire way, making sure Rin stayed warm. The parking lot was nearly empty and I was able to pull up right near the door. I walked inside with her, and Rin clung to me as we approached the front desk.

The receptionist gave us a warm smile, and her gaze softened as she took in Rin. "Dr. Myron is waiting for you. Exam room two."

I went back with Rin, but I didn't enter the room with her. I hesitated in the hallway, not sure if she'd want some privacy or if she wanted me there.

"Maybe I should go back to the waiting room?" I asked.

"Please stay," she said.

I nodded and stepped into the room. There was a gown out on the table, and I shut the door, knowing she'd need to change. I offered to turn my back, even though I'd already seen her half-naked today. Rin undressed in front of me, and the fact that she didn't even expect privacy broke my heart. Not more so than the rest of what her body looked like, though. If I'd thought her back was bad… My gut clenched. What Joe Banner had done to her made me want to hunt him down and put a bullet in his head. And if he'd done that to his own sister, I could only imagine what he did to the women not related to him. Then I wanted the name of every fucker who had ever laid a hand on Rin, and I'd make them pay too.

She handed me her clothes after she'd put on the gown and I folded them, then set them aside. I helped her onto the padded table, and she gripped my hands tight, not letting me move away. She was strong yet fragile. For her to have survived the things done to her, and still try to escape, took more courage than most people possessed. My hands tightened on hers when I felt a tremor run through her.

"When's the last time you saw a doctor?" I asked.

"A real one? Not since my dad took me to the clinic for whatever shots were required for school. Since then, Joe hired hacks to treat me and the other women in his stable."

"Dr. Myron is loved by all the women in the club. You have nothing to fear, okay?"

She nodded.

There was a quick knock on the door before it swung open. Dr. Myron came in, a warm smile on his face. Rin seemed to lean a little closer to me, and I hated that even a man as nice as Dr. Myron would make her feel afraid.

"You must be Rin," Dr. Myron said, holding out his hand to her.

She gripped mine tighter and I gave the man an apologetic smile.

"Sorry, Doc. She doesn't mean anything by it," I said.

He nodded. "Quite all right. Rin, Venom told me a little about what happened to you. Would you permit me to examine you and maybe run some tests?"

She refused to look at him.

"Would it help if I told you that I'm gay and very much in love with the man in my life?" the doctor asked.

Rin peeked at him and Dr. Myron nodded.

"It's true. I'm gay and not the least bit interested in the female body except from a medical perspective."

"Can Wraith stay?" she asked.

"If you want him here, that's fine with me," Dr. Myron said. "The exam will get a little… delicate. If you'd like him to step out at any point, just let me know."

"Rin, maybe it would be better if I left the room," I suggested.

"Please don't leave me," she said.

Dr. Myron moved closer and listened to her heart and lungs. He did a routine exam he'd give any patient, including checking her blood pressure and temperature. At my request, he did a full blood panel and ran a urine test for STDs. When he had her slide farther down the table and put her feet into some stirrups, I made sure I was standing near her head and couldn't see anything from the waist down, wanting to give her as much privacy as I could considering she refused to let go of my hand. I might have seen her undress and put the gown on, but this was different. Like the doc had said, it was a rather intimate exam.

The dark look that crossed Dr. Myron's face made my gut clench and I wondered what he'd discovered. He pulled Rin's gown down and removed her feet from the stirrups, but he kept her lying on her back. He stepped out of the room and returned a moment later with some sort of machine on a cart. It almost looked like a small computer.

"What's that?" I asked.

"I'm going to do an ultrasound. I just want to make sure there's no internal damage."

Dr. Myron pulled a sheet over Rin's legs, then lifted her gown to expose her belly. He squirted some gel on her, then used some sort of handheld thing and pressed it against her skin. I didn't know what he was looking for, but the tension in his shoulders eased a little.

"Any known pregnancies?" he asked.

"No," Rin said. "He made me take birth control, and the men were told to use condoms."

"And did they?" he asked.

"Most of the time, but not always," she said.

"Do you want to remain on birth control?" Dr. Myron asked.

"I don't know."

He nodded. "Well, I can call in something for you, and if you decide to take them you'll be prepared. I should have the results back on your lab work in about two to three days. Someone in the office will call and let you know if the tests were normal or if you need to come back for a follow-up."

He wiped the gel off her belly, pulled her gown down, and helped her sit up.

"Do you have any questions for me?" he asked.

"Not right now," Rin said.

"Do you know what type of birth control Joe Banner gave you?" Dr. Myron asked.

"I just know it was a pill. A small one. He had someone give me a shot the first time, and I had a bad reaction to it. Then I had a reaction to the next two pills he tried," Rin said.

Dr. Myron froze and his gaze sharpened on her. "You had a reaction to three types of birth control?"

She nodded.

"I'm not calling pills in for you. Can you describe the ones you were last taking?"

"They were blue, like a bright blue, and maybe the size of the head of a straight pin," she said.

"Rin, there are not birth control pills that I'm aware of that look anything like that. I don't think that's what you were given. Do you remember feeling anything after taking them?"

"Maybe a little lightheaded. Sometimes it felt like the room was spinning and my body would feel heavy."

"Did he make you take them every day?" Dr. Myron asked.

"No, only when I had to…" Her cheeks flushed.

"Rin, I think he was drugging you to make you more compliant," Dr. Myron said. "I'm going to take one more vial of blood and a run a test for date rape drugs. Do you remember when you last took one of those pills?"

"Two days ago."

"It might be too late depending on what he gave you, but I'd like to see if there are any traces left in your system. Let me get the blood drawn, and then you can dress and leave."

It didn't take long for the doctor to take more blood, something I'd always thought a nurse did, and then I helped Rin dress and we walked out to the truck. I didn't like being in town with her any longer than necessary, not with her half-brother possibly hunting her. I did go through a drive-thru to make sure she had something hot to eat. I didn't know when she'd had a meal last, and she was too damn skinny. It was obvious that Joe hadn't given a shit about his sister's health, and I doubted that regular meals had been part of her life since her dad had died.

We hadn't even made it back to the house before she'd devoured her meal. Without a second thought, I handed her one of the burgers I'd ordered for myself, and smiled as she chomped into it. The happy sounds she made as she ate filled the cab of the truck. Whatever it took, I would keep her safe and make sure she was cared for.

Chapter Three

Rin

When we pulled up to the gates of the compound, a tow truck was just pulling through. The guy at the gate waved us by and Wraith stopped by the clubhouse and rolled down his window, motioning one of the other Dixie Reapers over.

"What's up with the tow truck?" he asked.

"Ridley's car wouldn't start, and none of us can figure out what's wrong with it. She insisted on calling this new place in town. Camelot Towing." The guy snorted. "Ever heard of anything more ridiculous for a towing company?"

"Camelot Towing?" he asked.

"The guy's name is Lance. His wife's name is Gwen. They own the business together. Ridley met Gwen in town the other day at the coffee shop and I guess the company name is one of those cutesy things that women like," the guy said. I noticed he was trying to peer around Wraith and check me out.

"Bats, this is Rin," Wraith said, pointing to me.

"You settling down?" Bats asked. "Never thought I'd see the day."

My cheeks burned. "He's just helping me."

The humor left Bats' face. "You're the one everyone's talking about. The woman related to Joe Banner."

I nodded.

"You need anything while you're here, doll, you just give me a shout." Bats smiled. "Although I get the feeling Wraith will be keeping you close."

Wraith shoved Bats back and pulled away from the clubhouse, with the other man's laughter following us. Everyone seemed to think that Wraith was keeping me, but I knew men like him didn't end up with whores. Even if I hadn't chosen that life, it's what my brother had turned me into just the same. I didn't delude myself into thinking my life would end with rainbows, puppies, and a loving family of my own. Joe Banner had destroyed whatever chance I had for a happy life long ago.

The truck came to a stop outside his house and I climbed out, then waited at the front door for him. He might have welcomed me into his home, but that didn't mean I had the right to walk right in. Wraith pushed the door open and we stepped inside. The food I'd eaten sat heavy in my stomach. It had been a long time since I'd had something that substantial. Joe kept all of us barely fed, saying his customers preferred skinny women. I knew the truth, though. If he kept us half-starved, it was easier to handle us. When you weren't at full strength, it was hard to fight back. He'd also hooked most of the girls on hard drugs. They'd do almost anything for their next fix.

"Shit. We were supposed to go to Torch's place and pick up some clothes for you," Wraith said, running a hand through his hair.

"It's fine. It's not like I'm staying here long-term. If someone could just help me get out of the state, then I'm sure I'd be fine."

He folded his arms. "And how are you going to provide for yourself? Do you have money in your pockets to get you started? A place to stay? Food to eat? Not to mention it's nearly Christmas. You shouldn't be alone during the holidays."

"No," I said. "I'd rather starve on the streets than go back to Joe. And no offense, but Christmas hadn't meant something to me in a long while. It's just another day except with pretty lights in the store windows and holly on the light posts around town."

"Sweet girl, no one is making you go back to him. Not ever, okay? But running off on your own isn't the way to handle this." He sighed. "And Christmas should damn sure mean more to you than that. If anyone needs one day of happiness and hope, I think it's you."

"I'll stay for a few days," she said. "If I start getting in the way, tell me and I'll go somewhere else. You've been nice enough to help me so far, and I don't want to overstay my welcome."

He had a look in his eyes that said he would try to make me stay through the holidays. I had to admit that his tree was pretty, and it made me think of happier times. It had been a long time since I'd sung carols, opened presents, or sipped hot cocoa while staring at a lit tree. Part of me wanted those things again, but I didn't trust that I'd have that in the future. I'd rather not get it now and have to give it up again.

"Would you like a hot bath? I can run and grab the clothes from Isabella and Torch while you're soaking in the tub."

"Wraith, you don't have to --"

He held up a hand to stop me. "I don't ever do anything I don't want to. Well, unless Torch orders it. I'm helping you because I want to, all right? You're not a burden, Rin."

"No one's ever been nice to me before without wanting something in return." I cocked my head and studied him. "What is it you want from me, Wraith?"

"I just want you to be safe," he said. "I'm not asking you to repay me."

I nodded and let him lead the way to the bathroom. We passed one in the hallway, but he kept going. When we entered a large bedroom, I realized it was his room, and he was taking me to his bathroom. The tub was huge and he started filling it with hot water, then he retrieved a navy tee from his bedroom and laid it on the counter.

"I don't have any of that girly bath stuff," he said. "You can wear my shirt when you're done. After the day you've had, I'd imagine you wouldn't mind a nap."

I glanced longingly at the king-size bed in his room.

"I'll be back soon," he said. "Enjoy your bath, and try to relax, Rin. No one is taking you out of here against your will, and no one expects payment for helping you. You're safe."

I started to remove my clothes and he hurried from the room. It was strange seeing a man run the opposite direction when I got undressed. Usually they were unzipping their pants and expecting me to service them. The water was hot enough my skin turned red when I stepped into the tub, but it felt divine. Closing my eyes, I tried to relax like Wraith had said, and slowly the tense muscles in my body unclenched. My fingers started to prune after a while, and Wraith still hadn't returned. I got out and dried off, then pulled on the shirt he'd provided. His bed was far too tempting and I crawled under the covers.

I breathed in his scent and closed my eyes, feeling safe for the first time in so very long. I hugged his pillow and tried not to feel sorry for myself. After living with Joe for the last eight years, I was free. That's what I needed to focus on. My future was uncertain, but at least I would have one. If he'd sent me to Mexico, I knew it wouldn't have taken long for me to contract something that would have killed me, after making me miserable for whatever was left of my life. I doubted they asked their clients to use condoms, and while not all of Joe's had, the majority had followed the rules.

If my tests came back normal, I would consider myself very fortunate. I didn't feel sick, but that didn't mean one of those men hadn't given me something. Not that any of them would have cared if they were spreading disease. Self-centered bastards every last one, just like Joe. All he cared about was how much he could make off me and the other women. He didn't care if we were hungry, if we were in pain, or if we were sick. Money was all that mattered to him. And those who couldn't earn him cash disappeared.

Now I wondered if maybe they'd been sent to the brothel in Mexico too, or had Joe done something even worse to them? I shivered as I thought about how so much evil could be inside one person. I hadn't realized how much my parents had sheltered me until they were gone. Joe was quite a bit older than me, and he hadn't lived with us. Even the times he'd come to visit, I'd felt like something was off with him, like he wasn't quite right inside. Maybe even when I was little I'd sensed the darkness in him.

I heard the front door shut, then booted steps came down the hall toward me. Wraith stepped into the room, a large paper shopping bag in his hand that looked like it was nearly bursting it was so full. It was the kind I'd often seen women walking with as they left the mall. Even when my mom had been alive we hadn't been able to afford trips to the mall.

He set the bag down and came closer.

"You all right?" he asked. "Can't sleep?"

"I don't want to be alone," I admitted. "I used to crave the times I could be alone because it meant that

Joe didn't want something from me. Now the silence is... unnerving I guess is a good word."

"I can bring a chair in here and sit with you," he said, rubbing the back of his neck.

"Or you could lie down with me," I said, my heart pounding as I waited to see what he'd say. I'd never willingly asked a man to get into bed with me, but Wraith was different. I wanted to feel his strength surrounding me.

"Rin, you don't have to --"

"I know," I said, interrupting him. "Please? I've never... I've never been held by a man before, and I've certainly never asked one to lie down with me, not without my brother receiving payment."

I watched his throat bob as he swallowed hard, then he nodded. Wraith pulled off his boots, set his leather vest on the dresser, and pulled off his belt before he climbed into the bed beside me. He seemed tense, and I hated that I was making him uncomfortable. Slowly, I eased closer to him until my head was on his shoulder.

"Thank you," I said softly. "I know you don't really want to lie here with me, and I'm sorry I got into your bed without asking."

"Christ," he muttered. "Is that what you think? That I don't want to be here with you? That I'm mad you're in my bed?"

I nodded.

"Baby, I like you being in my bed a little too much. Seeing you in my shirt, all fresh from your bath, and curled up in my bed is making me want things I shouldn't. I'm here to protect you and nothing else. I'm just trying to convey that message to my dick."

My eyes went wide at his confession, and before I could second-guess myself, I slid my hand over his hip and nearly gasped at the feel of his hard cock pressing against the denim of his jeans. He groaned and I felt his body stiffen as I stroked him through the material.

"Rin…"

I unfastened his jeans and dipped by hand inside his underwear, then gripped his shaft, stroking it. Pre-cum smeared on my fingertips, and I wanted him far more than I'd ever wanted anything before. Being with him like this, knowing that I wasn't being forced to do something I didn't want, gave me a sense of power. My heart thrummed as I worked his cock. I wondered what he tasted like, but knowing there was a chance I could be carrying something, I wasn't about to put my mouth or my pussy on him, no matter how much I wished I could.

"Christ, Rin! You're going to make me come in my pants like a damn teenager."

"Then take them off."

"We shouldn't do this. You're a victim, Rin, and you need time to heal."

"Will?" I said, using his name for the first time. "Shut up and take off your pants. You're not forcing me to do this. For the first time in my life, this is my choice. Let me enjoy it."

He quickly stripped out of his clothes, then lay back naked, his cock pulsing and twitching with need. I stroked him some more, and marveled at the beauty of his body. He had scars too, but some of his looked like bullet wounds. There was also a stretch along his ribs that looked like he'd been raked over gravel and it had healed wrong, but to me, he was perfection.

"Please, Rin," he begged.

"I don't want to take a chance on giving you something," I said.

"Condom," he said, his voice a near growl as he grabbed at the drawer on the nightstand.

I released him long enough to open the drawer and pull out a condom. It was barely within the expiration date, but I knew something was better than nothing. I ripped the package open and rolled the latex down his shaft. He groaned and his hips flexed.

"You ever had someone make love to you?" he asked.

"No."

"Lie back, sweet girl."

I sprawled on my back and he knelt between my legs. My pussy was waxed smooth, something Joe had insisted upon for all his girls. Wraith parted the lips of my pussy and stroked my clit. Shockwaves of pleasure rolled over me and it didn't take much before I was coming. I'd never had an orgasm before, even though I'd had sex more times than I could count. As my body trembled, he gripped my thighs and pressed inside me. His cock stretched me wide, and it felt so damn good.

"If I hurt you, say something," he said.

"Feels good. Really good," I murmured.

"We're just getting started."

He shifted his hands to my hips and held on as he rocked into me. The push and pull of his cock inside me had me moaning and begging him for more. He seemed to know exactly what I needed and rubbed my clit again while he thrust into me over and over. Each plunge of his cock was harder than the last, and I'd have sworn he was going deeper than before.

"Come for me, baby. Squeeze my dick with that pretty pussy."

On the next stroke of his cock, I shattered, crying out his name as stars burst behind my closed eyelids. I tried to force them open, so I could watch as he found his own release. I'd never seen anything so beautiful as Will in the throes of passion. He slammed into me again and again, until he finally came with a growl. I could feel his cock twitching inside me as he braced his weight on one hand. The other was still playing with my clit, and even though I'd already come twice, I could feel a third orgasm building.

"That's it, sweet girl. Come for me again."

"Will, I can't... I..."

He leaned down and took my nipple into his mouth, then gently bit. It was enough to send me soaring and I screamed so loud my throat hurt. It felt like my body splintered, then tried to come back together.

"Shit! You're already making me hard again," he said, pressing his hips closer to mine.

He pulled out, removed the condom and tied it off before grabbing a second one from the drawer. He slid it down his shaft, then flipped me onto my stomach. I went up on my hands and knees, then cried out in sheer pleasure as he drove inside me in one hard thrust.

"You feel like fucking heaven wrapped around my dick," he said, taking me fast and hard. "Tell me what you want, Rin. You want me to play with your nipples or your clit?"

"Clit," I said, then gasped as he canted his hips and went even deeper, rubbing a different spot that felt too damn good.

His fingers stroked the hard nub between my legs as he powered into me from behind. I gripped his headboard, his thrusts forceful enough to push me up the bed. Using his hand, he pressed the center of my back until I flattened my chest against the mattress. It let him thrust in and out of me at a different angle, one that felt incredible. He strummed my clit like he was playing an instrument until I was screaming out another release.

"Yes! Will, yes! Don't stop! Please don't stop!"

He growled as he continued to hammer into me, the sounds of his hips slapping against me filling the air. When he came again, I felt a tremor rake his body. I was glad to know I wasn't the only one affected by what we'd just done. It had always been a job, just random sex that didn't mean anything and never felt good. But sex with Will? Oh, my God! My toes were curled, and I could have died happy with his cock still stuffed inside me.

He pulled out, then got up to dispose of both condoms. I collapsed onto the bed, my legs feeling like jelly. When he came back, he curled himself around me and pressed a kiss to my neck.

"You didn't have to do that," he said.

"I wanted to, and I'm not the least bit sorry. You're the only man I've ever wanted, and the only one to make me come. I will remember this moment for the rest of my life," I murmured, finally feeling sleepy enough to doze off.

"You act like you're going somewhere," he said. "Sweet girl, I have news for you. After what we just shared, I'm not letting you go. No one has ever made me feel like that before."

"Just sex," I said softly.

"No. That wasn't just sex," he said. "I know what just sex feels like it, and it's nothing like that. You're mine, Rin. Maybe Venom could tell when he met you earlier, and that's why he said what he did. I mean it. I'm not letting you go."

I cracked an eye open and looked at him. "What exactly does that mean?"

"It means you're mine. No one is allowed to touch you except me." He shoved his hand between my thighs. "And no one gets to fuck this pretty pussy but me. You're my woman. Do we really need to define it?"

"I don't guess so. Does that mean I have to wear one of those vest things? I've seen a few of your women wearing them around town. They all said Dixie Reapers across the back."

He laughed a little. "It's called a cut, and no, you don't have to wear one. Old ladies get those, which would be the biker equivalent of us being married. It's for life, Rin, and I honestly don't know that I'll ever be ready for something like that. But it doesn't mean I'm letting you walk out of here. Those women get a property stamp. I'm not asking you to get inked, just to stay here with me, be mine and only mine."

I hummed and closed my eyes again, snuggling into his embrace. "I think I'd like that. Being your property. Not going to ever ask for that, though. You deserve better."

He kissed my shoulder. "Sleep, sweet girl. We'll talk more after you've rested."

For the first time since my mom died, I fell asleep with a smile on my face and felt happier than I had in forever. I knew it was just the good sex talking, and he'd be singing a different tune by morning, but it was nice to be wanted, even if it was just for a little while. No, he hadn't offered me the forever thing the other women apparently had, but him wanting to keep me? No one had ever wanted that before, not with me. I didn't count my brother wanting to keep me, since I'd just been a source of income for him.

Chapter Four

Wraith

I'd spent the best night of my life with Rin in my bed. After she'd slept for a little while, I'd ordered dinner for us, then I'd spent the next five hours making love to her again and again. I hadn't been able to get hard so fast since I was in my twenties, and I sure as hell hadn't gone more than once a night in a few years. With Rin, it was like my dick hadn't gotten the memo that we were getting older and couldn't do sex marathons anymore.

Didn't mean I wasn't going to try. With her naked curves pressed against me, it was hard to ignore how hard my cock was. I reached into the bedside table drawer and pulled out another condom. I tore open the package and rolled it down my shaft, then pulled her leg across my thigh. She moaned in her sleep and pressed against me.

I slid my hand between her legs and stroked her clit. It didn't take long for her to wake up, and soon after that she was coming, coating my fingers in her cream. I kept rubbing that tight little bud, not stopping even as she cried out my name. When she was coming down from her third orgasm, I rolled so that she lay under me, her legs parted, and thrust deep and hard. Her pussy pulsed around me and I groaned at how fucking good she felt.

"Christ, Rin! You feel like fucking heaven."

She mumbled something but I didn't catch it. I gripped her hips and started riding her sweet little pussy, driving into her like a man possessed. I should have been gentler, sweeter, but I couldn't seem to control myself. For the first time in my life, I wished a condom wasn't necessary. I'd never wanted to take a chance and fuck a woman bare before, but there was nothing I'd like more with Rin.

I grunted as cum filled the condom, then felt like an asshole because she was just lying there. I pulled out, tossed the condom into the trash can I'd put beside the bed after our third round last night, then rolled her over to face me.

"Did I hurt you?" I asked.

"No." She gave me a drowsy smile.

"You scared me the way you were…"

"I couldn't move," she said. "You had me pinned too well, but it's okay. I still liked it."

"Jesus, Rin." I closed my eyes when I realized what I'd done. "I took you like…"

I couldn't even finish the sentence.

"Hey," she said softly, reaching up to touch my face. "Will, I love everything we do together in this bed, all right? You're not the men who paid for me. You could never be like them. I knew it was you and I was all right."

"I shouldn't have done that," I said.

"I'd say you could make it up to me, but I'm a little bit sore this morning."

I leaned down and kissed her, then nibbled my way down the column of her neck, between the valley of her breasts, and down her soft belly. When I pushed her thighs wide and settled between them, she sucked in a breath.

"Will, you don't have to…"

"I want to," I assured her.

"But what if… I mean, the test results aren't back, so…"

Yeah, it was risky. Really fucking risky, but my gut said that Rin was clean, and I wanted so damn badly to taste her. I spread her pussy open and looked at how pretty and pink she was before swirling my tongue around her clit. She cried out and her hips bucked, so I laid my arm across her hips and held her down. *Merry early Christmas to me*! I couldn't remember the last time I'd tasted something so sweet, or wanted someone as much as I wanted her. I licked, sucked, and nibbled at her, lapping up all the nectar spilling from her pussy. She tasted so fucking good, and the scent of her arousal was driving me fucking insane.

I sucked her clit into my mouth, drawing on it long and hard, then gently bit down with my teeth. It was enough to send her over the edge, and she screamed out my name so loud I wondered if the entire compound had heard her. When she lay panting and sated, I kissed and licked my way up her body, stopping to suck at her nipples.

"Will, I think you broke me. My legs don't work."

I chuckled. "Then I guess you should lie here while I shower and make some breakfast for us."

She nodded. "I like that idea. I'll just wait until feeling returns to my legs."

I kissed her, letting her taste herself on my tongue, then slid out of bed and went into the bathroom before the temptation of her body was too much to pass up. As the hot water beat down on me, I gripped my cock and wondered how the fuck I was still hard. It wasn't like I was some sixteen-year-old kid anymore. I was fucking forty but my dick didn't seem to care. Just the thought of Rin lying naked in my bed had me thrusting into my fist.

My balls drew up within seconds, and I was spraying the shower wall with cum. I cleaned up the shower and myself, then got out and did my damnedest not to look at Rin as I got dressed. I was already addicted to her and it hadn't even been twenty-four hours. What the fuck was wrong with me?

While she showered and got dressed, I thought about our amazing night together. I'd thought things were pretty perfect between us, and I was hoping I could convince her to just stay in my room. She didn't have to move to the guest room if she didn't want to, not when my bed was plenty big enough for the two of us. I'd liked waking up to her pressed against me, her pussy tempting me.

She came into the kitchen, yawning and looking like a sleepy kitten, and I hid a smile. Her feet were bare and she still had a slightly rumpled look. She was so fucking cute first thing in the morning.

"I'll let the club know you'll be staying here. They don't have to worry about finding a place for you," I said as I set breakfast in front of her.

She pushed the food around her plate, then looked up at me, her eyes flashing.

"I'm not good enough for you," she said, her chin lifting at a stubborn angle. "I'm dirty. Just a common whore. Last night was great, and I'll always remember our time together, but I shouldn't stay here."

"Rin, you're not dirty, and stop calling yourself a whore. Did you have to do horrible things you didn't want to do? Yes. You were abused, sweet girl. You think I'm going to hold that against you? Do I really seem like that much of an asshole?"

"You're not an asshole," she mumbled. "That's the problem. You're a good guy, Wraith, and you deserve so much better than me. Even if you only want me here short-term, I'm not the girlfriend type, or whatever you want to call it."

"Why do we have to label things?" I'd asked her that last night. What the hell was it with women and labels? Couldn't we just have fun together, enjoy one another without making a huge deal out of it? "I want you here, and that should be enough. I wasn't lying last night when I said I wanted you to be mine."

She shook her head. "Last night was wonderful, and I'll always cherish those memories, but you need someone… you need someone who would make a good mom, someone who can give you all the things you need and deserve. I'm broken."

"You're not broken, dammit! You're the strongest woman I know. And who the fuck said I was looking for a mom? I don't want kids, Rin. The rugrats running around here are cute and all, but I've never wanted any of my own."

Deciding I wasn't hungry after all, I pushed my plate aside.

I'd thought after our night together that things would be just as great today. Apparently I was wrong. I thought about the tree in the living room, and the plans I'd wanted to make with her for the holidays. They were crumbling to dust before my very eyes. With her current attitude, I didn't think she'd be here come Christmas Day, and for some reason, that left me feeling hollow. I really wanted to spend that time with her, see her face light up when she had gifts under the tree, maybe take her to the club party we had every Christmas Eve.

"I'm not strong," she said. "If I were strong, I'd have managed to get away before now. Maybe some part of me felt like… like maybe I wasn't supposed to have more than I already did."

"Rin, no one is supposed to be a whore. You weren't asked if that's what you wanted to do, that asshole half-brother of yours forced it on you. And trust me, I'm going to have a conversation with him about it, one that leaves him broken until he chokes on his own blood and dies."

She flinched and I realized that maybe that was a little more than she needed to know. Despite everything, she was still a woman with a gentle touch, and I doubted she'd ever hurt anyone in her life, not even when she was being tortured for having the guts to try to escape. I didn't know how to get through to her. She saw herself as damaged and tainted, but she wasn't. To me, she was beautiful, strong, and everything I'd ever wanted in a woman. I knew she could handle whatever shit the club went through, and as for being mom material… she'd be a kickass mom. That I didn't doubt for a second. And one day, maybe she'd meet the guy who would give her that, but it wouldn't be me. Even now, she was thinking of others before herself, and wasn't that a large part of what being a mom was about? It didn't mean I couldn't hold onto her until she was ready for that stage of her life, though.

"Rin, if you're mine, no one would fuck with you. If I tell my brothers I'm keeping you, then they'll defend you. No one would get past us, you'd be safe from everyone."

"Even the mayor?" she asked dryly. "Do you have any idea who Joe's clients are? Or just how many pockets he's lined to stay out of jail? He owns half the police force, if not more, and just about every city official. Including the mayor."

"Then we'll make sure town hall is cleaned out. I'm sure the citizens of this town wouldn't mind a fresh start, especially if they know their elected officials and the men and women who are supposed to protect them are condoning prostitution and sexual assault. Call it whatever you want, Rin. You didn't go to those men willingly. They raped you, and your brother pocketed the cash he earned off your pain. I'm not letting the fuckers get away with this."

I saw tears mist her eyes. I was up and out of my chair heading toward her when she swayed in her chair a moment. I rushed forward and pulled her into my arms, holding her against my chest. I rested my cheek on the top of her head and felt the wetness seep into my shirt as she cried.

"I'm going to protect you, Rin. Please stop fighting me. No matter what you say, you're mine, and there will never be another woman I want as much as I want you. I can't promise you forever, but I can give you today, tomorrow, and the day after that. Do I seem like the type of guy to beg?"

She shook her head and I dropped to my knees in front of her. I held her hands and smiled when I realized we were eye to eye even though she was standing. I'd never met someone pixie sized before. Yeah, the old ladies at the compound weren't exactly tall, but they were all bigger than my Rin.

"I don't kneel for anyone, sweet girl, no one except you. Just tell me that you'll at least think about it. Even if we just have a few weeks or months together, you need time to heal and figure out what you're going to do with your life. You can stay with me as long as you want."

"All right," she said. "I'll think about it, but I can't promise that I'll stay. I still don't think I'm right for you."

"I can take that for now."

She tucked her face against my neck and I held her tight. There were things we needed to share with one another, but I worried if she found out about my sister, then she'd think I was trying to right an old wrong by keeping her. That might have been what prompted me to help her in the first place, but after even spending an hour in her company, I knew it was more than that. She touched a part of me I'd long thought dead, and made me feel more alive than I had in a long-ass time. If I were a different man, I'd offer her forever. No matter how much she thought she wasn't worthy of me, the opposite was true. She deserved far better than me.

My phone buzzed against my hip and I pulled it off the holder. It was Torch.

Church in fifteen.

I knew the meeting would be about Rin, and I wondered what Wire had been able to find. It was probably too much to hope that her half-brother wasn't looking for her. A man like Joe Banner didn't give up easily, and he considered Rin his property. After the years of abuse he'd heaped on her, there was no way she was walking away without some repercussions, or Joe Banner being buried six feet under. I was more than happy to help with that last option.

"Baby, I need to leave for a little while. You have the clothes Isabella sent over; there's plenty of snacks and sodas in the kitchen, and I have about two hundred channels on TV. Make yourself at home and I'll be back as soon as I can."

"Everything all right?" she asked.

"Yeah, just some club business. Torch called a meeting."

She nodded. "You don't have to babysit me, Wraith. I'll be fine."

I leaned in closer to her. "Last night it was Will. Now I'm Wraith again?"

"Will should be reserved for the woman who's going to be a big part of your life, and I don't think that's me. It's better if I call you Wraith like everyone else."

She was going to leave. I didn't know when, or how, but one day she'd be gone, likely without so much as a goodbye. I could see it in her eyes, hear it in her voice. I'd have loved to stay and change her mind, but I needed to haul my ass to the clubhouse. If I was late, I'd either be fined or face some god-awful chore like cleaning the clubhouse bathrooms. I'd much rather pay than clean.

She pulled away from me and sat back down, playing with her food again. With a sigh, I pulled my keys from my pocket and went out to my bike. I started the engine, then stared at my house for a minute. I didn't know how to make her stay, not when I couldn't give her everything she deserved. Still, even asking her to stay, to move in with me, was a huge step for me. I'd never wanted more than a quick screw up against a wall or wherever was convenient. Rin was the only woman I'd ever made love to, the only one I'd been tempted to keep. I didn't know how to make her see the significance of that, or if it was even enough.

When I got to the clubhouse, it looked like all my brothers were already there, minus Saint, but Ryker was there. He wasn't a Reaper even though he lived inside the compound with his woman, so if he was included, then something big was going on. Maybe even bigger than Rin's problem. I turned off the engine, swung my leg over the seat, and made my way inside. The doors to Church were open and when I stepped through them, Torch gave me a nod. I scanned the room and saw that I was correct and everyone was present, except for Saint who it seemed was still unaccounted for, so I shut the doors and took my seat toward the end of the table.

"We have a few things to discuss," Torch said. "The first is that Saint has been missing for two days. A woman came here seeking his help yesterday and that's when we realized he wasn't here, and he's not answering calls. Wire tried to trace him and can't get a lock on his location. Anyone heard from him?"

"Not since day before yesterday," Flicker said. "He stopped by for a minute, and now that I think about it, he was acting a little strange. I didn't think much of it at the time, but if he's gone dark, maybe we need to look into it further. It's not like him to hide shit from the club."

Torch nodded. "Wire will keep trying to find him. In the meantime, if any of you hear something, pass it on. I'm going to assume he left of his own accord, but it's more than a little strange he didn't say anything to anyone and won't pick up the phone. He hasn't even responded to Isabella's voicemail, and the two of them are pretty close."

"He won't answer Kayla's calls either," Preacher said. "She's getting worried and I don't want her stressed out right now. She's not getting much sleep. The baby is up at all hours of the night."

I saw a few of the daddies in the club wince and nod with understanding. Just another good reason not to have kids. If I want a sleepless night, it will be from having too much fun, not changing diapers and shit.

"You said that was the first order of business. What's the second?" Savior asked.

"The woman who showed up at the gates yesterday asking for Saint is Joe Banner's half-sister. Her name is Rin and she needs our help," Torch said. "I'm going to let Wire tell you what he's found so far."

Wire flipped open a rather hefty file folder he had in front of him. "So, I think we're all familiar with Joe Banner, local pimp and a giant pain in the ass. He's lined the pockets of pretty much every official in town, both in town hall and the police department. I've actually got proof that quite a few of them use his services on a regular basis, including some county officials."

Wire glanced at me a moment, and I had a feeling I wasn't going to like what I was about to hear.

"The city manager and mayor are regulars, as are two judges. Some of the officers…" He slid some photos down the table and bile rose in my throat as I looked at them. It was my girl, and the things they were doing to her made me want to tear them in half with my bare hands. "Rin has a good reason to be scared. And that's part of why I've asked a guest to come here today. Officer Daniels is the only one who appears to be squeaky clean in the department. He's never broken the law that I can find, does his job, even received commendations at the last place he worked."

There was a knock on the doors and Wire got up to open them. Officer Daniels walked in and gave everyone a nod. Wire motioned for him to take a seat on the bench along the wall, then Wire sat back down with his file folder.

"Officer Daniels is more than willing to help clean house, but it's a town-wide epidemic and we're going to have a really hard fucking time getting rid of the trash," Wire said. "I have enough shit on some of them to have them hauled away by law enforcement."

"But you said the cops are corrupt," Venom said. "So who's going to arrest them? Officer Daniels? Won't the others just let them go?"

Officer Daniels stood up. "Permission to speak?"

Torch nodded.

"Wire found out that the police chief, as well as many of the higher-ranking officers, have a penchant for younger girls. As in fourteen- and fifteen-year-old girls. He has enough evidence to have them put away for a long time. The problem is that I don't know we can trust the county sheriff's office either, so I'm going after them at the federal level. Some of those girls came across state lines, which means the FBI can get involved," Officer Daniels said.

Tank's phone went off and he glanced at it, letting out a string of curses.

"Motherfuckers!" He stood up, his chair nearly falling over. "Those two pretty boys who helped out Josie heard what's going down, and they're on their way here."

"Agents Drey and Logan?" Flicker asked. "What the hell does the DEA want with a prostitution ring?"

Wire cleared his throat. "That would be my doing. Joe Banner isn't just into prostitutes. He's been selling date rape drugs of various types locally and statewide. According to some intel I gathered, he's planning to take things to the next step and become a major distributor for the entire southern region. Drey and Logan came to mind, and I thought they could be of assistance, but why are they messaging you, Tank?"

Tank snorted. "They're keeping tabs on Josie, making sure Jackal treats her right. I get a message once a month asking for an update. I think they're waiting on him to step out of line so they can go kick his ass. I've been tempted a few times to lie just so I can watch them take that little shit down."

"Don't like the brother-in-law?" I asked. "I thought the two of you were getting along now."

"We do, mostly," Tank said. "Doesn't mean I'm still not pissed about how he treated my sister in the beginning. I figure I should find ways to make him pay for at least the first ten years of their marriage."

"Jesus," Torch muttered. "It's been a fucking year, Tank. Let that shit go. The boy is doing the best he can. At least he's trying, and Josie seems content. Leave it be."

Tank grumbled but seemed to settle down.

"I know the club isn't exactly legit," Officer Daniels said, "and you probably don't want the FBI anywhere near this place, but we need somewhere to meet. The two agents I'm working with would like to hear things straight from Wire and Rin. If you don't want the meeting to take place here, then I can set up something around town, but it's not going to take long before that shit spreads through the gossip mill."

"And just who are these agents?" Venom asked.

"Agent Lupita Montoya and Agent Paxton Hughes."

"A woman?" I asked. "You want a woman to take down men who are known abusers and rapists of girls?"

"Can you think of anyone better?" Officer Daniels asked. "Hell, we'll likely have to hold her back. It wouldn't surprise me if she gelded them in front of everyone and saved the taxpayers some money when the assholes bled out."

Tank grinned. "I think I'm liking this Agent Lupita Montoya. I say we let her deball them. I'll bring the popcorn."

"Of course you'd get off on that," Venom said.

Tank shrugged. "I'm not the club enforcer without reason. Getting my hands dirty is half the fun. Watching a woman get *her* hands dirty while taking down a rapist? That would be like my birthday and Christmas all rolled into one."

"Now that we're reminded that Tank is a sick fuck," Torch said, "any other surprises, Wire?"

"I don't know that I would call it a surprise, but... when Joe couldn't find Rin, he needed a replacement. The deal with the Mexican brothel was apparently already set. A woman with dark hair, petite stature, and close to Rin's age was kidnapped from a neighboring town last night. She hasn't been found, but I did locate an email from Joe to his contact that the package was on its way."

"Son of a bitch," I said, slamming my fist onto the table. "Rin can't find out! If she thinks for one minute that someone else suffered in her place, she'll turn herself over to Joe."

Officer Daniels rubbed his jaw. "It's not that I'm not grateful you're helping out Rin Banner, but what's in it for y'all? I mentioned a woman needing help and no one seemed to care, not enough to do something. That was over a week ago. Now you're willing to go to any lengths to make sure she stays safe."

"She's Wraith's," Venom said.

Zipper rubbed his hands together. "When do I get to lay some ink on her?"

"You don't," I said. "I've told you I'm not taking an old lady. She's mine, but..."

Torch leaned back in his chair. "Son, she's either yours or she's not. If she's yours, then you need to ink her and we'll order a property cut. If she's not..."

I clenched my jaw until I thought my teeth might crack. What the fuck did it matter if I inked her or not? I wanted her, and she seemed content enough with me, if we could just get past the I-deserved-better-than-her bullshit. Why did everything have to have a fucking label? It was bad enough she was asking if I wanted her as a girlfriend, now my Pres was giving me an ultimatum? Claim her as my old lady or... or what?

"If she's not, then what? You kick her ass out of the compound and she's left to fend for herself?" I asked.

Torch folded his arms and the look in his eyes told me I'd crossed a line by snapping at him. I'd be lucky if all I had to do was clean toilets. Fuck! I looked around the table and every one of my brothers wore the same expression. I was in deep shit, but I wasn't so sure it was because of my comment to Torch. No, I had a feeling it was because I didn't want to commit to Rin. Seriously? These assholes wanted me to claim her for life after one night together?

"Is there a problem with claiming her?" Torch asked. "Is she not worthy to be your old lady because of her past?"

Something told me I was treading on thin ice.

"I don't care about her past. I mean, I care. I want to beat the shit out of the assholes who hurt her, but no, it doesn't bother me that she was a..." I clamped my lips shut. I didn't want to call her a whore because it wasn't true, no matter if she did say otherwise. Yeah, guys had paid to fuck her, but in my mind what they'd really done was pay to rape her, which just enraged me all over again.

"You can't say it, can you?" Venom asked. "Can't call her a whore?"

I saw Officer Daniels take a step forward out of the corner of my eye.

"You're going to call that poor girl a whore?" the officer asked with a bite to his tone.

Venom raised a hand. "I'm making a point, officer. I'd suggest you step back before you're assisted out of the clubhouse and not welcomed back. You're here by invitation, but it can be revoked at any time."

Officer Daniels' jaw clenched, and I could have sworn I heard his teeth grinding. Nice to know Rin had people in her corner, even if I didn't particularly like being backed into one when it came to her. I'd give my life for her if that's what it came down to, but making her mine forever? Putting my name on her body, being responsible for her for the rest of my life? I'd faced some scary shit overseas, but I couldn't think of anything that terrified me more than commitment, except maybe fatherhood. It wasn't that I didn't like kids, because I loved everyone else's. I just didn't want one of my own. I'd fucked up enough lives already.

"So what is it, Wraith?" Venom asked. "You can't call her a whore, but you refuse to officially claim her. You want to what? Play house until you're tired of her and kick her ass to the curb? What's she supposed to do then?"

I shrugged. I honestly hadn't thought that far ahead. I could see myself spending a lot of time with Rin, maybe even a few years if I were completely honest, but I knew a guy like me wasn't meant for the long haul. I might not know much, but I did know that I was doing her a favor by not making her mine in every way that mattered. I wasn't the one who deserved better. She was. She needed someone who would be there for her, who didn't fuck up peoples' lives and let their sister die in a gutter.

All right, so maybe my sister had more do with my shit with Rin than I'd acknowledged. She'd needed a better brother, one who was here when she was in trouble, and I'd failed her. What the fuck did it matter that I was serving my country when I'd come home to my only family being gone? If my parents had been alive, they'd have disowned me. They'd given me one job. Take care of my little sister. And I'd fucked it to hell and back.

Venom eased back in his chair. "I stand with Torch on this one. You either man up and claim her, the right way, or you stand aside and let someone else take over."

My back went ramrod straight and my shoulders tensed.

"What the fuck does that mean?" I asked.

"Keep that sweet little thing permanently?" Bats asked. "Doesn't sound like a bad deal to me. If Wraith doesn't want her, I'll claim her."

Gears leaned his elbows onto the table. "And if she doesn't want Bats, then I'll take her. Hell, maybe we should wait for Saint to resurface. The two of them have history. Maybe he wants her as his old lady."

I could feel my skin heating as fury flowed through my veins like lava. I glared at Bats and Gears, then turned my stare to Torch and Venom.

"Really? You're going to auction her off like some plaything? Any brother will do, right? Doesn't matter what the fuck she wants. You don't think she had enough of that shit with her half-brother? Men have told her what the hell to do and when to do it since her mom died." I glared at everyone at the table. "Fuck all of you."

I stood so fast my chair toppled and before anyone could call me back, I stormed out of the room and didn't stop until I got onto my bike. I gunned the engine and my tires spit gravel as I flew toward the gate. Diego was keeping watch and hastened to open it up before I went straight through the damn thing. I took a sharp right and headed out of town, letting the wind whip through my hair and not giving a shit how fucking cold it was. The highway beckoned and I accelerated until I was going at least ninety miles per hour. It was dangerous as hell, but right then I didn't much care. Maybe an adrenaline rush would do me some good.

I rode for what had to be a good two hours considering how far I'd traveled, then I pulled off to the side. My lungs ached and I breathed hard and fast, like I'd been running instead of riding. My head wasn't much clearer than it had been when I'd left but I knew one thing. I couldn't let them decide Rin's fate like that. She needed to make her own choice, and while I hoped she decided to stay with me for however long we lasted, if she wanted someone else I wouldn't stand in her way. All I wanted was for her to be happy. After everything she'd been through, she'd earned that right. Hell, even if she'd had the happiest of lives, she still had the right to decide what or who she wanted. It pissed me off that they were no better than Joe Banner, trying to sell her off to the highest bidder. Money might not have exchanged hands, but they were treating her like a whore and not like a woman who had a mind of her own.

I snorted. Maybe I should have turned in my man card and just kept riding. I sounded like a fucking sap, even in my own fucking head. Women were property in any club, and yet… were they really? Yeah, Venom acted like he owned Ridley's ass, but everyone knew she'd been the one to claim him. And Torch would walk over broken glass before he'd ever hurt Isabella's feelings. So maybe they were more than property, even if that's what we called them. I didn't understand how they could be so tenderhearted when it came to their women but obviously didn't give a shit what mine wanted.

Fuck. I was still calling her mine. And it felt right, dammit.

Turning my bike around, I stared down the road ahead of me, wishing that I had the answers I needed. Regardless, I couldn't leave Rin alone. With all the time that had passed since I'd hauled ass out of Church, they likely had told her what happened. The last thing I wanted was for her to think I was running from her. She was too damn sweet to chase anyone off. No, my brothers had pissed me off good and proper, but it was no excuse. I should have stayed, gone home to Rin, and at least told her I needed a little breathing room. Made sure she knew I wasn't trying to escape being around her. Then I could have left.

I gunned the engine and sped back toward the compound. I didn't know what the hell I'd find when I got there, but I hoped like fuck they'd left Rin alone. She didn't need more shit piled at her feet. I didn't expect the assholes I called brothers to really think that far ahead, though. Yeah, some of them had women, but they still fucked shit up with the fairer sex. Hell, it had taken Venom five fucking years to even propose to Ridley and they'd had two kids by then. He'd claimed her, inked her and made her his old lady, but everyone could have told him she wanted the ring to go with it. She'd have denied it if he'd asked, but even I had caught the wistful look on her face when she saw Isabella's wedding band.

And Preacher? Shit, he'd claimed Kayla and they'd had two kids before he'd ever gotten around to proposing. She'd turned his ass down the first time, but we all knew it was because she worried he couldn't handle the marriage thing a second time. Once he'd put a ring on her finger, he'd rushed her to the nearest courthouse, though. At least he'd figured shit out faster than Venom had.

And the fuckers thought they could tell me how to handle my woman?

The time going home dragged, but I finally pulled through the compound gates and went straight to my house. My ass was numb from riding four hours straight and I took a second to stretch out the kinks before going inside. And that's when I knew something was really fucking wrong. It was quiet. Too damn quiet. I went room by room, but I'd known the second I cleared the front door. Rin was gone.

"Son of a bitch!" I yelled, then planted my fist through the sheetrock in the front entry.

I stomped back out to my bike, but I didn't get far before Gears and Tank stopped me.

"Where the fuck is Rin?" I demanded.

"Gone," Tank said.

My blood turned to ice. "What the hell do you mean she's gone?"

I'd known it. The moment I'd stopped long enough to think for half a second, I'd known that leaving the way I had was the wrong thing to do. She'd probably blamed herself and had run off. If she got her hurt because of my stupidity… Who was protecting her?

"Torch loaded her and the clothes he'd given her into the truck and took off about two hours after you disappeared. We didn't know if you were coming back or not." Gears looked about two seconds from laying me out. "What the hell is wrong with you? You say you want her, but you don't. Not really. And leaving her here like that?"

"She looked… Hell, I think she half expected you would abandon her at some point," Tank said. "There was a moment of anguish in her eyes, then nothing but acceptance. Never seen anything so fucking sad in my life."

"Where did he take her?" I asked.

Gears shrugged. "He didn't say and we didn't ask. Torch and Venom had a meeting. Venom's in charge until the Pres returns. Torch came for her, loaded her up, and they were off. All I know is she's supposed to be somewhere safe. Isn't that what you wanted? Her to be safe? What do you care where that is? She's not your old lady, right?"

I'd never wanted to beat the hell out of my brothers as badly as I did right then. I settled for going back into my house and slamming the door so hard the wood cracked. Wherever Rin was, I hoped like hell they were right and she was safe. I didn't like the thought of her outside the compound. I'd fucked up. Again. I'd lost my sister before, and now if Rin died because fucking Joe Banner got his hands on her... No. That wouldn't happen. When Torch came back, I'd just pry the information out of him and go get Rin back. She belonged here, where I could watch over her. Anyone who said otherwise would eat my damn fist, even if they were my Pres or VP.

There were some things you just didn't fuck with. A man's bike and his woman were at the top of that list. The club had just fucked up, and I wasn't above letting them know it. Just because I didn't want an old lady didn't mean that I didn't want Rin. I gave a shit what happened to her, whether they believed that or not. It hadn't taken long for her to get under my skin, maybe only seconds. One look in her eyes and I'd been ready to take on the world if it meant she would feel safe.

Chapter Five

Rin

"Are you sure this is a good idea?" I asked Torch for what had to be the millionth time. "If Joe comes after me, then anyone who gets in the way could be hurt. Your club volunteered to take that on when you let me stay at the compound, but this…"

He looked around the room before focusing on me again. "Look, these are Ryker's people. I trust them to keep you safe, and you're way the fuck out of Alabama. I doubt your half-brother will come sniffing around here, but if he does manage to track you down, Spider and his crew won't let a damn thing happen to you. You don't have anything on you that could be traced, so I don't foresee any trouble."

I wrapped my arms around my waist and wished that Wraith was with me. I'd tried to put on a brave face, but I was honestly devastated that he'd run and didn't want me. Torch had explained that Wraith had been given a choice to claim me as his old lady or let me go… and he'd run. Guess that was answer enough. I'd known I wasn't the right woman for him, not even short-term, but I'd hoped like hell that I was wrong, that he'd *prove* me wrong. I should have known he'd be like every guy I'd ever met. Except for maybe Johnny, but he'd always had that hero complex.

I'd wondered if Torch had noticed that his missing Saint was here in Hades Abyss territory. I'd caught a glimpse of him briefly when we arrived, but then he'd vanished just as fast as he'd appeared. Either Ryker knew where Johnny was and he just wasn't saying for whatever reason, or the club had kept it from him. Either way, I had a feeling that was going to be another shit storm when everyone found out. Not that it was any of my business.

"You're safe, Rin," Torch said, his voice dropping and sincerity ringing in his tone. "I'd leave my daughter and my pregnant wife here without a second's hesitation."

"Thank you for helping me," I said. "I'm sorry if I caused trouble with your club."

He shook his head. "Wraith is fucked up in the head right now. Sooner or later, he'll realize what he's missing and try to find you. I won't give away your location until I know for sure that he wants you for the right reasons. He's a good man, but he has a troubled past. If he shows up, you make him tell you everything. Don't go running off with him until you know about his sister. Hear me?"

I nodded, but it made me extremely curious about Wraith's sister. He'd never mentioned having one. We hadn't been together but one night, but if Torch thought the woman was that important, I'd have thought Wraith might have mentioned her at some point. Especially since he'd asked me to stay with him for more than just a few days.

"This home belongs to Rocket. We thought you might be more comfortable with someone closer to your age, but you can stay with any of them. No one here has an old lady, so you're the only woman in the compound," Torch said.

The thought of being alone with all those men made my heart pound a little harder, but I reminded myself that I would be safe here. They were good men, despite their rough exteriors.

I thought about the small Christmas tree I'd noticed in Rocket's living room, and mentally compared it to the bigger one at Wraith's. I could have spent the month with him, stayed for Christmas and made some good memories. Even if I knew it would never last between us, maybe I could have had a few moments to cherish in the years to come. I could easily picture us cuddling with only the blinking tree lights casting a glow in the room, maybe even have sex under the tree. I wouldn't call it making love. No one would ever be that way with me, and I was fine with it. Mostly.

I'd given up that chance, though, when I'd agreed to leave with Torch. Maybe I should have fought to stay, forced Wraith to tell me how he felt. I just didn't think I could have handled hearing I wasn't enough, despite knowing it was true. So much for the holiday magic my mom had always talked about. She'd said that Christmas was a time for miracles and that anything was possible during the holiday season. I hated to disappoint her, but I'd been waiting on a miracle for a long time now.

Torch set a phone down on the dresser. "This is just one of those pay-as-you-go phones and it has a month of service on it. I programmed in my number, as well as Venom's and Gears'. If you need someone, you call one of us and we'll get here as quickly as we can. The GPS is turned off so no one can trace you when you make a call. Even if Banner got the number, he wouldn't be able to find you."

"Not Wraith's number?" I asked.

"I thought you might be tempted to call him. Not sure that's the best idea right now."

"What if he worries about where I've gone? Like you said, he's a good man. Even if he didn't want me long-term, he might be concerned about Joe getting to me."

Torch crossed his arms. "If Wraith is that damn worried, then I'll deal with it. You focus on healing. I'll have Dr. Myron forward your records to a doctor here, one the club uses. You need any medical care, don't hesitate to see a doctor. Either my club or the Hades Abyss will cover the cost."

"Thank you."

"I'm going to get a few hours' sleep, then head back. With Isabella being pregnant, I don't like leaving her for too long. Morning sickness seems to be an all-day sickness for her."

"Congratulations on the baby," I said.

My stomach cramped as I thought about how sweet babies smelled, and how I'd never have one of my own. No one would ever want a family with me. Not if they knew my past, and I couldn't very well lie to a man I wanted a future with.

"Rocket's in the living room if you need anything. Take care of yourself, Rin."

He walked out of the room and I sank onto the edge of the bed. New town, new club. New me? If I stayed in this area, maybe I could reinvent myself to some extent. I didn't have any job skills and I'd never had to survive on my own for more than a day or two. I needed to learn, though. It wasn't right for me to rely on other people to take care of me. At twenty-three, I was old enough to stand on my own two feet.

I got up and went to find Rocket. What I hadn't expected was to find Johnny sitting on the couch with him, and holding a small baby who couldn't have been more than a few weeks old. The way he cradled her, I could tell that she meant something to him. Did he have a daughter? No one had said anything about him having an old lady or steady girlfriend. Did they not know about the baby?

"Hi, Johnny," I said as I came into the room.

He looked up at me and smiled faintly. "Hey, Rin. Been a while."

"Girl?" I asked, noting the pink print on the yellow blanket.

He nodded. "My daughter, Delia."

"I didn't know you were with someone. No one said anything," I said.

"They don't know," he said quietly, staring at his daughter. "I met Rhianon a while back, but she was just a kid. Last time I saw her, she was eighteen and we hooked up. Delia is the result. She was Rocket's sister so I'm not sure how well that's going to go over with the club. Ryker is technically Hades Abyss and the Pres's son, so…"

"You haven't told your club that you have a daughter?" I asked.

"He didn't know," Rocket said. "Rhianon didn't want him to feel pinned down. She knew he was the type to take responsibility for them, and she didn't want that. When she died, I knew I had to call Saint and tell him about Delia."

"I'm sorry for your loss," I said.

Rocket shrugged. "Drunk driver. It's just one of those things."

Despite the way he blew it off, I could see the pain in his eyes and knew he missed her. Giving Delia to Saint was probably really damn hard for him. The baby was a tie to his sister that it was likely difficult to part with, but he'd done what he thought was right for both baby and daddy.

"How old is she?" I asked.

"Six weeks," Rocket said. "Rhianon died two weeks ago. Took me that long to get my head out of my ass and call Saint. He dropped everything and came running like I knew he would. Just didn't expect him to leave the Reapers in the dark about where he was or what was going on."

"I'll tell them," he said. "When I'm ready."

"You should let them know you're safe," I said. "I think they're worried about you."

Saint nodded. It was hard to think of him that way, after knowing him as Johnny my entire life. I knew they valued the names they'd earned with the club, though, and I didn't want to disrespect him. I'd slipped up and called him Johnny at first, but I'd try not to do it again. He hadn't given me permission to call him by his given name, and from what I'd gathered, that was a big deal.

"Torch is still here," I said. "If you introduced him to Delia and told him what you were dealing with, I bet he'd give you the time and space you need. He seems like a reasonable guy."

"Yeah, the Pres is awesome," Saint said. "I was just trying to wrap my head around the fact I have a kid, and that Rhianon is gone."

"How are you getting her home?" Rocket asked. "You rode your bike here."

"Looks like I'm buying an SUV and I'll get a trailer to haul the bike back," Saint said. "I'm going to need a lot of baby shit, aren't I?"

"I have most of what you need. You can take all her stuff with you," Rocket said. "I won't be needing it. I even have some pictures of Rhianon you can take, so that Delia can see what her mom looked like when she grows up. There's some jewelry…"

He trailed off and I could see he was fighting not to cry. It broke my heart that he'd lost his sister and was now giving up his niece. And poor Saint. He looked both completely in awe of his daughter, and terrified of her.

"I'll give the two of you some time," I said, edging toward the door.

"No. Stay," Saint said. "Rocket told me a little of why you're here, but I want to hear it from you."

I nodded and eased down onto a nearby chair. I started from the beginning, what had happened after my dad died, and everything just spilled out of me up until the point where Torch had brought me to Hades Abyss. Saint's jaw was tight and his lips had thinned. I could tell he was furious, but it wasn't until he spoke that I realized he was mad at himself.

"I knew you'd lost your parents, and I just… it never occurred to me that you were in trouble. I never heard mention of your half-brother getting custody of you. I'm so damn sorry, Rin. I should have done something."

"Saint, we weren't exactly close, and no one knew. I was too ashamed to tell them. Besides, we were both kids. What could you have possibly done back then?" I asked.

"I was already Prospecting when I was seventeen. Torch found me living in an alley in town. I'd walked out after my mom's latest tried to beat the hell out of me. I never should have left Kayla there, but I'd thought she was safe enough. Then she told me about mom's boyfriend sneaking into her room at night." He shook his head. "It was too late to go back home by then. I took care of her the best I could, but I didn't give a second thought to anyone who wasn't my blood or a brother."

"It's not your fault," I said. "No one at school knew. Or if they did, no one ever said anything to my face."

"And Wraith said you were his, but he wouldn't make you his old lady?" Saint asked. "That's bullshit. Did he... Did he fuck you and then refuse to man up?"

My cheeks burned. "I started it. Don't blame him. I don't regret what happened between us, even if it didn't end with rainbows and sunshine. Besides, it's not like I haven't slept with men before who didn't want more than that from me."

"No, Rin. You were victimized by men who paid your brother for the privilege of hurting you. It's not the same thing at all," Saint said.

"He said my past didn't matter, but maybe it did," I said softly. "Maybe he didn't want a whore for an old lady. I can't blame him for that."

Rocket nudged Saint. "Maybe you should claim her. The two of you are the same age. She needs help, and you have a daughter who will need a mother."

My eyes went wide and my jaw dropped. "Are you crazy?"

Rocket grinned. "Maybe. But just the thought of you and Saint together might make Wraith's head explode. Might be the nudge he needs to get his shit straightened out and admit you were more than a fuck."

"He said it meant something to him," I said. "But then he said he doesn't do forever. He wanted me to stay, just not as... not as an official someone in his life. I get it. I really do. I'm not the type of woman you keep forever."

"If he wanted regular pussy without putting some ink on her, he could have just asked one of the sluts to move in," Saint said. "Any of them would jump at the chance, just in hopes it would become permanent. No, it was wrong of him to ask that of you, especially with everything you've dealt with. I'm sorry, Rin, but Wraith is being an asshole."

He knew the man better than I did, but I didn't like thinking of Wraith like that. He'd been nice to me, had wanted to help me. He'd even defended me just seconds after us meeting. I was the one who fucked it all up by having sex with him. I'd just wanted to know what it would feel like to be with someone of my choosing, and I hadn't been disappointed. He'd made me see stars, had given enough orgasms to last a lifetime. Well, maybe not a lifetime because already I wanted more of them, but our night together had been amazing.

Saint handed Delia over to Rocket. "Watch her while I go talk to Torch. I'd planned to leave in a day or two, but I want to stick around until Rin is settled."

Rocket took the baby, who was dozing peacefully. "You have a room here for however long you want."

"I'm… I'm not kicking you out of the guest room by being here, am I?" I asked Saint.

He smiled a little. "No, I'm staying in Rhianon's room. She had Delia's baby bed in there. I like being close to her so I can hear her if she wakes up."

Saint stood and came to stand next to my chair. He didn't say anything, but he squeezed my shoulder before walking out. I heard the front door open and shut, then I was left alone with Rocket and the baby. I didn't know what to say to the man who was letting me stay in his home. He'd suffered a great loss and yet he was willing to help me. I hadn't known men like him, or like the other bikers I'd met, existed. I'd known Saint was good, and that's why I'd gone to him. I'd seen the ugly side of men for too long, but now I was getting to see that not all of them were bad. These tough men loved hard and deeply, whether it was their wife, their sister, or the tiniest baby I'd ever seen.

"You know, I was only partially kidding," Rocket said. "If Wraith thinks you're moving on to someone who's willing to commit, it might make him pull his head out of his ass. He'll either man up, or you'll know for certain that he doesn't really want you."

"I appreciate the thought, but I don't want to play games with him. He either wants me or he doesn't, and I think he's proven that he doesn't. It's fine." I tried to smile a little. "I'm used to it."

"Doesn't make it right, doll, and you should never get used to men being assholes to you. Next time some guy pulls that shit, kick him in the nuts."

I nearly choked on my laughter, then gave myself up to it. I laughed so hard I cried, until the tears weren't from the laughter anymore. I sobbed until my body shook and I didn't think I'd ever stop crying. Rocket set the baby into a playpen nearby and then came toward me. He knelt at my feet and took my hands in his.

"You cry as much as you want. Get all of it out, doll. You've been strong long enough. Now it's time to let someone else carry the load, all right? You're safe while you're here, from your brother, from Wraith, and anyone else who wants to hurt you."

"Th-thank you," I said, starting to hiccup from the force of my breakdown. "I haven't cried this hard in front of anyone since my mom died."

"Then I'd say you're overdue."

Rocket pulled me into his arms and I sank to the floor, letting him hold me as I let out all the pain I'd been bottling up over the years. But what hurt the most was that Wraith had run when his club had tried to force his hand when it came to me. I'd felt like trash before that, but somehow his reaction had made me feel even worse. Even knowing I wasn't worthy of him, some small part of me had hoped that I was wrong.

I was still crying when Saint returned. He halted inside the doorway.

"What the fuck? I'm gone twenty minutes and you make her cry?" he demanded.

"Not… not his fault," I said, trying to wipe the tears from my eyes.

"How'd it go with Torch?" Rocket asked him.

"Fine. He seemed surprised as hell, but told me I could stay as long as I needed and my spot would be waiting when I got back. He'd already given me a small house when I patched in, but he's going to have some work done it. Make it more appropriate for the home of a little girl."

Rocket nodded and I eased back onto the chair. He stood, gave me a long look, probably making sure I wouldn't fall apart again, then retook his seat.

"What if my half-brother shows up here?" I asked. "You have Delia to think about. I don't want to bring that kind of trouble here."

"But you were going to take it to the Reapers and all the kids there?" Rocket asked. "Try again. What's really bothering you about being here?"

Saint tipped his head and stared. "She feels like a burden and unworthy of our help. Isn't that it, Rin? Women like you don't deserve good shit to happen. Is that what's going through your head?"

"Maybe," I said.

"Right. So, first order of business, you need to see a counselor," Rocket said. "I've been seeing someone since my sister died. I can take you over there and introduce you. She's a nice woman and not the least bit intimidating. I know it might sound stupid, but I think it's helped me to have someone to talk to. She doesn't tell me the right or wrong way to grieve, but she's insightful and helps me figure shit out on my own."

"I don't want..."

Saint scowled at me. "Are you about to say you don't want to be a burden? Because I might not ever hit a woman, I will damn sure spank you if you utter that bullshit in my presence."

My eyes went wide and my jaw dropped a little. Well, that was definitely a side of him I hadn't ever seen before.

"If you want to see the counselor, go see her, Rin," Saint said. "I'll take you or Rocket can. Whichever one of us makes you more comfortable."

"I'll think about it," I agreed.

"Make yourself at home," Rocket said. "You don't need to ask permission to get anything from the kitchen, or use anything in the house. I want you to feel welcome here, Rin. If you want to add some personal touches to the spare room, you're more than welcome to. It's on the plain side and could probably use a woman's touch anyway. My sister was never interested in decorating."

"Um, the room is fine," I said. Honestly, it was nicer than the one I'd had living with Joe.

"That sack Torch carried in the only things you own?" Rocket asked.

"Yeah. His wife gave me a few things. I haven't even had a chance to really go through it. I just grabbed what was on top to wear on the way here."

"We're almost out of diapers and formula," Saint said. "I'm going to the store. Why don't you come with me? I've been using Rocket's SUV, so you won't have to ride on the back of my bike."

"Shit. I won't need the damn thing when you take Delia with you. Just go ahead and take it. It was more for Rhianon anyway," Rocket said.

"I'll buy it from you," Saint said. "No arguments. You can use the money for whatever the fuck you want. It's the least I can do after everything..."

Rocket nodded.

"You want me to go shopping with you?" I asked, my brown furrowed.

"You can get some stuff you might need. Toothbrush, hair shit, whatever girly stuff you need," Saint said. "Women like to smell pretty, right?"

I felt the blood drain from my face and he was suddenly kneeling in front of me.

"Hey, what did I say?" he asked.

"Sorry, it's just... Joe always made me shower with this special scent before I..." I swallowed hard.

"Buy whatever you want, Rin," Saint said softly. "If you want to use plain soap or men's bodywash, I don't give a shit. You get something that's yours, any scent or unscented thing you want, and don't worry about the cost. All right?"

I nodded. "Thank you."

"Kayla know you were at the compound?" he asked. "Does she know about what happened to you?"

"I don't think so. They wouldn't let me see her. I guess her husband didn't trust me or something."

Saint snorted. "Fucking Preacher. He screwed up big time with Kayla, but ever since he got her back, he's treated her like she's made of glass. If she finds out he kept her from seeing you when you needed help, she'll threaten to rip off his balls."

I had a hard time picturing the sweet girl from high school doing any such thing, but everyone had probably changed since those days. Saint had definitely changed. He still had that hero complex, but he was rougher. Tougher too I was sure. And he definitely didn't look like the boy I'd seen in the halls at school. I could see why Rhianon had lost her head around him, and likely her heart too. Someday, he'd make a very lucky woman a good husband. I hoped he found the perfect woman for both him and Delia.

I let him help me stand, and then I pulled my coat back on and followed him out to the SUV. If I was going to seriously think about starting my life over, I might as well get started now. The sooner I put the ugliness of my past behind me, the better. I just hoped it didn't come back to bite me in the ass.

If only I'd known that it wasn't my time with Joe that would come back to haunt me, but my one and only night with Wraith. Someone upstairs really didn't like me.

Chapter Six

Wraith

Four fucking weeks. It had been one month of hell since Rin had left, and I still didn't know where the fuck she was. And her shit stain of a half-brother was elusive as fuck. I'd tried to kill time, and keep my mind off Rin, by tracking Joe Banner. I'd done my damnedest to gather as much evidence as I could the old-fashioned way, hoping it would bolster whatever Wire had on the guy. We'd met with the FBI agents a few times now, and while they really wanted to talk to Rin, Torch still wasn't letting anyone know where she was.

And Saint… Fucking hell. Torch comes back from wherever he took Rin and suddenly knows where our missing brother is? And doesn't seem the least bit concerned that Saint wanted to stay gone for a while? It made my blood boil, knowing in my gut that Saint and Rin were together, probably holed up somewhere cozy while she hid from Joe Banner. Were they getting close? Did she let him touch her the way I had?

I'd already put too many holes in my fucking walls, but I wanted to punch something just thinking about Rin with another man. I normally wasn't prone to random acts of violence, but knowing that I'd hurt Rin, that I was the reason she'd left made me feel out of control. I hated myself, and I wasn't too fucking happy with my club either. If they'd stayed the fuck out of my relationship with her, then she'd be here now. Safe.

The damn Christmas tree in my living room mocked me with its cheerfulness, the lights twinkling like everything was all right. I fucking hated that tree right now, and everything it represented. Even though it was doubtful Rin was coming back, I'd bought a few gifts for her. Kayla had been sweet enough to help me wrap them, even if she had given me pathetic looks every few minutes. If she knew where Rin and her brother were hiding, she wasn't giving the information up, and I wasn't about to grill her about it. She had three kids running her ragged and didn't need the added stress.

There was a hesitant knock on my door and I stormed into the front entry, jerking it open. I blinked a moment and then tried to not look quite so fierce. Tex and Kalani's daughter, Janessa, stood on my front steps, shifting from foot to foot.

"What is it, Janessa?"

She'd been fourteen when Tex found her locked up in an asylum. Since then, she'd come a long way. If I remembered right, she was about to turn sixteen. The bubbly girl everyone was used to wasn't on my porch, though. She worried at her lower lip, her hands clenching and unclenching in front of her.

"Can I come in?" she asked, glancing around like she was afraid to be caught here.

I stepped back and let her in, wondering if she was in some sort of trouble. She shivered and rubbed her arms, her nervousness not abating even though I'd shut the door. She'd come by before, asking if she could earn money washing my bike or helping around the house. Sweet kid.

"What's going on, Janessa?"

"I overheard Mom and Dad talking," she said. Her gaze locked on mine. "I know I'm young and everyone thinks I'm silly, but I know what it's like to care about someone and not be able to have them. I'm too young right now, and I know that."

I held up a hand, but she barreled ahead.

"If you want to know where Rin is, I can tell you," she blurted.

My hand fell to my side. "What?"

She nodded. "I overheard them discussing Rin and Saint. I guess Ryker said something to Laken, and then she told Flicker. It spread from there. Torch took her up north. They're both holed up with Hades Abyss. You know, Ryker's club? They've been there this whole time."

I sagged against the wall. Rin was with Hades Abyss? And what the fuck was Saint doing up there? I ran a hand through my hair and mentally checked off all the shit I was supposed to take care of this week, but none of it mattered a damn, not compared to seeing Rin again.

"Are you going after her?" Janessa asked.

"Depends. Who's the guy you want but can't have?" I asked, wondering if I needed to school some little punk on the proper way to treat girls.

Her cheeks flushed. "He's part of Jackal's club and too old for me. At least, right now he is, but I'll be eighteen in two years. Daddy can't keep me here after that."

My eyebrows shot upward. "You're after a Devil?"

"He was just a Prospect when I met him, but I overheard Scratch when he was here over Thanksgiving. He said they'd just patched in a Prospect and his name was now Irish. It's Seamus, I know it is."

I wasn't getting anywhere near that. Tex would have his hands full soon, but I was staying the fuck out of it unless he asked for help. I wasn't exactly one to say that there was too much of an age difference between her and the guy she was crushing on. I hoped it was a crush anyway. I'd hate for her to get her tender heart broken by a member from a club that we considered family.

"You have some more growing up to do," I said. "But if he's the right guy, the one you're meant to be with, then he'll be there when you're ready. And if not, then maybe you're meant for someone else."

"Like you and Rin are meant to be together?" she asked, blinking wide, innocent eyes at me, but I wasn't fooled. The little shit.

"What Rin and I are is no one's concern but ours. And if the club had remembered that, then she'd be here right now."

"If you want her home by Christmas, you might want to hurry. You only have a few days."

"You're right, kid. Head home. I need to pack a few things and head out. I'll message Torch along the way and tell him I needed to clear my head. If I tell him where I'm going, he might alert Hades Abyss, and they could move Rin."

"I won't tell anyone. Swear," Janessa said, pretending to lock her lips.

"Go on home before your mom and dad start looking for you."

"Mom is busy with Noah and Clayton right now, and Dad disappeared the second Noah started throwing his blocks."

I tried not to laugh, I really did. Janessa even snickered a little before heading out the door. It was kind of funny watching Tex with his kids. Sometimes he stared at his sons like they were aliens. He'd missed the first fourteen years of his daughter's life, so fatherhood was still new to him. He wasn't doing a bad job, just seemed a little lost sometimes. Good thing he had Kalani.

I crammed some shit into a duffle bag, but when I got to my front steps I stopped. Shit. I couldn't go after Rin on my bike, not if I wanted to bring her home. It was too fucking cold to ride that much of a distance, especially since she wasn't used to it. If I took one of the club trucks, Torch was going to ask more than a few questions, and might even figure out where I was going. I wanted to pull my damn hair out.

I was still staring at my bike when Ryker pulled up in his woman's SUV.

"Get the fuck in," he said, nearly growling.

I could feel the anger coming off him and wondered what the fuck I'd done to piss him off. I tossed my bag into the backseat and sat up front next to him.

"I know where Rin is," Ryker said. "My fucking club kept that shit from me and I'm not happy. If you want her, I'm taking you to get her."

"Thanks."

He frowned and looked at the bag in the back. "You knew where she was, didn't you? You were going after her?"

I nodded. "Someone told me today, but I can't say who."

"Good. Then I can pretend I'm going to check on my dad and you just asked for a ride," Ryker said. "Then Torch can't kick my ass."

"You're not scared of Torch. You're worried your woman will decide to stay here with Flicker when the Pres kicks you out. Not like you don't have somewhere to go. Hades Abyss would likely welcome you back with open arms. You're still a member."

He nodded. "True, but Laken likes being here. And the Reapers have a ton of kids, so it's better for Gabriel. If I took Laken back to Hades Abyss, our kid wouldn't have anyone to play with. Everyone there is still single."

"Pretty sure you knocked up Laken without the benefit of marriage. You never know. Your brothers might have kids out there and not know it."

He snorted. "Wouldn't surprise me. Especially Fox or Shooter. Those two are complete hound dogs and screw anything with a pussy."

I gave him a pointed look considering how he'd met Flicker's sister and he just shrugged.

"I'm reformed," he said. "And before Laken, I'd always wrapped my dick. Maybe subconsciously I'd known she was it for me."

"Maybe."

We rode in silence for a while, then stopped for gas along the way. We were probably a few hours from the Hades Abyss compound when Ryker started talking again.

"You going to claim Rin?"

"Don't plan on it," I said. "She's better off without me."

He looked over at me, probably for longer than he should have since he was driving, but he didn't say anything. It made me wonder if he knew something I didn't. Yeah, Janessa had overheard her parents talking about Rin's location, but was something more going on? Had my fears about her hooking up with Saint been legitimate?

"Just don't freak the fuck out when you see her again," Ryker said. "Even my old man won't look too kindly on me bringing your ass with me if you flip out on everyone."

I clenched my hands into fists. What the fuck? Why would I flip out? What was going on with Rin that had him worried?

"And you should know, my source said that Rin's tests all came back fine. She wasn't carrying any STDs, since it seems you slept with her, and the doc had done a pregnancy test that came back negative. So she wasn't carrying a kid from some asshole who paid to use her."

Wait. "You know I slept with her?"

He gave me an are-you-fucking-kidding-me look.

"Right. Everyone knows I slept with her, then bolted like a dumbass without talking to her first. I know her running isn't completely on the club. I should have made sure she was all right before I took off, but Torch and Venom should have stayed the fuck out of it. What the hell does it matter if I claim her? Why can't she just stay with me?" I asked.

"Because she deserves commitment. And if you can't give it to her, then you need to let her find someone who can."

It sounded like he muttered *especially now* under his breath.

My phone started going nuts with text messages and calls. I mostly ignored them. What with Ryker giving me a ride, I'd completely forgotten to let Torch or Venom know that I would be MIA for a day or so. It would just depend how long it took me to convince Rin to come home with me. I wasn't going to leave without her, unless she'd hooked up with someone else. As badly as I wanted her back home with me, I wasn't going to take her by force.

I finally sent a message to both Torch and Venom letting them know I was fine, but I needed some space for a few days. Everyone knew I was pissed as hell about Rin being gone, and anyone who had seen my house had told me I needed to control my temper. I wasn't typically the type of guy to punch holes in walls. Hadn't ever done it until Rin came into my life. I just… she made me feel shit, things I'd never felt before. It scared the fuck out of me, and at the same time, I wanted her back because I felt like a piece of me was missing when she wasn't there.

Christ! I'd had her in my house one fucking night. One! Even I knew how fucked up that was. It wasn't like we'd spent days, weeks, or months together and fallen in love or some shit. We had insane chemistry together, and yeah, she'd made me forget every woman I'd ever fucked. All I'd been about to think about was how damn right she'd felt in my arms, and wrapped around my cock. Fuck! I'd never wanted a woman as badly as I wanted Rin. Even now, just remembering the way she'd looked at me that night, I started to get hard. I hadn't fucked anyone since she'd left, having no interest in the club sluts.

When we pulled through the Hades Abyss gates, Ryker didn't go to the clubhouse like I'd expected. He turned and drove past some homes until he stopped at one, pulling into the driveway. I saw Saint's bike, another Harley, and an SUV. Was this where Saint and Rin had been staying? And who the fuck was the Hades Abyss member they'd been crashing with? Shit. They hadn't made Rin be part of a threesome, had they? I didn't see her liking that shit one bit.

I nearly dove out the car, forgetting my bag in the back, and didn't even stop to knock on the door. I just barged in and started looking for Rin. What I found stopped me in my tracks.

Saint stood in the hall, a small blonde baby cradled against his shoulder, and Rin was retching in the bathroom with some asshole holding her hair and rubbing her back.

"Are you sick?" I asked, staring at the woman I'd thought about night and day for a damn month.

She blinked at me and paled even more. "Wraith."

The Hades Abyss asshole glared at me. "So you're Wraith. Nice of you to show up."

What the hell?

"No one would tell me where they'd stashed Rin. I've been trying to find her for four fucking weeks!"

"She's safe," Saint said. "But I think the two of you need to talk. Come on, Rocket. Let's give them some space."

Saint went to move past me and the little girl on his shoulder opened her eyes and blinked at me. Holy shit.

"You have a kid?" I asked, because she had Saint's eyes.

"Yeah. This is Delia," Saint said. "And now that you're here, I can take her home."

"Wait. You've been here this entire time waiting for me to show up? Why the hell didn't you just text me and tell me Rin was here?" I asked.

"Because she didn't want me to," Saint said and kept walking.

Rocket slid past me and I turned to face Rin again.

I stepped into the bathroom and knelt beside her.

"Hey, sweet girl. When you hide, you do it really fucking well."

She smiled a little, but still seemed a bit green.

"You got the flu or something?" I asked.

"Only if this flu bug lasts nine months." Her gaze focused on mine. "I'm pregnant."

I processed her words, then tried to stand, but she latched onto me.

"That asshole knocked you up?" I demanded. "I thought he was protecting you."

"Wraith. You're a dumbass," she said. "Rocket hasn't touched me in that way. You're the one who knocked me up. Even though the condoms you used weren't expired yet, they apparently weren't foolproof or you have super sperm."

My mouth opened and shut a few times, but it felt like the world was falling out from under me and everything spun for a moment.

"I got you pregnant?" I asked so softly I almost couldn't even hear myself.

"Yeah. It's why I didn't call you. You made it clear that you didn't want me and I didn't want you coming just because of the baby. We'll be fine. So now that you've seen I'm all right, you can go home."

I stared at her, noting the dark smudges under her eyes.

"I wanted to find you, but no one would tell me where you were. When I asked Wire to search for you, he told me to fuck off. The second I found out where you were, I packed a bag and came straight here. I want you to come home, Rin. You don't belong here."

"I don't belong with you either," she said. "You made that clear."

"Baby." I reached out and gripped her hair, feeling the silkiness between my fingers. "I didn't run that day because of you. I needed some time to clear my head because my brothers pissed me the fuck off."

"Torch told me. He gave you an ultimatum. You either claimed me or let me go, and you didn't want to claim me." She sighed. "I understand, and I understood then too. I've always known I'm not good enough for you, Wraith, and I never will be."

"Don't ever say that. I didn't…" I released her and landed on my ass, my legs sprawled on either side of her. "It's me, all right? I'm fucked up and I'm no good for you."

She studied me a moment but didn't say anything. I worried she was going to walk out, until she opened her mouth.

"This is about your sister, isn't it?" she asked. "Torch said if you showed up that I had to force you to tell me about her."

I swallowed hard and nodded. "Yeah. I fucked up, sweet girl. I didn't protect her like I was supposed to and she ended up dead. But not before…"

"Before what?" she asked.

"Not before they kept her drugged and let men pay to fuck her for days, maybe even weeks. When they were finished and she was nearly dead, they left her in the gutter. She died alone, lying in sewage like trash." I felt my eyes burn with unshed tears. "It's my fault. If I'd been there…"

Rin crawled over to me and rested her palms against my cheeks. "Where were you when it happened?"

"Overseas. I was in the military and was off fighting a war. I should have been home watching over her, not trying to be a hero. I failed the only person who mattered."

"You didn't fail her, Wraith," she said softly. "And how many people did you save while you were over there? I've seen the scars on your body. You got those in action, didn't you?"

I nodded.

"The men and women you saved, they mattered too. It's horrible what happened to your sister, and I'm so damn sorry you have to live with that, but it wasn't your fault." She caressed my cheek with her thumb. "Would your sister be happy knowing that you're carrying around all this guilt and not letting yourself be happy?"

"No," I said, knowing that was the truth. She'd have wanted me to be happy.

"Maybe I'm not the only one who needs to heal. Maybe you do too, and you need to learn to forgive yourself." She paused and a haunted look entered her eyes. "Was it my half-brother? Was he the one who... who whored out your sister?"

"The police never seemed to be able to solve the crime, but I've wondered if Joe Banner was behind it. Even if he was, it just gives me another reason to bury his ass. I don't blame you for his actions, Rin, but your brother has to be stopped."

"I know," she said. "Is... is your only objection to claiming me or this baby that you feel like you failed your sister?"

"I'm not a good man, Rin. I know you seem to think otherwise, but I've done some pretty bad shit in my life, including things that aren't legal. You'd be better off, both of you, if you just left and started a new life somewhere else. I'd thought I'd convince you to come back with me, stay with me for a while, but now..."

"Because of the baby your plans changed?" she asked.

"Yeah. You have more than yourself to think about now. I can't ask you to put your life on hold, Rin."

She dropped her gaze to the floor, then turned a sickly shade before she started throwing up again. I held her hair back, but felt awkward as fuck. What did I know about taking care of anyone? The thought of me having a kid was terrifying. I only hoped that one day Rin could forgive me for this. I'd ruined her damn life all because I hadn't been able to say no when I should have. She might have instigated things that first time, but I hadn't pushed her away, and I'd been the one to reach for her after that.

All the plans I had went out the window. For some reason, the thought of never seeing Rin again left me feeling empty and there was an ache in my chest, but this wasn't about me. It was about her, and what would be good for her and the baby. And I seriously didn't think that was me.

I could still take care of the problem of Joe Banner, though. Make sure he never got his hands on Rin again, or anyone else. There would likely be someone else who moved into his territory once he was gone, but if we took the corrupt officials down, then it would be easier to put a stop to them.

Chapter Seven

Rin

Wraith disappeared after I finished throwing up yet again. It seemed to be all I did these days. I'd thought I'd come down with a virus when Rocket had suggested I see the doctor. One little test and suddenly I'd felt fear like I'd never felt before. What did I know about raising a baby? I hadn't had a good role model after my mom had died, and I'd been so little when I lost her that I didn't remember much. Not as much as I would have liked. If I closed my eyes, I could still see her face or hear the sound of her voice, and I had a few memories of happy times with her, like the holidays. I did remember being happy, and that she hugged me all the time. I'd felt safe when she was alive. But was that enough to show me what it meant to be a good mom?

I didn't know where Wraith had gone, possibly straight back to the Dixie Reapers. I'd brushed my teeth, then huddled under a blanket on the couch, not really paying attention to whatever Christmas movie Rocket had put on. I'd found I liked the Hallmark movies, with their happy endings. It always seemed to work out for those women. Whatever man they wanted, whatever outcome they needed, it happened for them. Real life didn't seem to work that way, though, or at least it never had for me.

Yes, I was away from Joe Banner and no longer had to do what he said, but my life still wasn't my own. Now I had to focus on the baby growing inside me and figure out what my next step would be. I knew I couldn't stay here forever, but I didn't exactly have anywhere else to go either. I didn't have money or a job, so finding a place to live wouldn't be easy. There were always women's shelters, but I felt like there were women out there who needed those spots more than me. I was no longer living in a dangerous situation, but there were plenty of women who were.

The front door opened and Saint walked in. He'd left earlier to let Spider know that he was heading home with Delia. I knew Rocket, and probably the entire club, would miss the little girl. She was such a sweetheart. If my baby were half as good as she was, then being a mom wouldn't be so bad. I'd helped with her when I was able, though she'd scared me to death at first. I'd never held a baby before her. I'd been close to a few, and their baby powder scent always made me smile, but no one had ever trusted me to hold one.

"You heading home?" Rocket asked.

There was tension in his voice and I knew he would miss his niece, even if he was doing the right thing by letting Saint have her. The baby belonged with her daddy, but I hoped that Rocket didn't step away completely. I didn't see any reason why he couldn't visit, or vice versa. Now that Delia had linked the clubs together, surely they wouldn't mind making arrangements for the members of either club to go onto each other's territory. I didn't know enough about all this to really understand how everything worked. It had seemed like the clubs were friends.

Saint stared at me hard before looking at Rocket. "I am, but I'm wondering if I should take Rin with me."

"What?" I asked. "Why would you take me with you? Wraith doesn't want me. He's made that clear twice now. The club pushing me toward him isn't going to do anything but make him angry again. Just leave it alone."

"Rin, you don't have any family except the asshole who sold you to random men. Who's going to help you during your pregnancy or when the baby gets here?" he asked.

"I'll figure it out," I mumbled. Honestly, there wasn't much to figure out. It was go with Saint, hope Rocket let me stay longer, or live on the streets.

"Look, even if Wraith doesn't man up and take responsibility, that baby is still part of the Dixie Reapers," Saint said. "If you want to stay with us, I'm sure Torch could find a place for you to live. Maybe even give you a place of your own. There's some duplexes at the back of the property and several are empty. Some of the brothers preferred those over the houses, so you'd have someone nearby if you needed something."

"Saint, I --"

He held up a hand. "Look, Rin. I know you want to do this on your own, but you're going to need help whether you realize it or not. If you get a job, you'll need someone to babysit. I'm sure the old ladies would help you out when you needed it, or we could assign a Prospect to help you."

"Go with him, doll," Rocket said. "I think it would be good for you and the baby, and you never know. Wraith might come to his senses and realize that he wants you."

I wasn't going to hold my breath that would happen.

"When are we leaving?" I asked.

"As soon as you can get packed up. I'm going to take the essentials for Delia, and Rocket can either send everything else, or he can bring them down when he visits. I'm hoping he'll be down often to visit his niece," Saint said.

Rocket nodded and reached over to pat my leg.

"Go with him, Rin. You need family around you, and while the Dixie Reapers might not be your blood kin, they'll protect you and that baby. I think they're what you need right now, even if you don't want to admit it."

"All right," I agreed. "I'll go."

Saint smiled. "Get your things while I gather Delia's clothes and toys. I'll just take the playpen for now. I'm sure Ridley or someone else at the compound will have a baby bed I can borrow until I can go buy one."

"You can have this one," Rocket said.

"And where will Delia sleep when she comes to see you?" Saint asked. "I'm not cutting you out of her life. Keep some things here for when she visits. I'll take the important things like diapers and clothes, the playpen, and her car seat and stroller."

Rocket nodded.

There was a hint of relief in his eyes and I wondered if he'd been worried that Saint would keep him from seeing Delia. He obviously knew nothing about the man who had knocked up his sister if he'd thought that for even a moment. Yeah, Saint might have screwed up and gotten Rhianon pregnant, but he was definitely one of the good guys. He'd always been a protector, and he probably always would be.

When Saint left the room, I inched closer to Rocket.

"He's going to take good care of her," I said. "You made the right decision by calling him. He'll be a really great dad, and maybe one day, he'll find an amazing woman to help raise Delia. But I can promise that he'll never forget your sister, and he'll make sure you see Delia as much as you want. It's just the kind of guy he is."

"Yeah, I get that," Rocket said, smiling faintly. "Just hard to watch Delia walk out the door, knowing she's the only tie I have to my sister. My parents are gone, so she's the only blood I have left."

"And you still have her," I said gently. "She'll always be your niece, and I bet Saint makes sure she sees you often, even if he has to use an app on his phone or something. He's not going to let her forget you, or her mom."

"Thanks, Rin. You're a sweetheart, and if Wraith can't see that, then he's an idiot. If I were the settling down type, I'd keep you here."

"Thanks, Rocket, but I'll be fine without Wraith."

"Yeah, I know you will." He leaned over and hugged me.

I rested my head on his shoulder for a moment, and I realized that I would miss him when I left. For the last month, he'd been there for me. Only as a friend, but I'd never really had those, not in a long time. It was nice to feel wanted, even if just for a moment. I was about to pull away when the front door flew open and I heard arguing. I looked over my shoulder and saw someone shoving Wraith through the doorway.

"Talk to her, asshole," the other man said. "I'm not taking your ass home until you've given her a really good fucking reason not to claim her and that kid, and not some bullshit excuse of you not being good enough. You're a goddamn decorated war hero, and a valuable member of your club. Man the fuck up."

"Ryker," Wraith pushed back. "Fuck off!"

"It's Diablo while he's here," Rocket said, releasing me and standing up. "He's the Pres's son so treat him with respect while you're on Hades Abyss territory. Maybe you forget that when he's on your turf, but here you'd better damn well treat him like a patched member of this club."

"It's fine, Rocket," Diablo said, glaring at Wraith. "He's just being a stubborn ass."

"You mean all men aren't?" I asked, then slapped a hand over my mouth. It wasn't like me to say things like that, not where people could hear me.

Rocket chuckled. "She's not wrong."

"Hey, Rin, are you almost…" Saint trailed off when he saw Diablo and Wraith in the living room. "What the fuck is going on?"

"Is she almost what?" Wraith asked with narrowed eyes.

"I was going to ask if she was almost packed, but it seems she hasn't even started," Saint said.

"Packed?" Wraith asked, then turned an accusing glare at Rocket. "You're throwing her out?"

"Fuck no," Rocket said. "Saint's taking her home with him."

If a person could ever look like they were about to go off like a bomb, Wraith would have in that moment. His face flushed red and his hands clenched into fists. With a roar, he launched himself at Saint and all I could do was stare in open-mouthed shock as the man who professed to not want me attacked Saint.

I leapt off the couch when I came to my senses and tried to get between them, but Rocket put an arm around my waist and pulled me out of the way.

"Let them settle this, Rin. You try to get in the middle and you'll get hurt, then they'll both feel bad."

"He's right," Diablo said. "They need to work it out. Although, I think Wraith misunderstood what Saint meant by taking you home, unless you've decided to move in with him?"

I shook my head. "He said Torch would find a place for me to stay at the compound."

I winced as Saint and Wraith pounded on each other. They both had split lips, busted knuckles, and poor Saint was getting a black eye. I wriggled free of Rocket and picked up the nearest thing, a baby book, and launched it at Wraith's head. He whirled, then the anger drained from him when he saw I'd thrown it.

"Rin?"

"Stop fighting," I said. "You don't want me, or the baby, which means you have no say over where I live. I'm sorry you don't want me at the compound, but I'm going."

"You're not living with him," Wraith said, pointing at Saint.

"Wraith…" I moved closer. "Will, you can't dictate my life. You don't own me."

He came toward me, slowly, then gently reached up and stroked my cheek. "I can't watch you set up house with another Reaper, Rin. I just can't. You're supposed to be in my bed, not his. Not anyone's."

"Then I guess you have a decision to make," I said.

He ran a hand through his hair and looked like he was torn between bolting and tossing me over his shoulder to let everyone know I was his. I wouldn't have a problem with that second option, not at all. Not if he truly wanted me.

"Can we have some time to talk?" Wraith asked the other men in the room.

"Just let me get Delia. I'll let the club say bye to her while the two of you work this shit out. But, Wraith, if Rin wants to go to the compound, I'm taking her whether you like it or not."

A few minutes later, the door shut as all three men and a tiny baby stepped out into the cold December air.

Wraith tugged at his hair and began pacing.

"What scares you the most about claiming me?" I asked.

"I could fail you, and now there's a baby to think about too."

"Can I ask you something?"

He stopped and faced me.

"Did you have the club at your back when you lost your sister?" I asked.

"No. I patched in after that. I'd prospected for them before joining the military but once I shipped out I was gone for a while. Even when I came back stateside, I only went home to tend to Elisa's funeral."

"You have an entire MC behind you, Wraith. Don't you think if the baby and I needed something and you weren't around that someone else would step in and help?" I asked. "You let those kids put a tree up in your house and decorate it. You even left the ornaments all clumped together just the way they'd arranged them. Are you going to tell me you haven't done other things for the kids or the women in the club?"

"Of course I help when I can!"

It was like a light bulb went off. His eyes widened a moment, and he breathed hard. Then he was striding toward me, scooped me up, and carried me down the hall. He paused outside the bedroom doors, and I pointed to the room I'd been using. He kicked the door shut, then eased me down to stand in front of him.

"Just one question, sweet girl. Before you ran off and came here, you said you weren't good enough for me and you wouldn't even think of staying with me with or without strings attached. Now you want me to claim you. If this is about the baby…"

I pressed my lips to his. "It's not. I've been working on my self-worth since I've been here. It's still a struggle, but I'm getting better. I want you, Will, want to be a part of your life."

Maybe it was also a little bit that I hoped he was the Christmas miracle I'd been waiting for all this time. It was the holiday season, after all, and Christmas wasn't here just yet. I'd still get to spend it with Wraith, make new memories, and maybe we could start our own family traditions. I could do some of the things my mom had always done for the family on Christmas Day, and Wraith and I could figure out some new things that were just ours.

"And me pushing you away isn't helping," he said. "Rin, I never meant to hurt you, to make you feel unwanted. Fuck knows you're all I think about. I can't promise things will be perfect, but I'm willing to try if you are."

"I missed you," I admitted, my cheeks burning. "I tried not to, but every time I closed my eyes, I wished you were lying next to me. We might have only had one night together, but it was the best night of my life."

He hooked an arm around my waist and pulled me tight against his body. "I missed you too. So fucking much. And just so you know, I haven't been with anyone since you left, unless you count my hand. Even jerking off left me feeling unsatisfied."

My cheeks were on fire and I suddenly found it hard to look at him.

He tipped my chin up and I saw a smirk on his face. "Did you try to pleasure yourself, my sweet Rin? Did you touch that pretty pussy and make yourself come while you were thinking of me?"

"Yes. It didn't feel as good, though."

"Show me," he commanded and took a step back.

My hands shook as I undressed, but the hungry look in his eyes made me keep going. When I was naked, I lay back on the bed, placed my feet on the mattress, and spread my thighs wide. I grew even wetter as he unbuckled his belt, unzipped his pants, and pulled out his cock.

"Fuck, sweet girl. Part those pussy lips and give me a good look at what I've missed," he said.

I spread myself open and bit my lip as he tugged on his cock.

"Make yourself come. Show me how you played with yourself while we were apart," he said.

I circled my clit with my fingers, but I locked my gaze on the hand stroking his cock. Pre-cum slid down his shaft and I wished he was inside me, fucking me hard and deep. I felt so empty and knew my fingers would never be enough. I rubbed faster, my body tightening as I fought to come, but I couldn't seem to get there.

Wraith grunted and came closer. My eyes went wide as cum shot out of his cock and covered my pussy and fingers. His body trembled as he stared down at me, then reached out and ran his fingers along my pussy. He shoved his cum inside me, fucking me with his fingers. I moved my hand out of the way and he stroked my clit with his thumb. It didn't take much to make me come, just his hands on me was nearly enough to get the job done. I cried out his name as my body bucked and pleasure raced through me.

"Get me hard again, Rin. I want to fuck you."

I slid off the bed and knelt at his feet. He hadn't completely softened, even though he wasn't as hard as before. I lapped at him, licking off the remains of his cum before sucking him into my mouth. When men had come in my mouth, I'd always gagged at the horrid taste, but this was Wraith and I welcomed his flavor as it hit my tongue. I sucked and licked his cock, tonguing the tip, then swallowing him down. His hand tangled in my hair and he thrust deep, not stopping until I'd taken all of him.

I kept my gaze locked on his as he fucked my mouth.

"That's it, sweet girl. Take it all."

My hands tightened on his thighs as he took what he wanted, but I didn't feel cheap or dirty like I had in the past. I could see his desire for me blazing in his eyes. He didn't want to just get off with whoever was handy, he wanted *me*. I felt his cock harden even more and swell as he got close to coming, then he abruptly pulled out.

"Fuck! Your mouth is like goddamn heaven, Rin."

I stood on shaky legs, and he rubbed his thumb across my bottom lip.

"Was that okay? I didn't think... you didn't have a flashback or something?"

"I'm good," I said, meaning it. "I knew it was you and that this was different. I trust you, Will."

"Turn around and bend over the bed. Guess it's too much to hope you have lube stashed in here."

"Didn't need it," I said.

He grunted.

I turned to face the bed and bent over the foot of it, my ass in the air. I felt his hands as he lightly touched me at first, then he parted my ass cheeks and rubbed his cock between them.

"When we get home and have the proper supplies, I'm taking this ass. I'm going to make every part of you mine, Rin. You'll have my cum in every hole you have, and I'll bathe the rest of you in it too. I'm going to erase every bad memory if it takes me fucking you for days with only food and bathroom breaks."

"Please, Will. I need you."

He rubbed his cock up and down the crack of my ass a few more times before he shifted and I felt the head press against my slit. His hands slid down from my ass, then opened my pussy wide as he thrust deep.

"So fucking beautiful. I love watching you take my cock."

He continued to hold me open as he fucked me, going slow as if he were savoring the moment. I felt every inch of his cock slide into me again and again. I gripped the bedding and bit my lip so I wouldn't beg him for more. I wanted him to fuck me, to take me like he owned me. I didn't need slow and gentle.

"So good," he murmured. "You nice and warmed up, baby?"

"Yes. Yes! Please…"

So much for not begging!

I felt him pull back, and then he slammed into me hard and fast. I gasped and my eyes flew open wide. He gripped my hips and drove into me, the force of every thrust taking me up onto my toes. He was nearly savage as he pounded into me, as if he'd completely lost control. In my old life, I'd have been scared or at least trying not to cry from the pain, but all I felt was pleasure. I trusted him, and I knew now that he would never hurt me intentionally. My running from him had been a mistake, and I would make it up to him.

"Fuck, Rin! I'm already close to coming. Gonna fill this pussy up and watch my cum slide out of you."

He seemed to get even wilder, his strokes erratic. Will moved one of his hands between me and the bed, then used his fingers to rub my clit until I was screaming out his name. I felt the first splash of his cum as he slammed his cock into me over and over. My body felt heavy and sated as he finished, burying himself as far as he could.

He gently brushed my hair to the side and pressed kisses to my shoulder and neck. I could feel his cock twitching inside me and I wished we could stay joined a while longer. I knew he'd go soft sooner or later, then he'd pull out and I'd have that empty feeling again. I'd never felt it before, not until he'd spent all night making me come so many times my throat had hurt the next morning from all the screaming.

Will pulled out, then rolled me over. He propped my heels on the bed and spread me open. There was a possessive gleam in his eyes as he watched his cum slide out of me. I thought I was seeing things when his cock started to get hard again. I'd never known a man who could come and then be ready to come again so fast, but it seemed that Wraith stayed hard all the time. Not that I was complaining. The man had more stamina than anyone I'd ever known.

"You make me feel like I'm eighteen again," he said. "It's been a long damn time since I've been able to get hard again this fast. Only happens with you. It's like my dick knew all along that you were meant to be mine."

"Maybe you should listen to him more often," I said, smiling softly.

"Baby, if I did that, I'd be fucking you non-stop regardless of what room we were in or who might be watching."

He was still staring at my pussy.

"Do you want that? Would you get off on someone watching us?" I asked.

"Don't want anyone to see this gorgeous body but me," he said.

"So it wouldn't turn you on to take me to the clubhouse in a short skirt, no panties, and no bra and make me ride your cock in front of everyone?" I asked, knowing there were men who would love something like that. "Make me show everyone my breasts while I took your cock?"

"Fuck no!" His eyes became nearly feral as they lifted to meet my gaze. "I even think some asshole has been looking at your breasts or your pussy and I'll gut the fucker. It's just you and me, Rin. It will only ever be me and you. Do you need more than that?"

"No," I said. "I'm glad you don't want to share me."

"I don't know how much longer I can control myself with you lying like that, Rin. Makes me want to do all sorts of dirty things to you."

"Then do them," I taunted. Whatever he wanted to give me, I'd take.

"Rin…" He took a step back.

"Fuck me, Wraith."

His eyes narrowed when I didn't use his given name and I decided to poke the bear again.

"You know you want to. Don't you want to be balls deep inside me... Wraith?"

He growled and before I could even so much as gasp, he'd flipped me over and was smacking my ass with blows hard enough I knew they'd leave a mark. His hand came down hard on my ass cheek, again and again.

"I'm Wraith again?"

Smack. Smack.

"What's my name, Rin? When I'm fucking you, what name are you supposed to use?"

Smack.

"Will!"

He landed three more blows on my poor abused ass.

"You stay right there, exactly like that. Don't fucking move or you'll get another spanking. Understood?"

"Yes, sir," I said meekly, then glanced over my shoulder and damn near creamed myself from the look in his eyes.

He slammed out of the bedroom and returned a few minutes later with lube in his hand. I didn't know where he'd found it, and I wasn't sure I wanted to know. He kicked the door shut again, then liberally coated his cock before his thighs brushed the backs of mine.

"Hold your ass open, Rin."

I winced as I spread the cheeks, my skin still burning from the spanking he'd just given me. I squealed as he worked the icy cold lube into me, using his fingers to stretch me out. When I squirmed, he smacked my ass again, above my hands, three swats on each cheek for every time I moved. I'd never be able to sit long enough to make the drive home.

He removed his fingers and I felt the press of his cock against me.

"You know what to do, sweet girl. Let me in."

I pushed out as he pressed inside me. I'd never enjoyed anal sex, or any sex for that matter, until Wraith. Chills ran up my spine as he filled me, and I pressed back wanting all of him.

"Next time, I'm taking a video of my cock fucking your ass," he said, his voice deeper and huskier than before. "Then when we can't have sex I'll have something to jerk off to."

My eyes slid shut and I bit my lip so hard I almost drew blood.

"Fuck! You just damn near squeezed my dick off. You like that idea, baby? Like the thought of me filming us while I fuck you?"

"Maybe," I said, my cheeks feeling like they were on fire.

I felt his hands slide up my sides, then he cupped my breasts. As he drove into me, he pinched down on my nipples, and it was enough to set off an orgasm stronger than any he'd given me before. He kept pinching and tugging as he fucked my ass, riding me hard.

"Beg me for it, baby," he said, then growled as he slammed into me again.

"Please, Will. I want you to come inside me. Come in my ass."

He growled and drove into me three more times before I felt the heat of his release. His cock twitched and pulsed in my ass and I finally let go of my cheeks. He was still playing with my nipples, pinching, rolling, and tugging on them. He hadn't softened hardly at all and he started thrusting again. When he pinched down and twisted on my nipples right as his cock slid into me again, I nearly screamed the walls down I came so hard.

He bit my shoulder, his body pressing me down as he fucked me some more, even though I didn't think he'd come again. Apparently, I was wrong. He shuddered as he came, the weight of his body a comfort.

"Fuck, baby. I think you liked me pinning you like that."

"I did," I admitted.

"After what happened to you, I didn't think you'd like being tied down, or even just held down like that."

I looked at him over my shoulder. "I told you that I feel safe with you."

"Let's clean up, then I'll help you pack your things. I want us to be home for Christmas."

He pulled out and I winced a little. Not because he'd hurt me but because Christmas hadn't been a happy time for me in quite a while. I didn't want to tell him that's what I was thinking, so I let him believe I was sore.

He nipped my ass, then licked away the sting. "Sorry, sweet girl. I shouldn't have gotten so carried away with you."

"Never apologize for making me yours," I said as I turned to face him.

"I'll get Zipper to ink you when we get home. I don't need to ask the club for permission to make you mine. I think they'd throw my ass outside the gate if I came home with you and *didn't* ink you."

I smiled a little. I didn't have a clue what he meant by inking me, but I'd let him do whatever he wanted. If it meant I got to keep him, he could shave my head and make me walk around quacking like a duck.

We showered and packed my meager belongings, all of which were items that had been given to me or purchased when I'd first arrived. When it was time to head out, Diablo offered to drive us home. I had a feeling I needed to thank him, that he was at least partially responsible for Wraith coming after me.

I hummed along to the Christmas carols on the radio, happier than I'd ever been before. Until a large truck came out of nowhere and broadsided us. I screamed for Will, just seconds before my head slammed into the window. After that, everything went dark.

Chapter Eight

Wraith

I groaned and tried to open my eyes. A hand pressed on my shoulder and I realized I was lying flat, not still sitting upright in the SUV. Panic rose inside me as I remembered a truck hitting us, and I tried to move my hands, needing to find Rin.

"Rin," I said, my voice not sounding like my own.

"Easy," a female voice soothed, but it wasn't Rin. "I'm going to take good care of you."

"Fucking Christ, woman!" I heard Ryker yell. "I'm fine. Get your damn hands off me! My wife will kick your ass if you don't back the hell off."

I would have smiled if I'd been able.

The woman touching me was pulled away and I forced my eyes open to see an angry Ryker peering down.

"Where's Rin?" I asked.

"Gone. I slammed my head into the steering wheel and I guess I blacked out. When I came to, I could hear the sirens, you were knocked the fuck out and Rin wasn't in the car anymore. My seatbelt wouldn't release so I couldn't check the area to see if she'd gotten out, but the sheriff's department has assured me no one matching her description has been found."

I groaned as I tried to sit up and realized I was strapped down. I growled at the woman hovering nearby, an EMT judging by her uniform.

"Let me the fuck up," I said.

"You sustained a head injury and need --"

"What I need is to find my woman."

Her lips thinned. "Maybe she didn't want to be with you anymore and ran off."

Ryker snorted. "Yeah, I'm sure his pregnant fiancée just decided she was tired of his shit, so she arranged a car accident that could have killed her baby."

The woman turned and stormed off.

"What the fucking hell was that shit?" I asked as Ryker freed me from the straps holding me down.

"I saw her groping you in the pretense of checking for injuries," Ryker said. "I think she liked the size of your dick. Or maybe she's a groupie."

"Great. Now I'll need a shower to get her germs off me." I managed to swing my legs over the side of the stretcher. "No way Rin walked out of here. If that accident made both of us pass out, then it likely did the same for her."

"There's something you need to know," Ryker said and his expression was grim. "There was blood on the window where she was sitting. I think she hit her head pretty damn hard. If I had to guess, I think someone took her. I don't think that accident was the least bit accidental."

My gut clenched and I swayed as I stood up. A deputy made his way over to us, his swagger just making me want to deck the asshole. He glanced from Ryker to me, taking in our cuts before he sneered.

"You're lucky. The driver of the other vehicle seems to be fine," the deputy said.

"You mean the asshole who plowed into us?" Ryker asked.

"That's your accounting," the deputy said.

"Seriously?" I asked. "There's no stop sign on the highway, which means the guy had to come from a side road and those *do* have stop signs. You can't lay this on us."

A man with a bandage over his forehead and another on his arm stumbled over to us. His eyes were glassy with pain and there was a tinge of remorse in the depths.

"He paid me," the man said. "Some guy with blond hair offered to pay off some of my debts if I caused an accident when you drove through here. Gave me the model and make of your car, told me to watch for bikers with a dark-haired woman. I saw you before you left town and followed, then took a shortcut so I could get ahead of you."

I advanced on the man and he cringed away from me.

"Some asshole paid you to cause an accident?" I asked. "Did he take my woman?"

The man nodded. "I didn't know what he wanted her for, but I'm guessing he's not a good guy."

"You think?" Ryker asked, the sarcasm in his voice clearly adding a *"you're a dumb shit"* on the end of the sentence.

The deputy eyed the man who was confessing to his crimes. With a sigh, he pulled out cuffs and began the process of arresting him. I took that as a sign that we were free to leave. With the SUV pretty much totaled, I didn't see how we were going anywhere.

"Now what?" I asked Ryker. "You know who has her, and he's probably halfway back to Alabama by now. If that's where he's even taking her. They could be anywhere and we're stuck here without a ride."

"I texted my dad," Ryker said. "Spider said he'd send some help our way. I also sent a message to Torch and told him what was going on. We'll get Rin back for you."

"If he hurts her…" My jaw clenched.

"I know," Ryker said. "With the FBI involved, it might be harder to get your hands on him, though. You'll probably have to turn him over if we do find him."

I focused on him. "Would you turn him over if he had Laken? If you knew he was going to whore her out, or maybe just kill her, would you just hand him over to the Feds like it was no big deal?"

"No. I wouldn't, and I know you won't either."

We waited until the Hades Abyss arrived. Spider was leading the way, and I recognized Rocket. I hadn't dealt with the others much.

"This is Marauder, Bear, and Fox. You already know Rocket," Ryker said we he made introductions. "And of course Spider, my dad."

"We'll get your girl back," Spider said. "She's a sweet little thing and I hate to think of someone hurting her."

"Thank you," I said, meaning it more than I'd ever meant anything. If they could help me save Rin, then I'd do anything they asked. She was the most important thing in my life. And it had taken me long enough to realize that. If I got her back, then I'd do everything I could to not only keep her safe, but to show her how much I cared.

"I've called in some favors," Spider said. "Between Wire, Shade, and a hacker from another club, we'll have access to every camera feed between here and your compound. Do we know what vehicle he's driving?"

"No, but I know someone who does," I said, looking at the man now sitting in the backseat of the deputy's car.

"On it," Fox said, as he ambled over that direction.

"Seems kind of young for a VP," I said, hoping only Ryker could hear me. Fox looked to be mid to late thirties at the most. Wouldn't surprise me if he were younger.

"Don't be fooled," Ryker said. "That man has done some deep, dark shit for this country, and he earned that VP patch just by being his badass self. Age is just a number, but Fox? He has an old soul. The things he's done tend to age a person."

I nodded. Wasn't really any of my business.

"Who's this other hacker?" I asked.

"He's just known as Outlaw. Apparently, he got picked up at the age of twelve for trying to hack the CIA. He's not as good as Wire, but the three of them working together should produce quick results," Spider said.

"What club is he with?" I asked.

"Devil's Fury," Ryker said. "We've had a few dealings with them in the past. They're pretty decent guys. Their Pres, Griz, lost his old lady a while back. Cancer. Hades Abyss put together a rally, and we donated all the proceeds to the American Cancer Society in her name."

"We?" Spider asked with his eyebrow raised.

"All right, my club did while I was off serving my country," Ryker said.

"We should do something back home," I mused. "Something to maybe start an abused women's shelter in town. If there had been a safe place for Rin to go, maybe she could have gotten away from Joe Banner sooner."

"I'm sure Torch would love that idea. Especially if he didn't have to plan it."

I snorted. "You're not wrong on the planning part. We did a toy drive back before any of us had old ladies. That thing was a bitch to put together, but well worth it. Made lots of kids happy that year."

"We should have done one this year," Ryker said, frowning.

"We?" Spider asked again.

Ryker sighed. "For fuck's sake. I'm Hades Abyss, but I live with the Reapers. I help them more than I help you these days. I'm just waiting on you to kick me to the curb and tell me to patch in with them. I love you, Dad, and I respect our club but I haven't really been a part of it in a long fucking time. Yeah, I'm the go between, but I don't have to actually be Hades Abyss to do that."

Spider shrugged. "I figured you'd let me know when you were ready to break off from us. You're my son, Ryker. It's not like we're going to kick the shit out of you for trying to leave. In some respects, you'll always be one of us, but you're right. You're more Reaper now than Hades Abyss. And that's fine. I know you want to keep Laken and Gabriel in Alabama where they can see Flicker as much as they want."

"Torch told you that you could come visit any time you wanted," Ryker pointed out. "No one's keeping you from seeing Gabriel."

"I know, and I will. I'll try to be there more than I have in the past. My grandson is a year and a half now, and I know I need to make more of an effort to be part of his life. I want him to know his grandpa loves him," Spider said.

Fox came back over, a grim expression on his face. "Got the make and model of the car, and a partial tag. Sent all of it to Outlaw and he's sharing with the others. My bet is that Joe Banner is heading for home, or at least his home state. I say we hit the road and head toward Alabama until we get some news."

"You're welcome at the Dixie Reapers compound," I said. I didn't even have to ask Torch or Venom. I knew if they were willing to help find Rin, then they would be welcome to hang at the clubhouse for however long it took. The more help we had, the better our chances of getting her back.

"Those Feds still hanging around?" Marauder asked. "Heard you were helping them out."

"One of them is," Ryker said, smirking a little.

"Yeah, that Agent Montoya seems to like making Tank a bit crazy. I think she gets off on teasing him, then not letting him have any," I said.

"Everyone head out," Spider said. "I had Bear bring a truck since the two of you were without bikes. The three of you can ride together."

"Thanks," I said, hoping he could see the sincerity in my eyes. I needed them right now. Rin needed them. If we didn't get her back, then I wouldn't have a reason to keep breathing. I'd do it, because I knew that's what she would want, but I'd be a damn miserable bastard for the rest of my days.

I got updates from Wire and Torch on the way home, nothing concrete, but it sounded like they were closing in on Banner. With some luck, we'd know where he was going and maybe even if he still planned to sell Rin by the time we crossed the Alabama state line. I hated not knowing what she was facing right now. With her being pregnant, she didn't need all this stress. If Joe Banner hurt her in any way, he'd answer to me, the Feds be damned.

When we made it to the compound, we still didn't know much other than Banner's car had run a red light at the edge of town about an hour before we arrived. He wasn't being cautious, which meant he didn't think we'd catch up to him, or figure out he took Rin. If he was sloppy, I didn't think that boded well for Rin's well-being. Wire had caught another glimpse of the car from a camera in an ATM about four blocks from that light, heading south through town, but no one knew where he'd gone after that. It's like the car had just disappeared.

"What's between that ATM and the rest of town?" I asked. I hadn't been in the military for a while, but sometimes those instincts still kept my ass alive, and right now they were telling me that Banner had gone underground somewhere in town. Somewhere big enough to hide his vehicle.

Ryker looked at Wire's screens with his arms folded. We'd both holed up in Wire's "war room" that had an entire wall of monitors.

"Anything with large parking structures, or maybe underground parking that wouldn't have a live camera feed?" Ryker asked.

Wire paused mid-keystroke and started cursing. "Of course. The town hall. There's an underground garage not even a block from that ATM, and you said the mayor had used Banner's services before. I bet that little rat went straight to the corrupt town officials for help. They have cameras on site, but I was focused on the streets."

Wire's fingers began furiously tapping at the keys. I had no idea what he was trying to do, but the sounds of frustration he made, with some cussing thrown in here and there, told me he wasn't getting the results he wanted. His lips thinned and his jaw firmed as he turned to face me.

"They've blocked all the feeds inside the town hall. I have no doubt that's where your girl is. I know the Feds want to clean house, but... I think we need to handle this one our way," Wire said.

"I'll let Torch know that Wire found something. I'm sure he'll want to call Church and form a plan," Ryker said.

Wire gathered whatever intel he had. Both our phones went off at the same time. A message from the Pres was on my phone.

Church. Now!

When we stepped through the doors of the conference room we used for Church, our seats were open, but the walls were lined with Hades Abyss, Devil's Boneyard, and some new faces. Their cuts said *Devil's Fury*. I didn't know where they'd come from, or how they'd gotten here so fast, but if they were going to help get Rin back, then I had no problem with them.

Tank was missing and so was Flicker, both their seats still open. I heard a commotion outside the doors and they burst open with Tank striding through them. A Hispanic woman followed, her face flushed and her lips in a thin determined line.

"So I'm good enough to fuck, but not good enough to help?" she demanded. "I knew it was a good thing I hadn't let you into my pants. You're a giant walking dick just like most every other man I know."

"Hey!" Flicker protested. "Don't lump me in with him."

She glared at Flicker over her shoulder, but our Treasurer merely looked amused. If there was a joker in our group, it would be Flicker. Hardly anything ever seemed to get him down, unless you fucked with his family.

Agent Montoya faced off against Tank again, hands on her hips, and her booted foot tapping. "I may be FBI, but it doesn't mean I'm fucking useless. I'm going to help, and that's final."

Tank moved in closer to the petite woman, towering over her, as he stared down his nose. "No. Get the fuck out of here. It's club business, and you're not part of the club."

"You… You…" Fury flashed in her eyes. *"Que te la pique un pollo."*

Ryker coughed into his fist and turned his head, but not before I saw the humor in his eyes.

"What did she say?" I whispered to him.

"She said she hopes his dick is pecked by a chicken."

"That's… an interesting insult," I said.

Ryker shrugged. "Spain has quite a few sayings that don't necessarily make sense anywhere else. That one translated well enough."

Agent Montoya removed her FBI ID and dropped it onto the table.

"There," she said. "Now I'm not FBI. You either let me go with you to help save that girl, or I'll let the DEA march through the gates. I'm sure you don't want them to know about that stash you have in a warehouse on the back end of the property."

Torch scowled at Tank. "I thought you were watching her."

Lupita snorted. "He has to sleep sometime."

"Are we going to have a problem?" Torch asked. "Because I don't condone violence against women, but I will protect this club at all costs."

"No problem, as long as I get to go along. After learning what the mayor, city manager, and others have been up to, I want to do a little ass-kicking of my own," she said.

"Fine." Torch looked at Tank. "She stays. Now sit the fuck down and someone close the goddamn doors so we can get down to business."

Flicker pushed the doors shut and everyone took their places around the room. As Tank was sitting, one of the Devil's Fury moved in closer. Tank tensed for a second, until his gaze landed on the man's name stitched on his cut.

"Slash?" Tank asked.

Slash held out his hand. "Just wanted to shake the hand of my brother before things got started. And blood is welcome to call me Talon." His gaze landed on Jackal. "And that goes for my sister and her husband too."

"Brother?" Venom asked.

"We have the same asshole for a sperm donor," Slash said. "Abraxas has given me a wide berth over the years, and I have a good feeling he won't make it out of prison."

"Why is that?" Jackal asked. "Because if you can guarantee he's out of Josie's life, I'm sure she'd sleep better at night. She still sometimes has nightmares about her dad coming after her."

"Let's just say he's going to have a fatal accident," Slash said.

I noticed his cut said VP, even though he appeared to be younger than Tank.

Jackal nodded. "You make that happen, and we may name our next kid after you."

Tank's gaze locked onto Jackal. "What kid? You have two already. Are you telling me you knocked her up again? Your second kid is only a few months old!"

Jackal shrugged. "She doesn't like birth control."

"Then you'd damn well better go get neutered," Tank said, scowling at Jackal.

Slash slapped Tank on the back of the head. "That's not our decision, dickhead. Just because Josie is our sister doesn't mean we can dictate her life."

"What's this 'we' bullshit?" Tank asked his brother. "You haven't even met her."

"Not my fault," Slash said. "Apparently, you've known about me for a while and never reached out."

"So how did you know Tank was your brother?" I asked before I could think better of interfering.

Slash pointed to Wire, then another man. "Wire and Outlaw talk. When that shit went down with Josie, Wire decided to pass along a bit of intel to Outlaw. And I'm glad he did. Now I can make sure dear ol' Dad gets what he deserves, and the families of his victims can have some peace."

"While this is a touching reunion, we have a woman to save," Spider said. "You didn't call in three other clubs to sit down for afternoon tea."

Torch snorted, then called the meeting to order.

Wire passed out some of the intel he'd found not only on Joe Banner, but the city officials as well. Thankfully, I didn't have to see the pictures of my sweet Rin being violated. I knew Wire had them, but I was grateful he hadn't shared them with the entire room. Even though none of that had been in Rin's control, if she knew my club and the others had seen those photos, she'd be deeply embarrassed.

"It's my belief that Joe Banner has gone to ground at the town hall. The camera feeds have been shut down, or at least anyone outside the building has been locked out. Even I can't hack into them," Wire said. "Shade and Outlaw have been helping me, so you can thank them for some of this information. Since our clubs seem to be intermarrying, I guess I'll be working with them more often."

"One big happy fucking family," Slash murmured as he perused the documents.

"What can I say?" Jackal asked. "The Reapers' sisters seem to have a type. Any of you have single sisters? Maybe we should have a party when all this is over and you can just get the introductions out of the way now."

Venom, Torch, Spider, and a few others looked rather amused. Tank and Flicker were not, since it was their sisters who had hooked up with other clubs.

Saint shrugged. "Sorry. Mine hooked up with a Reaper. Guess she had better taste than Josie and Laken."

Preacher smirked at Saint's comment, since he was the Reaper in question that she'd married.

"Leave my sister out of this shit," Gears said. "Cleo's too damn young to be thinking about hooking up with some asshole biker."

"Mine too," Bats said. "Mary-Jane is a no-fly zone for all you fuckers."

I had the sudden feeling that neither of my brothers were going to get their wish on that one. If Cleo and Mary-Jane were anything like Josie, Laken, or Kayla, then they would no doubt end up hooking up with another biker. Hard to say if they'd stick with a Reaper or pick someone else. On the upside, the more our clubs intermarried, the stronger our alliances became because it made us family. Fuck with one club, you get them all. Once people started realizing that, we'd hopefully have fewer issues to deal with.

"Enough," Torch said. "If all of you want to start a dating service, do it after we save Rin. Time is of the essence and y'all are pissing me the fuck off."

Everyone shut up. Spider, the Pres of Hades Abyss, moved closer to Torch, as did Scratch, VP for Devil's Boneyard. Slash stayed near Tank.

"Devil's Fury was kind enough to send their VP, Slash, as well as a few other members. Badger, Outlaw, and Demon are here to give their assistance," Torch said.

Spider stepped forward. "Most of you know I'm the Pres for Hades Abyss. My son Diablo, who you know as Ryker, lives here with his woman, Laken. I brought Rocket, Marauder, Bear, and my VP, Fox. We'll do whatever we can to get Rin back. She's a sweet girl, and we're honored to have gotten to know her the past month."

Scratch cleared his throat. "Pretty sure all the Reapers already know my crew. I haven't had much dealings with Hades Abyss or Devil's Fury so there are a lot of new faces around the room. Jackal, Shade, and Havoc came with me."

"And now that everyone knows every-fucking-one else," Torch said, "we need to discuss our plan of attack."

"The building is mostly secure. I'm sure they'll have someone watching all the entry points, or at least the ones they know about," Wire said.

"What's that mean?" I asked.

"I'm hoping they aren't aware of the secret entrance to the underground parking garage. There's a grate in the south corner that leads to some underground tunnels. I did a bit of research and the town hall is one of the few buildings still remaining in town that was here back when the town was founded in 1902."

"Which means?" Tank asked. "Break it down for those of us dumber than you."

Wire snickered. "It means that building was used during Prohibition. The underground tunnels were a way to smuggle in illegal alcohol. It wasn't always town hall. The original town hall burned down in 1962. Instead of rebuilding, they took over an old clubhouse that had an underground speakeasy."

"The parking garage?" I asked. "It was a speakeasy?"

Wire nodded. "I pulled up the plans from when the building was renovated. While there's a section of the parking garage that was used for that purpose even back in the day, a big chunk was walled off and turned into the secret club. The alcohol was smuggled through that grate and no one ever knew. The upper floors were a legitimate gentleman's club that followed the letter of the law."

"Learn something new every damn day," Flicker said. "So how do we access that grate? Would those tunnels even be safe after all this time?"

"Hard to say," Shade said, joining the conversation. "We can't find anything on the tunnels being officially shut down, but it doesn't look like they've been maintained either. Unless it's being handled off the books. With some luck, they don't know where that grate leads, or that it will give us access to the building."

"The speakeasy closed up when the owner was arrested on other charges, and as far as we can tell, those tunnels haven't been used since," Outlaw said. "There's an old dirt road outside town. It goes through a wooded area, and the entrance to the tunnels is at the end of the road."

"A road that hasn't been used since Prohibition?" Torch asked. "How the fuck are we supposed to find it?"

"We think it's being used for other means now," Wire said. "It's not any of the newer maps, but it does still show as far back as the late seventies. That road had a purpose even after it wasn't used for smuggling alcohol anymore. I just don't know for certain if it's being used now."

Torch rubbed the bridge of his nose and looked like he was getting a headache. I knew the feeling because I could feel one building behind my eyes.

"I just want Rin back," I said. "If I have to find some supposed road that may or may not exist, then point the fucking way. I'm not going to let Joe Banner hurt her, or our baby."

Nearly every eye in the room locked on me, except for a handful of people who I suspected already knew Rin was pregnant and had kept that shit from me. I'd deal with them later.

"She's pregnant?" Flicker asked.

"Yeah. About a month along. I didn't find out until I went to bring her home. Thanks for that, fuckers," I muttered.

"Have Dr. Myron on standby for when we find Rin," Torch said. "Between the accident and the stress she's probably feeling right now, she'll need to be checked out when we get her back."

"On it," Preacher said, pulling out his phone.

"So we find this dirt road, follow it to the tunnels, and then what?" Venom asked. "I'd imagine that grate is sealed. Do we know if they welded the damn thing shut? Are we going to make it all that way only to not be able to get through?"

"I can't answer that for sure," Wire said.

"I might could help with that," Rocket said. "Just need an acetylene torch. If that grate is welded shut, I'll cut a hole in it big enough for us to get through."

"Any cameras on that grate?" Torch asked.

"No," Wire said. "At least, there aren't any in the security plans. Without being able to access the camera feeds, I can't say for certain they don't have cameras up that aren't on the building schematics the security firm has on file. Even if I couldn't get to the cameras, I was able to hack into the plans."

"There's a portable acetylene torch out in the old barn," Tank said, giving the Reapers a pointed look that translated into *that place where we torture and kill assholes*.

"I'll get it," Saint said. "Anything that needs to be carried can go into one of the trucks."

I could tell that Saint felt partially responsible for what happened, the guilt in his eyes gave it away. But if he'd left the same time as us, then his daughter could have been in an accident. Thankfully, he'd taken off ahead of us.

"You're staying here," Torch said. "You have a new daughter to guard, and I want you to keep an eye on Isabella and Lyssa. Get Diego to drive the truck. I'll have King watch the gates."

"I'm not leaving Kayla and the kids unprotected. Some more people need to stay behind. Not to mention, if every man in this room goes, we're going to be noticed," Preacher said.

"My crew is going," Spider said, "but I can remain behind and watch over Laken and my grandson."

"I'll stay with Darian and the kids if Bull wants to go," Scratch said. "If Venom is going, then Ridley and the girls can some stay with us too."

"Venom should stay here since I'm going," Torch said.

"I'm going," I said. "No one's keeping me here while Rin needs me."

"We already figured that," Torch said.

"I'm going too," Tank said.

"At the risk of overstepping," Shade said, "what if the Devil's Boneyard remained behind with a handful of Reapers to keep the women and kids safe while the rest of you go find Rin? You'll need people hidden in the vicinity of the town hall in case anyone tries to run, or if Joe Banner tries to leave with Rin, you'll need eyes outside the building that can keep everyone abreast of what's going on."

"I think I like him," Bull said. "Good idea, Shade."

"Wraith, Rin belongs to you. Who's going with you in the tunnels?" Torch asked.

"I'll take Hades Abyss with me, you, and Tank. If everyone else that's going would be our eyes outside the town hall, that would be great," I said.

"I'm going too," Agent Montoya said. "She might want a woman there."

"Then it's settled. Everyone grab what you need and we'll meet at the gates in fifteen," Torch said, then slammed down the gavel, ending Church.

Ryker bumped my shoulder. "We'll get her back."

"You know I was including you in the crew that goes with me, right?" I asked.

"Yep. I'm still technically Hades Abyss so I figured that meant me too. We'll get her back, and we'll make the fuckers pay who are responsible for hurting her. Now or in the past," Ryker said.

I eyed his Hades Abyss cut. "You going to show me why they call you Diablo?"

"Let's hope no one ever sees that side of me, but it's there when needed."

I nodded and we filed out. In the end, we took two trucks and everyone else rode their bikes. We stopped about a half mile from the tunnels, in case they were being watched and Wire had been wrong about them being an unknown. By the time we'd hiked in, made it down the three-mile-long tunnel, and came to the grate, I was a mass of nerves and fury. The longer it took to reach Rin, the angrier I got, just thinking about what they might be doing to her.

Joe Banner was a dead man, and so was every other fucker in the building. I wouldn't rest until I knew the name of every man who had ever harmed Rin and I'd bled them dry.

Chapter Nine

Rin

I knew Wraith would come for me, just as soon as he figured out that Joe had taken me, or where we were. I had faith he'd rescue me. My asshole half-brother had taken me when I'd been unconscious after the accident. Otherwise I'd have fought tooth and nail to stay away from him. I'd woken bound and gagged. Now I was tied to a chair, my legs spread so my ankles could be fastened to the back legs, and my arms tied behind me. He'd removed the gag, though. Guess he didn't care if anyone heard me scream.

We were in some sort of conference room, and Mayor Fuckstick, along with some other assholes I recognized, were present. If they thought I was going to accept whatever they had planned, they'd better come up with a new plan. The second they untied me, I was going to start fighting, and I wouldn't stop until they either knocked me out or I managed to escape. The baby growing inside me was counting on me, and I knew Wraith was too.

One of the guards for town hall came closer, a leer on his face as he eyed me. Someone had cut off most of my clothes and I only had on panties, since I seldom wore a bra. In my old life, I could have hardened myself enough to ignore the fact I was naked. I wasn't that same woman, though, and it bothered me that they could look at my naked body. I wanted to cover myself and scream that only Wraith got to see me without clothes, but I knew that wouldn't do me any good. I had to act unbothered by my naked state. Emotions could get me killed, at least if they knew how I felt. I had to lock that shit down and keep it hidden.

The guard reached out and squeezed my breast until tears gathered in my eyes and I knew I'd have bruises.

"Why leave the panties on?" he asked Joe. "We could have played some if she were naked."

"Her mouth is available," Joe said absently, as he looked at something on the mayor's computer.

I nearly gagged at the idea of the guard, or any of them, putting their cocks anywhere near my mouth or any other part of me. No way I was going to take that shit anymore. I'd done it to survive before, and I knew if I had to, I would endure it again. If for no other reason than to give Wraith time to come for me. But if they raped me and he found out, I also knew none of them would live for very long. I'd seen what he'd done to the Prospect who had just felt me up over my clothes. I could only imagine what brand of justice he'd give anyone who went further, especially now that he'd decided I was his.

The guard rubbed my lips. "That what you want? My dick in your mouth? You want me to free you and we go have some fun over on the conference table? Spread you out and play a little."

Bile rose in my throat, but I knew this was a chance I couldn't pass up. I pasted a fake smile on my face.

"We can play. But not like this. I'd need my hands."

Joe glanced at me, but must not have thought I was a threat because he turned away again just as quickly.

The guard started undoing the knots holding my hands tight behind my back, then worked on my feet. It felt like needles were stabbing me as feeling rushed back into my limbs and I staggered as the guard pulled me up to my feet. I hadn't counted on not having complete control of my body, and I panicked for a moment. The guard led me over to the table and I saw two other men in the room start to unfasten their pants. My heart hammered in my chest and I tried to survey the area without being obvious. No one was by the doors to my far right. If I could break free, maybe I could make it? I didn't know where the doors led, but anywhere was better than here, right?

I meekly let the guard drag me where he wanted, and as he picked me up and set me down on the table, I knew I had to act quickly. He tugged on my panties and I took the moment to nail him in the balls with my bare foot. His eyes went wide as his face turned purple and he hit the floor. The other two men watching us had their pants down around their knees and their dicks in their hands. I made a mad dash for the doors to the right and I heard them shouting behind me, but I didn't dare stop to look behind me.

I ran, my feet pounding against the hard, cold floor, as I raced toward what I hoped was the front of the building and freedom. I could feel the dried blood on my body from the accident cracking as I flew through town hall, or tried to. A surprised cry left my throat as someone tackled me from behind and I slammed into the floor. The air left my lungs and I gasped as I tried to breathe.

One of the other men had pinned me down. As he flipped me over, I felt his dick brush against my thigh and I started fighting again.

"Such a little hellcat," he said, interest and fire lighting up his eyes. "I like it when they fight. Makes it more fun. Go ahead and struggle."

He was pulling at my panties with one hand while he held my wrists over my head with the other, and seemed immune to my squirming and kicking. The right hook that came out of nowhere got his attention, though. I was surprised to see it was a small hand that landed the blow. My gaze jerked up, and I saw a pretty Hispanic woman sneering at the asshole who was about to rape me.

"You like it when they struggle?" she asked, her voice dripping venom. "I'll play with you. Not that there's much to play with," she said as she looked at his cock.

He growled and released me as he launched himself at the woman. I didn't know who she was, but she seemed to be able to take care of herself. I scanned the area, wondering where she'd come from, when I saw a bunch of bikers storming toward me. When I saw Wraith, I started crying and ran for him.

"Rin!" he yelled as he came closer, then his arms were going around me and I let the sobs loose that I'd been holding back. "Baby, I'm here. Are you all right? Where are you hurt?"

"I -- I'm fine. The blood is from the car accident. I'm a little sore, but I think I'm all right. They tried to hurt me, but I didn't let them."

He cursed and shrugged off his cut, then pulled his shirt over his head. He put his tee on me, pausing before he covered my breasts, and I heard him curse. I looked down and saw bruises in the shape of fingers forming on the breast the guard had squeezed. Wraith pulled his cut back on over his bare torso, then tipped my chin up.

"Who touched you?" he demanded.

"The guard in the conference room. Then…" I looked over where the woman was fighting the man who'd tackled me to the floor. My eyes went wide when I saw her pull a deadly-looking blade and stab the man right between the legs.

"Seems Montoya has that one taken care," Ryker said from behind Wraith. "Give me Rin and go after the guard. I know you need to handle it."

Wraith pressed a kiss to my lips, then passed me to Ryker. "Go with him, baby. He'll keep you safe while I take care of things here."

"No, Wraith… Come with us," I said.

"Not yet, sweet girl," Wraith said, his jaw firm and his gaze determined.

"I'll come with you," Rocket said, materializing next to Ryker.

"Please, baby," Wraith said. "I need to take care of this. I need to know for certain they aren't coming for you again, and while I trust my brothers and everyone who came to help, I need to handle it myself. I'm sorry, Rin. I told you I wasn't a nice man and you deserve better."

I blinked back tears and reached up to place my hand on Wraith's cheek. "You're an honorable man, Wraith. And I love you."

I saw him swallow, his Adam's apple bobbing, then he kissed me hard and ran toward the conference room.

The man Montoya had cornered was screaming as she ripped his stomach open and… I turned and retched on the floor.

"Okay, enough excitement for you," Rocket said as he and Ryker led me away.

"I'll make sure some of the others come inside to help clean house," someone said, but I didn't recognize them.

It was freezing outside and my bare feet hurt from being on the icy ground. Rocket sensed my dilemma and lifted me into his arms, carrying me to a truck that was parked at the curb.

"When did those get here?" Ryker asked.

"I figured we'd be going out the front, so once I cut through that grate, I sent a text to the Prospect waiting with the trucks to bring one here. I didn't think Rin would be going home on the back of a bike," Rocket said.

"Good thinking," Ryker said.

"I have my moments," Rocket said.

Rocket eased me down onto the backseat of the truck, and the heat blasting from the vents felt really, really good. I held my hands out toward them and inched closer. I worried about Wraith as I looked over at the building. I knew he could handle himself, especially with all the backup he seemed to have, but I didn't want this to come back and bite him in the ass. If he went to jail because he defended me, I didn't know what I'd do. Having a baby was scary enough, but having the man I loved locked up in prison? I wasn't sure I could handle that.

"He'll be fine," Rocket assured me.

It felt like we waited forever, but at the same time it almost seemed like time had stood still, and when Wraith came out of the building, he was covered in blood and bits that I didn't want to try to identify. He paused outside the truck and placed a bloodstained hand on the window. I rolled it down, shivering as the cold air blew into the truck.

"I'm going to head back to my bike, then get cleaned up at home. Someone will stay with you until then, all right?" he asked, watching me closely.

"Okay." I wanted to ask what he'd done inside, but I wasn't sure I wanted to know. A piece of what looked like brains was stuck to his shoulder, and I refused to even look at the rest of the gore clinging to him.

"Rin, look at me. My eyes, not my body," he said.

My gaze locked with his.

"You're safe, baby. Joe Banner, and everyone else in that building, have been taken care of. No one is ever coming after you again. Got it?"

I nodded.

He turned to Rocket. "Get her home safely. I'll get someone to drop some clean clothes by the clubhouse for me and I'll clean up there."

"You got it," Rocket said.

Rocket and Ryker both rode back to the compound with me, a Prospect I'd never met behind the wheel, and when we cleared the gates, I breathed a little easier. It was amazing that a place I'd hardly seen could feel like home. But that's how I felt as we entered the gates and the Prospect driving pointed the truck toward Wraith's house.

Someone had left a change of clothes on the coffee table for me, and I picked them up and went straight to Wraith's bathroom. At first the hot water felt good, and loosened up any tight muscles I had from the accident, but eventually it started to cool. The dried blood cracked and slid down my body in chunks, swirling down the drain. Head wounds always bled a lot. What was left made the water turn pink as it slowly liquefied. I scrubbed at my skin, wanting to wash away the touch of those men, not stopping until I'd rubbed myself raw. The water was turning so cold my teeth were starting to chatter. The shower door was jerked open, and I screamed until I realized who was with me.

"Easy, baby," Wraith said. "It's just me."

He pulled me from the shower, turned off the water, then helped me dry off. He held up the clothes and I shook my head, reaching for him. I tugged at his cut, until he removed it, then I tried to pull his shirt over his head. The cut was spotless, and I wondered if he'd removed it when he'd dealt with the men at town hall.

"Sweet girl, what are you doing? You should see a doctor and rest. You still have a cut on your forehead and who knows what other injuries you might have. You might need stitches."

"I need you, Will. Please. I need…" I didn't know how to put it into words. I didn't care about the cut on my head, or anything else right then. What I needed was to feel like I was his again, to replace the horrible events of the day with something good.

Understanding filled his gaze and he nodded, then stripped out of his clothes. Wraith picked me up and carried me into the bedroom. I noticed the door was already shut, but after he laid me down on the bed, he went and locked the knob.

His touch was light as he caressed the bruises on my body. "I'm sorry I didn't protect you better."

"It's not your fault, Will. None of this was your fault. My half-brother was an evil bastard, just like those men today. You're not responsible for other peoples' actions. Only your own."

"I slaughtered them," he admitted. "Made them scream and beg for mercy. I didn't end their lives quickly."

"You weren't in there very long," I said.

His gaze narrowed. "Rin, you were waiting in the truck for almost an hour."

I blinked up at him. "But it felt like minutes."

"Maybe you're in shock," he murmured and he started to back away.

"No!" I yelled, reaching for him and latching onto his biceps. "Don't leave me."

"I'm not leaving," he said softly. "Tell me what you need, Rin. I'll give you anything you want. Whatever will make you feel better."

"Touch me," I said softly. "Touch me and make me forget."

He used light, sweeping strokes to caress me from my neck to my knees, his lips leaving a trail of kisses along my body. He licked at my nipples and took his time, making me feel cherished and important. In that room, tied to that chair with the men leering at me, I'd felt like trash. Here with Wraith, I wasn't a common whore, a body to be used. I was his, and I had value other than a price for someone to fuck me.

My body warmed under his expert touch, and soon I was begging him for more.

"Please, Will."

He moved farther down my body and I spread my thighs to give him room. He lapped at my pussy, then parted the folds to tease my clit with his tongue. I fisted the bedding as he licked and sucked, driving my need higher. He breached me with one finger, then two, as he lavished attention on my clit. He gently bit the nub and it was enough to make me come. I cried out his name as I twisted and thrashed, wanting the feelings to never stop.

When my body started to tremble as he licked at my clit some more, I knew that I wouldn't be satisfied until he was inside me. In every part of me. I needed him to claim me thoroughly, to wipe out every bad memory.

"Will, I... I need you to do something for me. You may not like it."

He came up over me, and I felt his cock brushing against me.

"What is it?" he asked. "Want me to stop? We don't have to go any further."

"No, it's not that. I need..." I licked my lips. "I need you to take control."

"Control?" he asked slowly.

"Yes. I need you to... I need you to claim me, to not hold back. You need to be forceful, even though I know you don't want to, and you might need to tie me down at one point. I need to purge all the bad memories, Will. I need you to replace them with good ones. I trust you not to hurt me."

"Claim you," he said. "What if I scare you?"

"If I can't handle it, I'll let you know."

"How?" he asked.

"A safe word?" I asked, thinking about some books I'd read. "Rabbit. If I say rabbit, then you need to back off and let me get my bearings."

He nodded. "I can do that."

I leaned up and kissed him, my lips softly brushing his.

"I trust you, Will. I know it's just you and me in this room, and that you won't let anything or anyone hurt me. Not even you," I said.

"I need to get a few things."

"I'll wait here," I said.

He got up and covered me with a blanket before he pulled on a pair of jeans and left the bedroom. I was a bit nervous, especially the longer he took to return, but he came back a while later with a small tote bag. I couldn't tell what was in it, but I hadn't lied to him. I really did trust him and knew he'd never do anything to hurt me. Not on purpose anyway. He'd caused me emotional pain before, but I hadn't exactly stuck around for him to explain things so he wasn't entirely to blame.

Will jerked the blanket off me and stared down at my body.

"Are you sure you're ready for this?" he asked. "What we've done so far… it's mild compared to what I'd like to do to you. I've held back because I didn't think you could handle it, not with your past."

"I'm sure," I told him, and I meant it.

"All right."

Will set the bag down and removed his boots, shirt, and jeans. I didn't remember him putting boots on, or a shirt, and wondered if he'd had them in the front of the house. Had he left the house to go get the supplies he'd brought back? I eyed the bag again, curious about what was inside, but he drew my attention back to him with a snap of his fingers.

Will pointed to the floor at his feet.

"Kneel," he commanded.

My heart started racing as I climbed out of bed and knelt at his feet, looking up at him and waiting for my next instruction.

Chapter Ten

Wraith

Christ! I couldn't believe I was about to do this. I'd wanted to handle Rin with care, but she'd asked for more. Yeah, I'd pinned her under me that one time, but I'd felt like a complete ass afterward. If this was what she needed, to be used, to be claimed by me, then I'd do it. And when were done, I'd let Dr. Myron examine her and I'd have Zipper ink her. No more playing around. She was mine, and I wasn't letting her go. Not now, not ever. She'd sealed her fate when she'd said she loved me. I should have said the words back, and I would when the time was right. Seconds before I murdered a group of men hadn't seemed like the right moment, and this wasn't it either.

She stared up at me from where she knelt at my feet, and I stroked my cock. Yeah, I was fucking hard even though I was at war with myself for what I was about to do. I'd be lying if I said I hadn't pictured this, though. I'd wanted it, craved it, but no way would I ever have asked her to give over this much control to me, not after all she'd suffered.

She licked her lips as her gaze dropped to my dick.

"You want this?" I asked, still stroking my shaft.
"Yes."
"Yes, what?" I asked. If she was going to throw out things like safe words, I wondered just how far she was willing to go.

"Yes, sir," she said, her voice breathy as her eyes dilated.

Oh hell. It was turning her on, which just made my dick even harder. My naughty little girl.

"Lick it," I said, pointing the head of my cock toward her mouth.

Her tongue flicked out and she lapped the pre-cum off the slit. I hissed in a breath as her little tongue darted out again to lick up more.

"Open."

Her jaw dropped and I fed her every inch of my cock, not stopping until she'd taken all of it.

"That's it, baby. You like my dick in your mouth, don't you?" I fisted her hair as I thrust in and out. My hand tightened. "You're going to take it all, aren't you? Every damn inch, and you'll swallow every drop of cum I give you. Because you're my good girl, right?"

She hummed, and the glazed look in her eyes told me I wasn't scaring her, just making her hot. Her nipples were tight little buds and I knew just what I'd do with them.

I thrust harder, going deep, but she never gagged and didn't try to pull away. I shoved my cock into her mouth again and came, grunting as my release spurted into her hot little mouth. She sucked me dry and when I pulled out, she lapped up the rest from my shaft and around her lips. Such a little tease. She'd be using that tongue again at some point.

"Sit on the edge of the bed. Legs spread. Hands behind your back," I said.

"Yes, sir," she said and scurried to obey.

I reached into the bag and pulled out some nipple clamps that had a thin sliver chain running between them. Her eyes went a little wide as I clipped them into place, and she moaned as I tugged on the chain. With her legs spread, I could see her pussy clench and I smiled, knowing she wanted me as much as I wanted her.

"You want me to claim you? To mark you as mine?" I asked.

"Yes, sir," she said softly.

"Spread your legs wider," I said.

She parted her thighs more and I started stroking my cock again. Her lips parted and I could hear her ragged breathing as she watched me get myself off. It didn't take much as I locked my gaze on her slick pussy and thought about how wet she'd be when I fucked her. I started coming and I let my cum spray across her breasts, down her belly, and the last drops landed on her pussy.

Even though I'd come twice, I knew I could go a few more times. I felt like an eager teen who couldn't get enough. I moved in closer and pointed to my dick.

"Get me hard again. No hands, just your mouth."

"Yes, sir."

As tall as I was compared to her, all she had to do was lean forward and open her mouth. She took me inside, sucking long and hard until my cock started to stiffen. When I was fully erect again, I pulled free of her mouth.

"Crawl up the bed and place your hands on the headboard. Wrap your hands around the spindles," I said. "Ass in the air."

She gasped and scurried up the bed. But she'd forgotten one thing.

I kneeled behind her and my hand cracked down on her ass. She yelped and looked at me over her shoulder. I spanked her twice more.

"Forget something, baby?"

"Y-yes, sir."

I reached into the bag again and pulled out some faux fur-lined cuffs. I fastened her to the headboard and waited a moment to see if she'd panic, but she didn't. Gripping her hips tight, I thrust deep into her slick pussy. I rode her hard, our bodies slapping together. She was so fucking hot and tight, and incredibly wet. I'd almost go so far as to say she was wetter than she'd ever been with me.

I reached between her legs and parted the lips of her pussy. I kept stroking in and out of her and I could tell she was getting close.

"Ready to come, sweet girl?" I asked.

"Yes, sir." She moaned. "Please, Will. Let me come."

I pinched down on her clit and slammed into her harder. "Now, Rin! Come for me."

She screamed as her pussy clenched my cock and her release coated me. I took her harder until I shot load after load of cum into her. If she weren't already pregnant, that damn sure would have made it happen. My breathing was ragged and sweat slicked my skin. I ran my palm down her spine and felt her tremble under my touch.

"You okay, baby?" I asked softly. "If it's too much, if I'm being too rough…"

"No!" She looked at me over her shoulder. "Keep going, Will. We're not done. You haven't claimed all of me yet."

I looked down at the temptation of her ass and fuck if I didn't start getting hard just thinking about getting to fuck her there. I grabbed some lube and worked on loosening her up so I wouldn't hurt her. I took my time, enjoying the sounds she made as I worked my fingers in and out of her. My cock was still buried in her pussy as I prepped her, and I felt it twitch and jerk in her tight channel. Yeah, I was more than ready to fuck her again.

When I knew she was ready, I pulled out and spread her ass cheeks wide. Placing the head of my cock against her tight little hole, I slowly pushed inside her. Rin moaned and her back arched as I went deeper.

"That's it, baby. You can take all of me, can't you?"

"Please, Will. More."

I gave here everything I had, and once I'd bottomed out inside her, it was like something inside me snapped. I held her open and fucked her hard and deep, watching as she stretched around the width of my cock. It was fucking beautiful. Her cries of pleasure spurred me on, and my sweet little vixen came twice before I unloaded every drop of cum from my balls, filling her tight little ass.

"Mine," I said, slapping her ass cheeks until they turned red. "This is my ass."

"Yes, yours," she said.

I plunged my fingers into her pussy, thrusting them a few times. "My pussy," I said.

"Yes!"

I reached for the chain running between the nipple clamps and tugged on it several times, triggering another orgasm that had her screaming my name.

"All of you is mine, isn't that right, Rin? Completely mine. Mine to fuck." I leaned down and brushed my lips across her shoulder. "Mine to love."

I heard her breath catch.

"You love me?" she asked so softly I almost didn't hear her.

"Yeah, baby. I love you. Didn't realize it until you said the words, but that's the emotion I've been fighting this entire damn time. I think I loved you the moment I saw you sitting there, all broken and scared, yet still fighting."

I slipped free of her body, then unlocked the cuffs and removed the nipple clamps. I carried her into the bathroom and we showered together. As much as I wanted my scent on her, we had other things to do than stay in bed all day. After our shower, I realized she only had one outfit to put on. I'd been so focused on finding Rin that I hadn't even thought to grab her bag of clothes from the wrecked SUV, and I doubted anyone else had thought about it either. At least, I didn't think they had. No one had said a word about getting her things. I wondered how much she'd fight me about a shopping trip. After everything she'd been through today, and all that I'd just put her through in the bedroom, she probably needed rest more than anything else.

I took her hand when we reached the front door and lifted it to kiss her fingers. "Just a few more things to do, then we can have hot chocolate, turn on the tree lights, and watch whatever movie you want."

"Better watch it. I've found I have a love for sappy Hallmark movies," she said.

"If you want to watch sappy movies, I'm all right with that."

Truthfully, after damn near losing her today, I'd give her whatever the fuck she wanted. If she wanted to paint the damn house pink, I'd have a Prospect outside painting it pink. Even though I knew the men who had been at town hall were never coming after her again, there were still others out there. Men who would have to be dealt with sooner or later. Wire had compiled a list, and Shade was helping him gather the latest intel on each individual who had ever hurt Rin. One by one, I'd put them in the ground, but I wasn't about to let Rin know that. She'd figure it out eventually, if she paid attention to the news, but she'd stressed enough already.

"Where we are going right now?" she asked as we stepped out onto the porch.

"I'm going to have Dr. Myron take a look at you. I just want to make sure everything is all right with you and the baby. Honestly, I should have taken you straight there after we got cleaned up earlier, but…"

"But I distracted you," she said.

"Yeah." I smiled. "I don't regret it either, but I feel like an ass since I didn't exactly put your well-being ahead of getting you into bed."

She tugged on my hand until I turned to face her.

"Will, I needed that. What we shared in the bedroom helped me. Don't let anyone, including yourself, make you feel guilty for not taking me directly to Dr. Myron's office. You did something for me that he couldn't."

I lifted a brow. "I sure as fuck hope he wasn't going to help you with that."

She playfully slapped my bicep. "You know what I mean."

Yeah, I knew what she meant, and it humbled me that she trusted me that damn much. Someone had left one of the club trucks in my driveway with the keys in the ignition. I was grateful since I really didn't want Rin on the back of my bike while she was pregnant. We made it to the doctor's office without any difficulty since the traffic was pretty much nonexistent, and the receptionist sent us straight to the back.

My phone rang while we were waiting and I answered when I saw it was Torch.

"What's up, Pres? Everything all right?" I asked.

"Not fucking hardly. That dumbass FBI agent decided to take the blame for the mess you made," he said.

"Uh. You mean Montoya?" I asked.

"Yeah. She turned herself in to her superiors, but not before she sent a message to Tank that she'd call in a favor later for cleaning this up now," Torch said.

What the fuck?

"They're going to throw her ass in prison," I said.

"Probably, but she doesn't seem to care. She said that getting Rin back and making sure those men never drew breath again was more important. I think she's going to try to pull some strings and get a light sentence," Torch said. "I don't know if she's calling in favors or what the hell she's doing, but maybe she has some powerful people in her corner."

"Fuck."

"Yeah. My sentiments exactly," he said. "Try not to upset Rin with the news, but I didn't want you to hear it from someone else."

He ended the call and I stared at the ceiling a moment before focusing on my woman again.

Rin sat on the padded table, swinging her feet, as we waited for the doctor to show up. Some people might think she didn't have a care in the world, but I could see the nervousness in her eyes. She placed her hand on her belly every few minutes, and I could tell she was concerned about our baby. I was too for that matter. She hadn't given me a chance to take care of her physical injuries, but hopefully I'd given her some emotional and mental healing. Dr. Myron would probably have a few things to say about taking so long to come see him, especially when he saw her head injury.

"Everything okay?" she asked.

"It's going to be fine, baby. Nothing for you to worry about right now."

She didn't look convinced, but she didn't press me for details either. Thank fuck for that at least. I knew she'd blame herself, even though none of this shit was her fault. I'd find a way to help Montoya, even if I didn't know how right this second.

When the doctor came in, he narrowed his eyes first at Rin, then at me.

"Before you say anything, she needed me and I wasn't going to tell her no," I said. "I took a chance on her injuries not being severe."

Dr. Myron shook his head and started examining Rin, asking her questions as he listened to her heart, checked her eyes, and gave her a thorough checkup. He had her lie back and pressed on her belly, then he cleaned her cut and put a bandage over it.

"Well, you don't seem to have anything broken, don't need stitches, and as far as I can tell the baby is all right," Dr. Myron said. "It's too soon for an ultrasound, and you can't hear the heartbeat just yet. If you start spotting or have heavy bleeding, go straight to the ER and call me. Otherwise, try to get some rest and limit your stress."

He gave me a pointed glare and I got the message. No sex. At least not for a few days. Hell, I'd gone a month without so a few days wouldn't be a problem. Getting Rin to cooperate might be difficult, though.

I tipped my head toward the hall, and Dr. Myron and I stepped outside for a moment.

"I want to have her inked. How long do I need to wait?" I asked.

Dr. Myron folded his arms. "I know how you Reapers can be once you find the woman you want to keep, but while she's pregnant I would advise against tattoos. If you absolutely have to have your name on her, get a bunch of custom-made temporary tattoos that she can reapply when one wears off. The good ones last a week or more."

I raised my eyebrows and Dr. Myron rolled his eyes before lifting his sleeve to show a tattoo around his wrist.

"It's not permanent. Yet. I wanted to see if I'd like having something like that on my body before I made a decision, so I bought a handful of temporary tattoos. I'll wear it for a month and make a decision, then see Zipper if I want to get one," he said.

"All right. Thanks, Doc."

When I opened the door, Rin was looking at me in curiosity. I crooked my finger, and she got down off the table and came toward me, slipping her hand into mine. I knew that move would get my ass handed to me with some women, but Rin didn't take offense. Since Dr. Myron had said she needed to rest, I knew a shopping trip wasn't a good idea. I'd write down her sizes and get someone to pick up a few essentials until she was able to pick out her own stuff.

"Time to go home, baby," I said as I boosted her into the truck.

"I like the sound of that," she said, smiling.

Yeah, I did too. Before I pulled out of the parking space, I shot off a text to King.

Get two orders of ravioli from that Italian place Zipper and Delphine like and drop it by my house.

He responded right away. *Anything else?*

I tried to remember if I actually had the hot chocolate I'd promised her. Probably not since I'd barely been existing while she was gone.

I sent another text to King. *Hot chocolate. Either instant or get some from the coffee shop.*

He responded just as fast. *On it.*

I put the truck into gear and headed for home. Rin was asleep, her head resting against the window, by the time I pulled up to the gate. A new guy I hadn't seen before was standing guard.

"Who the fuck are you?" I asked, as we came to a stop.

He glanced at my cut, then held my gaze. Kid couldn't have been more than twenty-one or so.

"Cal. My brother and I just started prospecting today."

I stared at him. "When the fuck did anyone have time to vet you for prospecting? It's not like we just take on anyone."

"Saint vouched for us," he said, pushing his shoulders back. "He knew us from before, me and Fenton. We're twins."

"What's Cal short for?" I asked.

"Calder." He motioned to the gate. "I can let you through."

"You don't know me, but you'll me through?" I asked.

His gaze flicked down to my cut again. "You're Wraith. They told me what you did today. I don't want any trouble."

I leaned back and glanced at Rin who was still sleeping.

"I won't let anyone in who doesn't belong," Cal said. "I promise your woman will be safe. Wire already left a list of men who are not only not permitted inside, but they're to be detained immediately for hurting your girl."

"Fine. Open the gates."

What the fucking hell? I knew we were short on prospects, but since when did we just randomly add people without some sort of discussion? I'd have to hope that Torch and Venom knew what the hell they were doing because if Cal or his brother fucked up and got Rin or my kid hurt, I wouldn't stop to ask questions, I'd just start taking heads.

He opened the gate and I pulled through, going straight to the house. After I parked and shut off the truck, I tried to wake up Rin, and she blinked at me sleepily before closing her eyes again. I figured she was crashing after all the shit she'd been through today.

I got out and went around to the passenger side, then lifted her into my arms. Carrying her into the house, I walked back to the bedroom and eased her down onto the king-size bed. I slipped off her shoes, then covered her with a blanket. Looked like that movie watching would have to wait, along with dinner.

I stared down at her, watching her sleep, and something inside me warmed. She was safe. At home where she belonged, and tucked into my bed. There was only one thing missing. Walking over to the dresser, I pulled out the bottom drawer and removed a small box from the back. It held the few things I owned that had been my parents. I opened the lid and took a moment to look over the items tucked inside, picking up a picture of my family. We'd all been happy that day.

Digging farther down, I pulled out a small box and flipped the lip open. My mother's engagement ring winked up at me. She'd been buried with her wedding band, but I'd kept this, thinking I'd give it to my sister when she was older. With Elisa gone, I was the only one left, and I knew that my mom would have wanted Rin to have her ring. It was a marquis-cut canary diamond on a white-gold band, and I knew it had set my father back a lot of money.

I plucked it from the velvet box and carried it over to the bed. I sat on the edge of the mattress and reached for Rin's left hand. Hesitating only a moment, I slid the ring onto her finger, smiling a little when I realized it was a perfect fit. She'd likely wake up and wonder what the hell it was doing on her finger, but I'd ask her the important question over dinner tonight, or breakfast tomorrow if she slept all night.

She was mine, and I was never letting her go. I might not be able to ink her right now, but that didn't mean I couldn't mark her.

Epilogue

Rin

It was Christmas Eve, and the Reapers had thrown a huge party earlier in the day, a family event that even the kids had enjoyed. The sun had set a while ago, though, and now a different event would take place in the clubhouse. I smoothed my hands down the silk sheath dress that Isabella had brought over this morning. When I'd woken the morning after my ordeal and found a ring on my finger, Wraith had dropped to his knees and asked me to marry him.

I'd said yes, but I hadn't realized he'd want to do it quite so fast, but here we were, about to get married on Christmas Eve. I couldn't think of a better present than the gift of a new family. I was gaining a husband, but more than that. The Dixie Reapers weren't just a club, they were family. Some by blood, but all of them by choice, and they'd all welcomed me with open arms.

My eyes teared up and I sniffled as I fought not to cry.

"You're going to ruin your makeup," Ridley said as she finished pinning my hair.

Darian snorted. "Do you think Wraith gives a shit about her makeup? As long as he can call her his by end of the night, that's all that matters. She could go out there in a burlap sack and birds nesting in her hair and he wouldn't give a shit."

Ridley snickered and I had to agree that Darian wasn't wrong. Wraith had done a complete one-eighty, and now that he'd decided I belonged to him, he wasn't stopping until I was his in every way possible. He'd already given me a cut that said *Property of Wraith*, and now we were getting married. As soon as the baby was born and I was finished breastfeeding, I'd be inked with his name too.

"I heard about Montoya," Ridley said, glancing at me briefly. "In case you're wondering, they're not giving her hard time, and she's going to some swanky place that's hardly even like a prison."

Darian growled. "What they should have done was give her a damn medal. She took out the trash or at least helped. We all know it was Wraith who did the most damage, but she won't let him or anyone else come forward. She's determined to put her neck on the block for the club, even though I don't know why."

"Something tells me we'll find out sooner or later," Ridley said. "There! All done."

She stepped back and I looked at the mirror Wire had hung on the back of the door for me. I could hardly believe the beautiful woman looking back was me. I didn't know Agent Montoya, but I owed her a debt. Because of her, I hadn't been violated that day, and I was here, getting married to the man I loved. Somehow, I'd find a way to show her my gratitude.

"Come on. Wraith looks ready to come get you himself," Kayla said from the doorway. Wire had let us borrow his room at the clubhouse to change into my dress and get ready. Not that there was a ton of room with all his computer equipment, but it was the thought that counted.

I walked down the hall with Ridley, Darian, and Kayla following me. They branched off to stand with their families as I walked across the room to join Wraith. Preacher had offered to do the honors of marrying us and he smiled as Wraith took my hand. I stared at my groom, who was dressed in his usual attire. He'd claimed suits and tuxedos were for civilians. It didn't matter to me what he wore.

Preacher cleared his throat and stared at me. My cheeks flushed as I realized he'd already started the ceremony and I'd been too busy daydreaming.

"I do," I said.

Wraith winked at me.

"Do you have the rings?" Preacher asked.

Tank handed over a white-gold band for me and a titanium band for Wraith. He'd said anything as soft as gold wouldn't last long. Apparently, he was rough on his hands. I wasn't sure I wanted to know the details about that.

We exchanged rings and when we shared our first kiss as husband and wife, the room erupted in cheers. His tongue tangled with mine and his hand tightened at my waist.

"Can you start the honeymoon after you've left the clubhouse?" Venom asked.

Wraith drew back and smiled down at me.

"Don't even think it," I told him. "They prepared a celebration for us and we're staying for it."

His gaze narrowed a moment.

"I said no, Wraith."

Zipper came up and slapped him on the back. "See, married all of thirty seconds, and she's already acting like a wife. Better get used to it."

"Fine. Half an hour," Wraith said. "And no more."

I honestly didn't care how long we stayed, but I knew they were passing around a camera so I'd have pictures of my wedding and reception. If we ran off right away, then we wouldn't be in any of them, and I wanted to make an album so I could look back one day and remember everything I was feeling right now.

"I love you," I told Wraith, pressing my lips to his again.

"Love you too, sweet girl. Thank you for not giving up on me, and for giving me a second chance."

"Thank you for saving my life," I countered.

He shook his head. "I didn't do the saving. It was you who saved me."

I curled against him, his arms going around me. I could hear the thump of his heartbeat.

"Merry Christmas, Will," I murmured.

"Merry Christmas… Wife."

I smiled as we danced and mingled with our family, and knew that this would be the most perfect Christmas ever.

Harley Wylde

When Harley is writing, her motto is the hotter the better. Off-the-charts sex, commanding men, and the women who can't deny them. If you want men who talk dirty, are sexy as hell, and take what they want, then you've come to the right place!

An international bestselling author, Harley is the "wilder" side of award-winning Sci-Fi/Fantasy Romance author Jessica Coulter Smith, and writes Gay Fantasy Romance as Dulce Dennison.

Harley on Changeling: changelingpress.com/harley-wylde-a-196

Jessica on Changeling: changelingpress.com/jessica-coulter-smith-a-144

Dulce on Changeling: changelingpress.com/dulce-dennison-a-205

Changeling Press E-Books

More Sci-Fi, Fantasy, Paranormal, and BDSM adventures available in E-Book format for immediate download at ChangelingPress.com -- Werewolves, Vampires, Dragons, Shapeshifters and more -- Erotic Tales from the edge of your imagination.

What are E-Books?

E-Books, or Electronic Books, are books designed to be read in digital format -- on your desktop or laptop computer, notebook, tablet, Smart Phone, or any electronic ebook reader.

Where can I get Changeling Press e-Books?

Changeling Press ebooks are available at ChangelingPress.com, Amazon, Barnes and Nobel, Kobo, and iTunes.

ChangelingPress.com

Printed in Great Britain
by Amazon